P9-CER-357

Underworld

BOOKS BY MEG CABOT

Abandon
Underworld
Awaken

Airhead
Being Nikki
Runaway

Allie Finkle's Rules for Girls series

The Princess Diaries series
The Mediator series
Vanished series
Avalon High series

All-American Girl
Ready or Not
Teen Idol
How to Be Popular
Pants on Fire
Jinx
Nicola and the Viscount
Victoria and the Rogue

Insatiable
Overbite
Heather Wells series
Queen of Babble series
The Boy Book series

MEG CABOT

Underworld

Point

Copyright © 2012 by Meg Cabot, LLC.
All rights reserved. Published by Point, an imprint of Scholastic Inc., *Publishers since 1920.*
SCHOLASTIC, POINT, and associated logos are trademarks and/or registered trademarks of
Scholastic Inc.

If you purchased this book without a cover, you should be aware that this book is stolen
property. It was reported as "unsold and destroyed" to the publisher, and neither the author nor
the publisher has received any payment for this "stripped book."

No part of this publication may be reproduced, stored in a retrieval system, or transmitted in
any form or by any means, electronic, mechanical, photocopying, recording, or otherwise,
without written permission of the publisher. For information regarding permission, write to
Scholastic Inc., Attention: Permissions Department, 557 Broadway, New York, NY 10012.

Library of Congress Cataloging-in-Publication Data

Cabot, Meg.
Underworld : an Abandon novel / by Meg Cabot. — 1st ed.
p. cm. — (Abandon)
Summary: John Hayden, a death deity, takes seventeen-year-old Pierce Oliviera back to the
Underworld against her will to keep her safe from the Furies, but her family is still at risk and
she, herself, may never escape his captivity.
ISBN 978-0-545-28411-0 (hardback)
[1. Supernatural—Fiction. 2. Gods—Fiction. 3. Mythology, Greek—Fiction. 4. Erinyes (Greek
mythology)—Fiction. 5. Future life—Fiction. 6. Family life—Florida—Fiction. 7. Florida—
Fiction.] I. Title.
PZ7.C11165Und 2012
[Fic] — dc23
2012003370

ISBN 978-0-545-04063-1

12 11 10 9 8 7 6 5 4 3 2 1   13 14 15 16 17 18/0

Printed in the U.S.A.   40
First Scholastic paperback printing, April 2013

The display type was set in Yolanda Duchess.
The text type was set in Adobe Garamond Pro.
Book design by Elizabeth Parisi and Kristina Iulo

> *"Before me there were no created things,*
> *Only eternal, and I eternal last.*
> *All hope abandon, ye who enter in!"*
> DANTE ALIGHIERI, *Inferno*, Canto III

Pierce keeps having the most terrible nightmares." My mom used to say this to all the doctors we saw right after the accident. "She talks in her sleep — sorry, sweetheart, but you do — about a boy following her. Sometimes she even wakes up crying. It doesn't seem normal. I've never had dreams that vivid."

That's because the worst thing that's ever happened to you, Mom, I'd wanted to tell her, *is your divorce from Dad. You never died, got resuscitated, then had a boy follow you back from the realm of the dead.*

Only I couldn't say this to my mother. Nothing good ever seemed to happen to anyone who found out about my problems, which had more or less caused my parents' divorce, even if Mom didn't know it.

"Often while we're sleeping, our mind is busy working out solutions to problems about which we've felt stressed while we were awake, though our dreams might seem completely unrelated to what's really bothering us," the doctors explained, one by one. "In Pierce's case, of course she isn't *actually* being followed by anyone in real life." This showed how much the doctors knew. "That's just how whatever is causing her anxiety manifests itself in her subconscious . . . the way some of us will dream that we're late for a class, for instance. It's perfectly healthy, and a sign that Pierce's subconscious is functioning normally."

You know what I'd like? To dream that I'm late for a class.

Instead, I'm always dreaming that someone is trying to kill me, or someone I care about. That's because people *are* trying to kill me, as well as the people I care about, in real life . . . so often, as a matter of fact, that there are times I can't tell when it's really happening, and when I'm only dreaming about it.

Like now, for instance. For a dream, this one felt pretty realistic.

I was clinging to the wooden railing of an old-fashioned sailing ship. High winds whipped my dark hair, causing loose tendrils to stick wetly to my face and neck. They tugged at the long white skirt of the silk ball gown in which I'd somehow become dressed, tangling it around my legs, making it hard for me to keep my footing on the rain and salt spray-slickened surface of the deck.

The sky above me was black as night . . . except when lightning sliced through the thick dark clouds, revealing the frighteningly whitecapped ocean waves crashing against the ship's hull below me, churned by a violent storm.

My heart pounded as I held the railing, but not with fear for my own safety. I knew I could turn around and go below, where it was warm and dry. Only I didn't want to. Because every time another bolt of lightning illuminated the sky, I saw *him* in the water, being cast about like a piece of driftwood. With every surge of the rough waves, he was pulled farther and farther out to sea, away from the boat.

Away from me.

"John," I cried. My voice was hoarse with emotion, and from overuse. It seemed as if I'd been screaming his name for hours, but no one would come to our aid. It was just us, and the storm, and the seething sea.

"Swim," I begged him. "Just *swim* to me."

For a moment it seemed as if he was going to make it. He was close enough to the side of the ship that I could see the single-minded determination in those gray eyes, mingled with the fear each of us was trying not to show the other. His strong, muscular arms rose from the ink-black water as he tried desperately to make his way back to the side of the ship.

For every stroke he took forward, however, the angry waves pushed him another two strokes back.

I looked around frantically for a rope, something, anything, to throw to him, but there was none. So instead I leaned out as far as I could, reaching down to him with one hand while gripping the railing with the other.

"I can pull you up," I assured him. "Just take my hand."

He shook his head, his dark hair slick with rain and seawater.

"I don't want to take you with me." His voice was as deep and rough as the ocean. "I'd rather die than let you die."

I'd rather die than let you die.

This made no sense. John Hayden *was* Death. He couldn't die. And every single one of his previous actions had indicated that he most certainly *did* want to take me with him, to the Underworld, over which he ruled. Why else had I spent so much time running from him?

Persephone, the girl in the myth the ancient Greeks used to explain the seasons, hadn't run fast enough from Hades, the Greek god of death, so he was able to chase her down in his chariot when he came across her hanging out with some nymphs in a field one day, and take her to the Underworld to be his queen.

Persephone was lucky. Her mother happened to be Demeter, the goddess of the harvest. Demeter went on strike, refusing to allow anything on earth to grow until her daughter was released. What fun is it being a god or goddess if all the humans are too busy starving to death to worship you? Hades was forced to let Persephone go, and after the longest winter imaginable, springtime finally blossomed across the land.

In reality, spring doesn't come because of some girl being released from the Underworld. It comes because of the earth moving into the astronomical vernal equinox.

But I get it. People have always been desperate for stories that explain why bad things happen to good people, myths with happy endings to give them hope. They don't want to know that when we die, what lies beyond may not be all harps and halos. No one wants to listen to someone like me, who comes back from the dead and says, "Hey, guess what? All that stuff they've been telling us is a load of bull." It's more comforting to trust the storytellers, to believe that fairy tales really do come true.

Still, when John said that thing in my dream about how he'd rather die than let me die, even though I knew that could never be, I realized something: *I* wanted to believe in the fairy tales, too. My subconscious — just like all the doctors had tried to reassure my mother — had worked out the resolution to a problem that had been bothering me for a long time. What I really wanted was to run *towards* John, not away from him.

Only now that I'd finally realized it, he was about to drown.

No wonder my heart gave a lurch like it was my own life I was watching disappear right in front of me.

"Take my hand," I begged him.

I sounded like someone possessed. I *was* possessed, with the fear of watching the sea swallow him up before my eyes. It figured that the minute I'd finally admitted to myself how much I loved him, I was about to lose him. Maybe this was my karmic punishment for having taken so long to figure it out.

A wave lifted him, as if in answer to my prayers, and suddenly, miraculously, he was so close, our fingers touched.

The look in his eyes turned into something like hope. I leaned out even farther to grasp his wrist, feeling his hand lock around mine. I smiled, overwhelmed with love and joy, daring to believe he was safe, and the ending to my own story might be a happy one after all.

Then from out of nowhere came another one of those powerful swells . . .

. . . and I saw the hope in his eyes die.

"Don't let go!" I shouted, knowing in my heart that this was exactly what he would do. Even as I said the words, I felt his fingers loosen from around my wrist. He was releasing me on purpose, not wanting to pull me down into the cold waves with him. . . .

A second later he was ripped away from me by a wave so big, it tossed him like a toy. I screamed his name, clinging to the wooden rail, my tears indistinguishable from the rain pelting my face, a hole as big as the sea seeming to split open inside me. Only when lightning streaked the sky did I see him again, a tiny, shadowy figure crested atop a swell a dozen yards away. He raised an arm as if to say good-bye.

Then the water closed over him. I was alone in the storm, and he was gone forever.

And round about I moved my rested eyes,
Uprisen erect, and steadfastly I gazed,
To recognise the place wherein I was.
DANTE ALIGHIERI, *Inferno*, Canto IV

My pulse still pounding from the dream, I opened my eyes. My hair was stuck damply to my face and neck, my fingers so tightly clenched into fists that it hurt when I tried to straighten them.

Wait. It *had* been a dream, right?

If so, then why, when I licked my lips, did I taste salt water? And why did that slant of light filtering through my bedroom curtains look so unfamiliar?

Because they weren't my bedroom curtains, I realized. The curtains in my bedroom weren't long and white and ghostly. They didn't hang from ornately carved stone arches. There wasn't a stone arch to be found in the house my mom had bought in a gated community in Isla Huesos, where we'd just moved from Connecticut, thanks to my parents' divorce being finalized and

7

my expulsion from the Westport Academy for Girls for decidedly unladylike behavior.

Nor would Mom's decorator have chosen medieval-looking tapestries picturing satyrs chasing half-clad nymphs around as a design motif.

That's what lined the wall opposite the stone arches, though, as well as sconces lit by actual flames. . . .

No way would Mom have okayed those (total fire hazard), *or* the enormous four-poster canopy bed in which I lay.

It wasn't until a deep, masculine voice said my name — in a voice so loud, I startled — that I realized I wasn't in the bed alone.

"Pierce."

The boy from my dream wasn't dead at the bottom of the ocean. He was in the bed next to me. Not only was he in the bed next to me, but he was holding me in his arms. The reason my name had sounded so loud was because my head was resting against his chest.

Which was shirtless.

Mom would *definitely* not have okayed this.

Suddenly, it all came rushing back. Underworld. I was in the *Underworld*.

And this time, I wasn't dead.

I gasped and sat up. Instantly, his strong arms released me.

"It's all right," John said, sitting up as well. His tone was gentle. So were his hands, going to my shoulders to soothe me. As gentle as if I were the bird I'd once watched him bring back to life.

Except that I knew the enormous power behind those callused fingers. I'd seen them stop hearts as easily as they'd started one.

"Pierce, you were having a nightmare," he said.

Nightmare? It took me a second to make the connection — the nightmare from which I'd just woken, about him drowning. He didn't mean the one that was unfolding right now before my disbelieving eyes as I looked down at our legs, entwined on top of the exquisitely embroidered white comforter.

Because while I wasn't wearing anything I'd have chosen for myself — I was dressed in the same kind of long flowing white gown as the nymphs in the tapestries — at least I was fully clothed.

I couldn't say the same for him. He had on jeans — though they were so formfitting, he might as well have been naked. The black denim molded itself to him like a second skin.

Nightmare . . . or quite excellent dream? I guess it depends on how you looked at it. His shirt was many feet away, tossed carelessly across the low white divan by the fireplace.

His bare chest and shoulders were surprisingly tan for someone who'd spent most of the past two hundred years trapped below the surface of the earth, allowed out only for short periods of time in order to commit felonies, such as kidnapping girls (admittedly, he'd done this to protect me from being murdered, but it was still illegal). His skin was the same gold as a lion's coat, just as warm and smooth . . .

. . . a fact to which I could attest only too well, as I'd apparently slept with my face pressed against it all night long.

I'd also been weeping against it, if there was any truth to his next statement.

"You were crying," he said, smoothing some of my dark hair from my forehead. "Do you want to tell me about it?"

"Not really," I said, feeling mortified as I remembered all those times my mother had mentioned my crying in my sleep. I lifted a wrist to wipe my cheeks. He was right. They were wet.

Crying in my sleep in front of him. *About* him. Great.

I knew I had bigger things to worry about — so big, I didn't know how I was ever even going to begin to deal with them — but I had never spent the night with a boy before. Then again, I'd never been in love with any boy but him.

I'd been wrong about his skin. When I looked more closely, I realized it wasn't entirely gold. There were fine, pale lines criss-crossing it here and there. What *were* those lines? A closer inspection was going to be necessary.

"You know you don't have to worry about her anymore, don't you, Pierce?" he asked, his dark brows lowered with concern. "I know it will take awhile to sink in, but you really are safe here with me. It was just a dream."

I wished I could share his confidence. I knew from experience that though dreams don't leave scars — at least not ones that anyone can see — they sometimes leave an ache that can prove every bit as painful.

And now that I'd gotten a better look at them, I could see that's what the pale white lines were that occasionally crisscrossed the otherwise golden skin of his body: scars from long-healed wounds.

I bit my lip. I knew who'd inflicted those wounds, and why. It was one of those worries that felt too big for me to deal with right then. Remembering the monster from which he'd saved me — more frightening than any ocean swell — by sweeping me from the cafeteria of my new school in Isla Huesos and bringing me to his world, I realized I was probably going to have post-traumatic stress for life. How does someone deal with finding out that her own grandmother hates her so much that she's tried to kill her . . . *twice*?

Apparently, she dreams about her boyfriend drowning right in front of her, then gets a little distracted from that dream when she wakes to find him tantalizingly shirtless on top of the bed beside her.

"But other people got hurt besides me," I said, as much to remind myself of this fact as him. "Do you really think bringing me here is going to make them just . . . *stop*?"

Because the rest of my worries were about precisely this.

"I don't know," he admitted, dipping his head to press his mouth to the back of my neck. I felt an immediate *zing* all along my veins, like his lips were carbonated or something. "This is the first time I've ever been in love with a girl who the Furies were trying to kill. But I do know there's nothing you can do to stop them. This is exactly where you belong. Where you've *always* belonged. And where I hope you'll consider staying . . . this time."

This time. Right.

"Well," I said. *Love.* He *loved* me. Hearing that word fall so casually from his lips might help a little with the post-traumatic stress. "This is certainly better than world history, which is where I'd be sitting if I were back in Isla Huesos right now." If school hadn't been canceled due to the giant hurricane bearing down on the island, anyway.

"History was a subject in which I was particularly good in school," he assured me, his mouth sliding down my throat, towards the gold links of the necklace he'd given me.

"I don't doubt it," I said.

"I can tutor you," he said, continuing to press kisses to my throat, "so you don't fall behind."

"Wow, thanks," I said. "That's such a relief."

He laughed. I wasn't sure, but it might have been the first time I'd ever heard him do so. It was a good laugh, throaty and rich.

The only problem — well, not the *only* problem, because there were *many* problems, I was quickly realizing, with our situation — was that he was wrong. Not about world history, obviously. I was certain he'd be good at anything he tried. I meant about the Furies.

I was never going to believe there wasn't a way to stop the evil spirits — angered by where they'd been sent after passing through the Underworld, and who'd managed to return there — determined to seek vengeance on John . . . as if where they'd ended up was *his* fault, and not their own.

But when John's merest touch sent my blood fizzing as if I'd just downed a six-pack of soda, it was hard to concentrate, particularly on forming an argument with him about the Furies, or whether or not it was true the Underworld was "exactly" where I belonged.

If that were true, that meant other things had to be true, as well . . . like that my grandmother was possessed by one of those Furies, and that she really had wanted to kill me for the sole purpose of causing John pain.

This was no foundation on which to build a lasting relationship. It wasn't as if my parents were going to like him much, either, if they ever got the chance to meet him. I wasn't sure my dad would consider *any* guy good enough for me, but a death deity who'd kidnapped me from my school cafeteria — even to protect me from Grandma — was never going to be high on his list.

And what about what Richard Smith, the sexton of the Isla Huesos Cemetery, had said to me that rainy day in his office about why John might have given me the necklace Hades had forged for Persephone?

Clearly there had to have been some kind of mistake. Persephone had been the daughter of Zeus and Demeter, and the goddess of springtime. I'd been kicked out of one of the most exclusive girls' schools on the East Coast for assault, my GPA was marginal at best, and I was probably the only seventeen-year-old girl in the entire state of Florida who'd yet to pass her driver's license exam. How did any of that qualify me for the position of Queen of the Underworld?

Persephone and I did have something in common, however. Our boyfriends had the same job . . .

. . . a reality that was impossible to ignore when the deep, sad sound of a marina horn cut through the stillness of the morning air. I recognized it immediately from my last visit to his home, and knew all too well what it signified.

"They're waiting for me down at the beach," John said with a groan, dropping his head to the indentation between my neck and shoulder.

These words chilled me far more than any nightmare ever could. *They*, I knew, were the souls of the dead, who gathered by the shore of a massive underground lake just on the other side of the walled courtyard beyond the stone arches, to wait for the boats that would ferry them to their final destination. . . .

John was the person who decided which boat they would board. The horn I'd heard signaled that a boat was arriving to pick up the latest batch of passengers.

I shivered, feeling suddenly cold. A dankness seemed to cling to every of inch of my body, despite the fire in the hearth and the warm tenderness of his touch. He must have noticed, since he reached for my hand and pressed it against his naked heart.

"Pierce," he said, as if I'd wounded him somehow. "Don't look like that."

"I didn't mean to." I felt foolish. But I couldn't help remembering my last visit to his world, when I'd been one of those souls, waiting on that beach to be sorted. "It's not your fault. It's just . . . that *horn*."

He kissed the palm of my hand. "I'm sorry," he said. All the laughter was gone, both from his eyes and his voice. "Sorry for all of this — sorry for your nightmares, sorry for what your mother must be going through, not knowing where you are, and sorry most of all for the times when I . . . well, when I didn't behave around you as I ought to have. You weren't far from wrong last night when you called me . . . what was it? Oh, right. A wild thing." The entreaty in his eyes was difficult to resist. "But you know I only ever acted that way when you were putting yourself in danger . . . or when you were acting as if you didn't care about me."

With the hand that wasn't holding mine, he reached up to trace the links of the gold necklace I wore around my neck.

"For so long, I thought you hated me," he went on, his eyes hooded by his long, dark lashes. They were completely wasted on a boy. "If I had known that you never stopped wearing this after I gave it to you, I might have been a little less . . . agitated."

I felt myself blush, and not only because his wandering fingers had strayed dangerously close to the neckline of my gown, seeming to search for my own heart.

"Well, I think you've figured out by now that I never hated you," I said, steering his hand firmly to the less intimate territory of my waist. "And I know you didn't mean to be so wild then, John. I'm not sure about now. . . ."

My primness brought a smile back to his lips. With his heavily muscled frame, those scars, and that long dark hair that had a tendency to fall into those absurdly light eyes, I was certain few girls would have called him handsome, much less cute.

I was equally certain, however, there wasn't a single girl my age who'd have been able to resist him. There was something so ruthlessly masculine about him that it was impossible not to feel a kind of magnetic attraction.

Especially when he smiled. Smiling, he went from the brooding juvenile delinquent the girls back at Isla Huesos High School might have whispered about, to the misunderstood hottie they'd definitely have slipped their number if he'd asked for it . . . and maybe more.

I couldn't help feeling as if in escaping with him to the Underworld to avoid being killed, I'd gotten myself into a whole different level of trouble.

"Pierce, I know how many questions you must have," he said. "And I swear I'll answer them all — the ones I can, anyway — as soon as I get back. But for now, just know that I mean to — I'm *going* to — make this place feel like home to you, if you'll give me the chance."

Home? The *Underworld*? A gigantic underground cavern where the sun never shines, wracked by perpetual damp, to which dead people show up every five minutes?

I raised my eyebrows. "Okay. But first, maybe we should talk about —"

Boundaries. That's what I meant to say. But he distracted me again.

"I know you never liked school," he went on, the corners of his mouth still irresistibly turned up, "or you wouldn't have gotten yourself thrown out of your last one. I know, I know . . . that was mostly my fault." He grinned down at me. I don't know what he was finding so amusing. He certainly hadn't been laughing about what had happened with my study hall teacher at the time. "But anyway, there's no school here. You'll like that. But there's still plenty here with which to entertain yourself while I'm working. I can get you all the books you need to graduate from high school, since I know that's what you said you wanted. In the meantime, there are all *my* books. . . ."

I'd seen his books. Almost all of them had been written before his birth, which had been more than a century and a half before mine. Many of them were books of love poems. He'd tried to read to me from one of them the night before, in order to cheer me up.

It hadn't worked.

I thought it more polite to say "Thank you, John," than "Do you have any books that aren't about love? And young couples expressing that love? Because I do not need encouragement in that direction right now."

"And you have this whole castle to explore," he said, an eager light in his eyes. "The gardens are beautiful. . . ."

I glanced skeptically at the billowing white curtains. I'd already seen the gardens outside them. Deathly black lilies and poisonous-looking mushrooms *were* beautiful, in their own way, especially to people like my mother, an environmental biologist who had a fondness for exotic plants and trees.

But I'd always preferred ordinary flowers, like daisies — the kind that grew wild, not cultivated in a garden. What chance did a poor, wild daisy have against a sophisticated black lily?

The night before, when I'd still been determined to escape and had tried to climb the garden walls, I'd seen that John's castle was on a little island, surrounded by water. There were no boats to cross it. Even if I could find one, the only place to go was the next island. That was the one where he worked, though. And there was no way to get from there to where I wanted to go, back to the land of the living.

"But you should know I've told my men that if they do see you anywhere you're not supposed to be, they're to bring you straight to me." Had he read my thoughts? He must have noticed the owlish look I gave him, since he added, his voice growing hard, "Pierce, it's for your own good. There are dangers here that you —"

"You told me there's no one here who can hurt me," I interrupted. "You said I'm safe here."

"You're *safer*, because I can protect you," John said. "But you have a heartbeat, and you're in the land of the dead —"

"*You* have a heartbeat," I pointed out. I'd felt it beating, as strong and steady as my own, beneath my hand. He certainly seemed fit for someone who was supposed to have died so many years earlier, not to mention so violently in my dream.

"Yes," he said. "But that's different. I'm . . . Mr. Smith already told you what I am."

I thought it strange that he didn't want to say the words *death deity* out loud. It wasn't like I hadn't noticed he had gifts that were unlike a normal nineteen-year-old boy's.

Then again, I was having communication difficulties of my own, so maybe we were even. I decided to drop it.

"So Furies can find me here, too?" I asked instead.

"They can," he admitted, sounding more like himself again. "But it will be much harder for them to attack you in a fortified castle in the Underworld than in your high-school cafeteria. Still, even with me around, *and* a necklace that warns when Furies are coming," he added, tugging on the chain I wore around my neck so that the large round diamond at the end of it slipped from the bodice of my gown, then tumbled into his palm, "that doesn't mean you're invincible, Pierce, whatever you might like to think."

I sucked in my breath defensively. "But Mr. Smith said —"

"Mr. Smith is a fine cemetery sexton," he said, holding the diamond up so that it caught the light filtering in from outside the stone arches. Whenever John was around, the stone glowed a deep silver gray, the same color as his eyes, but when people like my grandmother, who definitely did not have my best intentions at heart, were present, it turned a warning shade of black. "And I'll admit he's been better at his job than any of his predecessors. But if he's got you under the impression that just because this necklace was forged by Hades to warn Persephone when Furies were present, it also has the power to defeat them, you're wrong. Nothing can defeat them. *Nothing*. Believe me, I've tried everything."

His scars were testament enough to that.

Imagining what he must have endured — and remembering what he had gone through in my dream — caused tears to gather under my eyelashes. One of them escaped and began to trickle down my cheek before I could wipe it away without him noticing.

"Pierce," he said, looking alarmed. Nothing seemed to discomfit him more than the sight of my tears. "Don't *cry*."

"I'm not," I lied. "I've seen what the Furies have done to you, and it's so unfair. There's got to be a way to stop them. There's *got* to be. And in the meantime, can't I at least go back to warn my mom about what's going on? Even if it's only for five minutes —"

His expression darkened. "Pierce," he said. "We talked about this. Your mother is in no danger. But *you* are. It's too risky right now."

"I know, but I've never been away from her for this long without her knowing where I am. She's got to be freaking out. And what about my cousin Alex? You know he lives with my grandmother, and now that Uncle Chris is in jail, Alex will be with my grandmother *all alone* —"

"*No*, Pierce," John said, so sharply I jumped.

Thunder crashed, seemingly directly overhead. Technically, where we were — hundreds of miles beneath the earth's crust — there shouldn't have been any meteorological phenomena. But it was one of John's many special gifts that, when he felt something very deeply, he could make thunder — and lightning — appear . . . with his mind.

I blinked at him. He might have liked to believe otherwise, but it was clear the wild part of him was far from tamed. And as much as John might have wanted to pretend that this place was my home, it wasn't.

The palace was a prison. He was the warden . . . even if he was a warden who was only holding me captive for the best of reasons, to keep me safe from my own relatives.

"You don't need to shake the place down," I said reprovingly. "A simple *no* will suffice."

He looked a little sheepish. When he spoke again, it was in a much gentler tone.

"I'm sorry. Force of habit." He gave me another one of his heart-stopping smiles, then extended his palms. "I know something that will make you feel better."

If I hadn't been looking down at that exact moment, I wouldn't have believed my eyes. I'd have thought he'd made a sleight of hand, pulled it from his sleeve like a magician.

He wasn't wearing any sleeves, though, and he was no magician. He'd almost killed two men in my presence using nothing but his fingertips. He traveled back and forth between two dimensions, his world and mine, far more easily than other people commuted to and from work, because he didn't need to use public transportation, or even a car. He just blinked, and *poof.* It was done.

"There," he said. "What do you think?"

As turtle-doves, called onward by desire,
With open and steady wings to the sweet nest
Fly through the air by their volition borne.
DANTE ALIGHIERI, *Inferno*, Canto V

I . . . I don't understand," I said, looking down at the small white creature that nestled in his hands.

"She's for you," John explained, still smiling. "To keep you company when I'm away. I know how you love birds."

He was right about that. I had a weakness for animals of any kind, especially the sick and injured. It was how John and I had met, in the Isla Huesos Cemetery, when he'd come across me weeping inconsolably over a wounded bird. I'd been all of seven years old, but he'd been exactly the same as he was now — the age at which he'd died and become the death deity of the Underworld beneath Isla Huesos.

In an effort to stop my childish tears, he'd taken the bird's limp body from me. A second later, it had flown off, its life magically restored by him.

How could either of us have known then that it was my grand-mother who had purposefully injured the creature, using it to lure me into meeting John not only that first time, but a second time, as well?

That second time, since I had been fifteen and not a child, a different kind of magic had occurred . . . the kind that can happen between any two people who find themselves attracted to each other.

The only problem was, that time it had been me, and not the bird, who'd died. And it was here, in the Underworld, that we'd encountered each other.

Back then, I'd been much too frightened of this place — and of him, and of my feelings for him — to think of staying.

Everything was different now, I realized. Now I only felt frightened of losing him the way I had in my terrible nightmare . . .

. . . and of how quickly he was able to banish that feeling with his kisses, the way he had when I'd woken in his arms. But that fear was a whole other issue.

I guess, considering our history, I could hardly blame him for believing that a pet bird would banish all my fears. The bird in his hands now looked very much like the one from the day we'd met . . . some kind of dove, but with black feathers beneath her wings and tail. My mother would have known exactly what type of bird she was, of course. It was from her that I'd inherited my love for animals.

"Is this the same bird . . . ?" I let my voice trail off. Doves don't live that long, do they? This one looked as bright-eyed and alert as the one that day in the cemetery. She was even cooing softly.

Unlike that day in the cemetery, however, when John uncupped his hands, this bird didn't instantly unfold her wings and fly away. She stood and peered about, taking in her surroundings, including me. I couldn't help letting out a soft "Ooh!" of delight.

John smiled, pleased that his gift was a success.

"No, that was a wild bird that returned to its mate after we released it. This one is tame, see?" He held out his finger, and the bird butted her face against it, smoothing her feathers. "But she does look a little like that bird, which is why I thought you'd like her. Why? Would you prefer a wild bird?" His eyebrows constricted. "I could find one for you. But then it would have to stay in a cage to keep it from flying away. I didn't think you'd like that. . . ."

"No," I said hastily. I wouldn't like that. Then there'd be two of us who were prisoners.

But I thought it better not to say this second part out loud.

"That's good," John said, holding the bird towards me. "You'll have to think of a name for her."

"A name?" I stretched out a finger, as John had done, to see if the bird would rub her head against it. "I've never named an animal before. I wasn't allowed to have any pets growing up. My father always said he was allergic."

Now John's eyebrows lifted. "Allergic? Even to birds?"

"Well," I said, thinking of the oil spill my dad's company was responsible for, and had recently had to clean up. "Allergies are sometimes an excuse he uses for anything messy he doesn't want to have to deal with."

Instead of rubbing my finger with her head, the bird stretched out her wings, fluttered them a few times, then flew away. I let out a cry of dismay, thinking that she wasn't as tame as John had thought, and that she was going to escape.

She flew only as far as the other end of the room, however, landing on the back of one of the thronelike chairs positioned on either side of the long dining table.

"She's hungry," John said, with a grin. "You must be, too. Breakfast is waiting. I'm sorry I don't have time to eat with you before I go, but I think you'll find everything here you need. . . ."

For the first time since waking, I noticed that something in the room where I'd fallen asleep was different, besides the fact that there was a boy on the bed with me. The table was covered in silver platters laden with fruit of every variety; plates of perfectly crisp toast dripping with butter; golden brown muffins arrayed in ivory baskets; soft boiled eggs sitting in jeweled cups; icy pitchers of juice; and pots of aromatic tea and coffee. They had all appeared as magically as if brought by an invisible waitstaff.

"John," I murmured, rising from the bed and going to stand by the table, staring down in astonishment at the gold-rimmed china plates and intricately embroidered napkins in sapphire rings. "How did all of this get here?"

"Oh," he said casually. "It just does. Coffee?" He lifted a gleaming silver pot. "Or do I seem to remember you being more partial to tea?" His grin was wicked.

I gave him a sarcastic look — it was a cup of tea I'd thrown into his face to escape from the Underworld the last time — then sank down into the chair where the bird was perched. I realized I was starving. I'd had nothing to eat since lunch the day before. And even then, I hadn't eaten very much due to having gotten some bad news: Furies had murdered my guidance counselor, Jade.

Though I looked for them, I didn't see any pomegranates amongst the ripe pieces of fruit piled high in silver bowls at the center of the table. Gleaming strawberries, glowing peaches, and glistening grapes. But not a single piece of the fruit Persephone ate that — at least according to the version of the myth we'd been taught back at the Westport Academy for Girls — supposedly doomed her to an eternity in the realm of the dead . . .

Even before meeting John, I'd often wondered if Persephone had eaten those six pomegranate seeds on purpose, knowing that for six months of every year for the rest of her life, she would have to return to the Underworld — and to Hades, her new husband, of whom her mother Demeter most definitely did not approve.

Pomegranates were considered by the Greeks to be the "fruit of the dead." As a native of Greece, Persephone would have known that.

Maybe life with Hades — even in the Underworld — had been preferable to life with her overprotective mom and those nymphs. Could Persephone simply not have wanted to hurt her mom's feelings by saying so out loud?

It had to be safe to eat all the food on John's table. He wouldn't have offered it if it wasn't.

"Thanks," I said, gratefully accepting the cup of tea. "So you're telling me that a spread like this appears here *every* morning?"

"Yes," he said. "It does. Also one at lunch, and again at dinner."

"But who cooks it?" I asked, imagining an underground kitchen staffed by tiny, invisible chefs. "Who serves it?"

"I don't know," he said, with a disinterested shrug.

I couldn't help laughing. "John, food magically appears here three times a day, and you don't know where it comes from? You've been here for almost two hundred years. Haven't you ever tried to find out?"

He shot me a sarcastic look of his own. "Of course. I have theories. I think it's part of the compensation for the job I do, since there isn't any pay. But there's room and board. Anything I've ever wanted or needed badly enough usually appears, eventually. For instance" — he sent one of those of those knee-melting smiles in my direction — "you."

I swallowed. The smile made it astonishingly hard to follow the conversation, even though I was the one who'd started it. "Compensation from whom?"

He shrugged again. It was clear this was something he didn't care to discuss. "I have passengers waiting. For now, here." He lifted the lid of a platter. "I highly recommend these."

I don't know what I expected to see when I looked down . . . a big platter of pomegranates? Of course that wasn't it at all.

"Waffles?" I stared at the fluffy perfection of the stack before me. "None of this makes any sense."

He looked surprised. "Is there something you want that isn't here? Simply name it."

"It's not that," I said. "It's just . . . you *eat.*"

He hadn't joined me at the table since the horn from the marina had sounded again, and he'd sunk down onto the couch instead to put on his boots. But he'd grabbed a piece of toast, downing it as he did up his laces. "Of course I eat," he said, around the toast. "Why wouldn't I eat?"

"I've seen the crypt where your bones are buried on Isla Huesos," I pointed out. "It says 'Hayden' — your last name — right above the door."

He looked very much as if he was willing a change in the topic of conversation.

"What of it?" he asked tersely.

"Why do you need to eat if you're dead?" I asked, the questions bursting from me as I ate. "How can you have a heartbeat, for that matter? Why is there a Coffin Night for you back on Isla Huesos when you not only have a crypt, but you seem very much alive to me? What did you do to end up in this job, anyway?"

"Pierce," he said in a weary voice. He'd pulled a black tablet from his pocket and was typing swiftly into it. I recognized it as the same device he'd used the day I'd shown up at the lake, to look up my name and find out which boat I was supposed to be on . . . a boat he'd then made sure I'd missed. "I know I said I'd answer your questions, but I was hoping to make it to the end of the day without you hating me."

"John," I said. I got up and went to sit next to him on the couch. "You could never do anything to make me hate you. What is that?" I nodded at the device in his hands. "Can I have one?"

"Definitely not," he said flatly, putting it back in his pocket. "And I remember a time when you most definitely did hate me." He stood up. He'd been intimidatingly tall in his bare feet, but in his work boots, he towered above me. "That's why I'm not discussing my past . . . at least for now. Maybe later, when you . . ." He broke off whatever he'd been about to say, and finished instead with, "Maybe later."

I felt my heart sink, then chided myself for it. What had I thought, that John was some type of angel who'd gotten the job as a reward for good behavior? He'd certainly never displayed angelic-like behavior around me . . . except when he'd been saving my life.

What did someone have to do to become a death deity, anyway? Something bad, obviously. But not *so* bad that they got sent straight to wherever it was truly evil people, like child murderers, ended up. From what I knew about John, being a death deity seemed to require a strong character, swift fists, a willingness to adhere to a certain set of principles, and a basic sense of telling right from wrong. . . .

But could it also require something I hadn't considered? Something *not* so desirable?

"You can't have any worse skeletons in your closet than I do," I said, with a forced note of cheeriness in my voice, watching him pull a fresh black shirt from a wicker hamper. "After all, you've met my grandmother."

He pulled the shirt over his head, so I couldn't see his naked chest anymore, which was both a good and bad thing. But I also couldn't see his expression as he replied, in a hard voice, "Be thankful everyone in my family is dead, so you'll never have to meet them."

"Oh. I . . . I'm sorry," I said. I'd forgotten the terrible price he'd had to pay for immortality . . . like watching everyone he'd ever loved grow old and die. "That . . . that must have been awful for you."

"No, it wasn't," he said, simply. His shirt on, he turned to look at me, and I was startled by the bleakness of his expression. "In a way, you're lucky, Pierce. At least your grandmother is possessed by a Fury, so you know why she's so hateful. There's no explanation for why the people in my family were such monsters."

I was so shocked, I didn't know how to respond. People aren't supposed to say those kinds of things about their families.

The important thing was to forgive, my father had once told me. Only then could we move forward. . . .

"Except my mother," John added. From the same hamper he'd drawn the shirt, he pulled out a leather wristband, covered in some lethal-looking metal studs, and began to fasten it . . . a safety precaution of his profession, I supposed. Some departed souls needed more encouraging than others to move on. "She was the only one I . . . well, it doesn't matter now. But she was the only one who ever cared. And so she was the only one I ever missed."

Oh, *God*. My mother. I hadn't thought about it before, but suddenly the reality of my situation sank in: I was going to have to watch my *mother* get old and die.

Although, even people who weren't trapped in the Underworld had to face that burden . . . watching their parents age and inevitably die. The difference was, those people aged along *with* their parents. Together they enjoyed the holidays, went on vacations, helped one another through the hard times and celebrated the good.

Was I ever going to get to do any of those things? Could lords of the Underworld and their consorts even *have* children? I was pretty sure I'd read that Hades and Persephone had never reproduced. How could they? Life couldn't grow in a place of death. Even the plants in John's garden, exotic as they were, were a bit gloomy looking . . . not from lack of care, but because mushrooms and black flowers were the only flora that seemed to thrive in a place constantly shaded from the light of the sun.

Still, if John was going to continue to rain down spine-shattering kisses on my neck and roam around without a shirt, I needed to make sure that was really true about Hades and Persephone. I didn't know how much longer my resistance to his charms was going to hold out, especially after that dream. The last thing I needed was an accidental pregnancy resulting in a demon Underworld baby. My life had already gotten complicated enough.

What I was starting to think I needed more than anything was my own bedroom.

"Well," I said, trying to keep my tone light as I walked over to put my arms around his neck, though I had to stand on my toes to do so. "That wasn't so bad, was it? You told me something about yourself that I didn't know before — that you didn't, er, care for your family, except for your mother. But that didn't make me hate you . . . it made me love you a bit more, because now I know we have even more in common."

He stared down at me, a wary look in his eyes. "If you knew the truth," he said, "you wouldn't be saying that. You'd be running."

"Where would I go?" I asked, with a laugh I hoped didn't sound as nervous to him as it did to me. "You bolted all the doors, remember? Now, since you shared something I didn't know about you, may I share something you don't know about me?"

Those dark eyebrows rose as he pulled me close. "I can't even begin to imagine what this could be."

"It's just," I said, "that I'm a little worried about rushing into this consort thing . . . especially the cohabitation part."

"Cohabitation?" he echoed. He was clearly unfamiliar with the word.

"*Cohabitation* means living together," I explained, feeling my cheeks heat up. "Like married people."

"You said last night that these days no one your age thinks of getting married," he said, holding me even closer and suddenly looking much more eager to stick around for the conversation, even though I heard the marina horn blow again. "And that your father would never approve it. But if you've changed your mind, I'm sure I could convince Mr. Smith to perform the ceremony —"

"No," I said hastily. Of course Mr. Smith was somehow authorized to marry people in the state of Florida. Why not? I decided not to think about that right now, or how John had come across this piece of information. "That isn't what I meant. My mom would kill me if I got married before I graduated from high school."

Not, of course, that my mom was going to know about any of this. Which was probably just as well, since her head would explode at the idea of my moving in with a guy before I'd even applied to college, let alone at the fact that I most likely wasn't *going* to college. Not that there was any school that would have accepted me with my grades, not to mention my disciplinary record.

"What I meant was that maybe we should take it more slowly," I explained. "The past couple years, while all my friends were going out with boys, I was home, trying to figure out how this necklace you gave me worked. I wasn't exactly dating."

"Pierce," he said. He wore a slightly quizzical expression on his face. "Is this the thing you think I didn't know about you? Because for one thing, I do know it, and for another, I don't understand why you think I'd have a problem with it."

I'd forgotten he'd been born in the eighteen hundreds, when the only time proper ladies and gentlemen ever spent together before they were married was at heavily chaperoned balls . . . and that for most of the past two centuries, he'd been hanging out in a cemetery.

Did he even know that these days, a lot of people hooked up on first dates, or that the average age at which girls — and boys as well — lost their virginity in the United States was seventeen . . . *my age*?

Apparently not.

"What I'm trying to say," I said, my cheeks burning brighter, "is that I'm not very experienced with men. So this morning when I woke up and found you in bed beside me, while it was really, super nice — don't get me wrong, I enjoyed it very much — it kind of freaked me out. Because I don't know if I'm ready for that kind of thing yet." Or maybe the problem was that I wasn't prepared for *how* ready I was. . . .

"Ready for —?" He broke off, and then frowned as if it had all become clear. "Wait." He dropped his arms from around my waist and took a step away from me. "You think I spent the night with you?"

"Didn't you?" I blinked back at him. "There's only the one bed. And . . . well, you were in it when I woke up."

Thunder boomed overhead. It wasn't as loud as the violent cracks that had occurred in my dream. Although the rumbles were long enough — and intense enough — that the silverware on the table began to make an eerie tinkling sound.

And my bird, who'd been calmly cleaning herself on the back of my chair, suddenly took off, seeking shelter on the highest bookshelf against the far wall.

I realized I'd just insulted my host, and no joke was going to get me out of it this time.

"For your information, Pierce," John said, his tone almost disturbingly calm — but his eyes flashed the same shade as the stone around my neck, which had gone the color of the metal studs at his wrists — "I spent most of last night on the couch. Until one point early this morning, when I heard you call my name. You were crying in your sleep."

The salt water I'd tasted on my lips. Not due to rain from a violent hurricane, but from the tears I'd shed, watching him die in front of me.

"Oh," I said uncomfortably. "John, I'm so —"

It turned out he wasn't finished.

"I put my arms around you to *try to comfort you*, because I know what this place can be like, at least at first. It's not exactly hell, but it's the next closest place to it. You wouldn't let go of me. You held on to me like you were drowning, and I was your only lifeline."

I swallowed, astonished at how close he'd come to describing my dream . . . except it had been the other way around. I'd been *his* lifeline; only he'd let go of me, sacrificing himself so that I could live.

"Right," I said. "Of course. I'm sorry." I couldn't believe how stupid I'd been, especially since my mother had always worried so much about my talking in my sleep. On the other hand, I *had* been upfront with him about my lack of experience when it came to men. "But this is good, see?" I reached out to take his hand. "I told you I could never hate you —"

He pulled his hand away, exactly like in my dream. Well, not exactly, because he wasn't being sucked from my grasp by a giant ocean swell. Instead, he'd dropped my fingers because he was leaving to go sort the souls of the dead.

"You will," he assured me, bitterly. "You're already regretting your decision to — what was it you called it? Oh, right — cohabitate with me."

"No," I insisted. "I'm not. All I said was that I want to take things more slowly —"

That had nothing to do with him — it had to do with *me* and my fear of not being able to control myself when he was kissing me. It was too humiliating to admit that out loud, however.

35

"We can take *things* as slowly as you want, but you know it's too late now to change your mind, Pierce," he said, in a warning tone.

"Of course," I said. I could see I had approached this all wrong. Where, when you actually needed one, was one of those annoying women's magazines with advice on how to handle your man? Although that advice probably didn't apply to death deities. "Because the Furies are after me. And I promised you that I wouldn't try to escape. That isn't what I was —"

"No," he said, with an abrupt shake of his head. "The Furies have no part in this. It doesn't matter anymore whether or not you try to escape." He was pacing the length of the room. A muscle had begun to twitch wildly in the side of his jaw. "I thought you knew. I thought you understood. Haven't you read Homer?"

Not again. Mr. Smith was obsessed with this Homer person, too.

"No, John," I said, with forced patience. "I'm afraid we don't have time to study the ancient Greek poets in school anymore because we have so much stuff to learn that happened since you died, such as the Civil War and the Holocaust and making files in Excel —"

"Well, considering what they had to say about the Fates," John interrupted, impatiently, "Homer might possibly have been of more use to you."

"The Fates?" The Fates were something I dimly remembered having been mentioned in the section we'd studied on Greek mythology. They were busybodies who presided over everyone's destiny. "What did Homer have to say about them?"

John dragged a hand through his hair. For some reason, he wouldn't meet my gaze. "The Fates decreed that anyone who ate or drank in the realm of the dead had to remain there for all eternity."

I stared at him. "Right," I said. "Only if they ate pomegranate seeds, like Persephone. The fruit of the dead."

He stopped pacing suddenly and lifted his gaze to mine. His eyes seemed to burn through to my soul.

"Pomegranate seeds are what Persephone happened to eat while she was in the Underworld," he said. "*That*'s why they call them the fruit of the dead. But the rule is *any* food or drink."

A strange feeling of numbness had begun to spread across my body. My mouth became too dry for me to speak.

"However you feel about me, Pierce," he went on, relentlessly, "you're stuck here with me for the rest of eternity."

O blind cupidity, O wrath insane,
That spurs us onward so in our short life,
And in the eternal then so badly steeps us!
DANTE ALIGHIERI, *Inferno*, Canto XII

I didn't hate him.

After the way the sight of him being carried away by that wave in my dream had gutted me, I knew I'd never be able to hate him.

Check yourself before you wreck yourself. That's the phrase that had been tattooed on my guidance counselor Jade's wrist. I tried always to remember it, not just because she was dead now, and that was partly my fault, but because sometimes when I got angry, bad things happened. People got hurt.

In the past, it had always been John who'd inflicted that pain. This time when I got angry, it was John who got hurt.

Which was probably why, by the time he left, I was the one sobbing on the very same couch where he'd claimed to have spent the night. I wasn't crying because I hated him. I was crying because I hated myself.

"You knew," I'd accused him, when I'd finally found my voice after he'd made his revelation. "And you didn't tell me. The whole time I was sitting there eating all those waffles, you didn't tell me. You . . . you tricked me!"

"I didn't trick you," he'd insisted. "I thought you knew!"

I was quickly discovering that the expensive private school education for which my father had insisted on paying was worthless. All of the information I'd been taught at the Westport Academy for Girls back in Connecticut was either erroneous or useless to me in my current life as the consort of a death deity.

"*You* eat," I'd said to him accusatorily. "I saw you eat. And *you* leave here all the time. I've seen you in Connecticut, in Isla Huesos . . ."

"Did I say you can *never* leave?" he'd demanded.

"No. But —"

"But every time you do, you'll see your friends and family moving on with their lives, while you'll never age, and always have to come back here . . . to me." His tone became embittered. "I can see how thrilled you are by that prospect."

Tears *had* sprung into my eyes — not at the idea of spending eternity with him, but of watching my mother grow old and die before my eyes. I felt weepy every time I thought of it.

Seeing the tears, he'd softened, adding imploringly, "Pierce, you were hungry. You had to eat. If I *had* said something about it, what would you have done . . . gone without food?"

"Yes," I'd said, without thinking. "Of course."

All the softness left him then. Even his shoulders tensed. "You realize you just said you'd rather starve to death than be with me?"

He was right. I'd been so caught up in my own emotions, I hadn't noticed how insensitive I was being to his. I reached for his hand.

"John, I'm sorry. That didn't come out the right way," I said. "What I meant was —"

"I think your meaning was clear," he'd said. Overhead, thunder boomed again, though not as loudly as before. It sounded resigned . . . kind of like his demeanor. "Maybe you're right, and I did trick you. In any case, now you have the answer to your question, don't you . . . why I was the person chosen for this position."

It was hard not to admit that his dark side seemed a little darker than I'd previously suspected.

Still, that didn't change the fact that he'd saved my life when it would have been easier for him not to. Why go to all these lengths to keep me from feeling the pain of death again when he could simply have let me be murdered and be at his side as a spirit? I couldn't believe he was bad . . . not as bad as he seemed to want me to think he was.

"John, I'm sorry for what I said before," I'd said, meaning it. "But you've got to admit it — there isn't anyone . . . any *rational* person — who'd want to live in this place forever if there was the slightest chance they didn't have to."

"That's the difference between you and me, then," he said. I could see that he was trying to act as if he didn't care, but there was a hurt in his eyes that no amount of sardonic posturing could hide. "I *would* want to live in this place forever, if it meant living here with you. And though I suppose that means one of us isn't particularly *rational*, it looks as if I'm getting my wish. So I recommend you get used to the idea, Pierce, and learn to live with it. And me."

A second later, he'd jerked his hand from my fingers, and then — exactly like in my dream — he was gone.

That's when I flung myself onto the couch.

I knew crying was stupid. I hated doing it, and it never solved anything.

I couldn't help it, though. Never mind that thanks to some mysterious beings called the Furies, I was apparently powerless to keep completely innocent people like Jade from being hurt at the hands of monsters like my grandmother. Never mind that thanks to another mysterious force called the Fates, I was apparently going to have to live in the Underworld for all of eternity, just because I'd eaten some waffles.

The thing that hurt the most was that I'd injured John. The weight of *that* knowledge made me cry hardest of all . . .

. . . until I realized a small amount of that weight was literal. And it was sitting on my head.

"*Oh, my God,*" I cried, sitting up.

The bird gave an indignant flutter of her wings, then flew over to the dining table, where she started pecking at crumbs I had left

41

behind. Which was preferable to her trying to make a nest in my hair, I supposed, but not by much.

"Better knock that off," I said, drying my eyes. "Or you'll never be able to leave here, either."

The bird lifted her head to look at me inquisitively, as if determining my moral worth, then turned back to her meal.

That stung. Even though she was right.

I remembered the hopeful expression that had been in John's eyes when he'd given her to me. It had been almost exactly like the one he'd worn when he'd given me the necklace, nearly two years earlier.

She's for you, he'd said. *To keep you company when I'm away. I know how you love birds.*

I knew that by giving this bird to me to care for, he'd been hoping to replace the ache in my heart I felt for everyone I was missing back home. Perhaps he'd hoped to do something else, as well: remind me that *this* was my home now, and that there were those in it who needed caring for even more, perhaps, than the people I'd left behind.

"Maybe," I said to the bird, "I can start by taking care of you, and then move on to taking care of him. He's always needed a bit of caring for, don't you think? Though he's never liked to admit it."

I knew things had gotten bad — *really* bad — if I was talking to a bird. What did it matter, though? There was no one to hear me.

"It can't hurt. And maybe something good will come of it. We can only hope, right?"

On the word *hope*, the bird finally looked up at me, and started cooing.

"Oh, God, no," I said, mortified. "Please don't tell me you want to be called Hope. That's a total cliché for a bird that lives in the Underworld."

The bird lifted her wings and took off down the hall.

I decided I'd better follow her, not because I thought there were any dangers lurking for her in the bathroom (where she was headed, and through which I already knew from experience there were no escape routes), but because I needed to pull myself together, anyway.

I could see why the bird liked it in there. The massive sunken tub was fed by a naturally occurring hot spring — hot water came bubbling out from the bottom — and a steaming waterfall poured constantly from a crevice in the stone ceiling, through which moss and vines grew. Hope — though I refused to call her that, except in my head — fluttered around while I bathed, dipping her head in and out of the water, her coos echoing off the stones.

Really, all I'd hoped to find was a toothbrush, some shampoo, and maybe something to wear other than the dress I'd slept in. Possibly because the Underworld was so uniformly grim, the Fates — or whoever it was that provided the food and other amenities — had decided it was better not to scrimp.

John had said at breakfast that anything he ever wanted or needed badly enough usually appeared. Was that why all the things I needed were right there, smelling heavenly and feeling so soft to the skin? I wanted them, and so they were provided? John certainly didn't strike me as the type to moisturize. And he only ever smelled like the wood that was burning in the fireplace, not orange blossoms and lavender.

Or were those things there because John had wanted me, and so they came along with the package?

Was that the explanation for what I found in the large walk-in closet adjoining the bathroom? On one side were John's clothes, all hung with an orderliness that bordered on the obsessive (unlike the haphazard arrangement of his books).

On the other were dozens of the long flowy white dresses that John liked seeing me in so much. Some were silk and some were cotton, some long-sleeved and some with no sleeves at all, but all of them were exactly my size.

"Great," I said through gritted teeth to the bird. I had nothing against dresses. What I did mind a little was being limited to a choice of nothing *but* dresses. I supposed the wardrobe selection was symptomatic of the time during which John had lived, so it wasn't entirely his fault, since rights between men and women hadn't been so equal back then.

I chose what I thought was the most modern-looking of all the dresses hanging in the closet — there were shoes, too, of every kind. Each fit my foot as snugly as if I'd been measured for it — then found a full-length, gilt-framed mirror in the hallway just off the main room, where the bed and dining table stood. The bird was perched on the frame.

It was no use.

"I really *do* look like Snow White, don't I?" I asked the bird when I saw my reflection.

Well, just because I was dressed like a princess didn't mean I had to act like one . . . or at least, not one who slept all the time. I could act like a brave princess. Maybe even like the ones who escaped from the castles in which they were imprisoned, like Rapunzel or Princess Leia.

"Right?" I said to the bird.

The bird cooed contentedly from her perch. She was probably as aware as I was that John had nailed shut all the doors back to my world.

"Yeah," I said. "Don't even tell me. I already know. Every single one of those princesses ended up marrying either one of their rescuers or their captor, like Belle from *Beauty and the Beast*, and Persephone."

Except unlike Belle, Persephone wasn't fictional. I had her necklace to prove it.

If only she'd left behind some other useful tips on being the consort of the ruler of the Underworld.

Which wasn't why I started going through John's shelves. I was looking for a book on birds so I could figure out what to feed Hope. Which wasn't her name.

His books — which numbered into the hundreds, maybe even thousands — were so poorly organized I figured I might as well start sorting them by category. I was taking his advice, and getting used to it. And him.

If, while organizing his things, I happened to discover something that might be useful for navigating life in the Underworld, or that revealed a little something about John's past, so what?

"I'm new here," I said to Hope. "I don't know the rules."

I did find quite a lot of stuff inside all the boxes John kept scattered around, some of it beautiful — bolts of silk fabric, strands of pearls, numerous brass instruments, a few of which I could identify as nautical equipment, including a compass, a folding telescope, and what appeared to be a ship's bell. It was inscribed *Liberty, 1845.*

Mr. Smith had told me that the necklace John had given me had last been seen on the manifest of a ship that had disappeared in a hurricane in October of 1846 . . . the same hurricane that had caused the Isla Huesos Cemetery to flood, and every coffin in it to wash out to the sea, and in which, he'd hinted, John had died.

But John *wasn't* dead. So I wasn't sure how accurate Mr. Smith's information was.

It wasn't until I lifted the lid to a small crate behind which Hope had cowered the whole time John and I had been arguing that I saw anything I thought might be of value to me.

It was a book bag. *My* book bag.

Inside were all of the things I remembered stuffing casually into it the morning before my life changed so dramatically, before John hurled me into the realm of the dead in order to save my life. My wallet. My econ book. My jean jacket for when I got cold during school from the incredibly strong institutional air-conditioning. My notebooks, pens, house keys, makeup bag, pill case, hairbrush, sugarless gum.

I was so happy to see these familiar things, tears filled my eyes. Only . . . what possible use was I ever going to have for my debit card in a place where there was no ATM? My wallet, I realized, was useless here. So was my econ book. Even my cell phone, still in the special pocket where I stored it. It was beyond sweet that John had kept it all so safely tucked away, but . . .

"My cell phone," I said breathlessly to Hope, who blinked back at me.

I don't know what made me switch it on. It wasn't as if I expected to see anything but the message I got: No service.

On the other hand, as I stood there holding it, thinking of my family and how upset they must be over my disappearance — all except my grandmother, of course, who was probably telling them horrible lies about where I'd gone and with whom — it occurred to me that just once, it might be nice if the Fates did something for *me*. It had been nice to find my book bag, but *they* hadn't saved it. John had.

And I hadn't found it with their help. It had been thanks to Hope.

Obviously I was on my own in the Underworld, at least where the Fates were concerned.

I was about to switch off my cell phone — thinking I'd save the battery so at least I could look at pictures of my mom and dad and uncle Chris and cousin Alex when I was feeling sad — that I looked down and noticed a film was playing on the screen.

Only I hadn't pressed anything on the keypad.

I'd downloaded a few films onto my phone, but this wasn't one I recognized. It was a video of my cousin Alex.

I'd only moved to Isla Huesos a short time before, and had just been getting to know my mom's side of the family, with whom my dad had never gotten along. I'd never made a video of Alex, and to my knowledge, he'd never sent me one.

Even if he *had*, I doubted this was the type of film he'd make.

47

In it, Alex was struggling to get out of some kind of box, beating on the sides of it as if he were trapped.

There was no sound. No matter how much I messed with the volume, I could hear nothing, though Alex's lips were moving.

A terrible suspicion began to creep over me. Alex didn't have theater as one of his extracurriculars, and he'd never expressed an interest in film to me.

The suspicion turned to fear.

The lighting was excessively dim, but Alex's face appeared dirt-smeared. Through the smears ran pale tracks of what I realized were tears.

That's when I knew: Alex wasn't acting.

And he began: "What fortune or what fate
Before the last day leadeth thee down here?
And who is this that showeth thee the way?"
DANTE ALIGHIERI, *Inferno,* Canto XV

I don't know how long I sat there, dumbly watching Alex struggle inside the box. I couldn't quite understand what I was seeing, much less *how* I was able to see it, or why.

All I knew was that someone I cared about was in serious trouble. This wasn't something I was about to ignore — especially given what had happened to Jade, and before that, my best friend Hannah, back in Westport. Both of them had died . . . maybe not directly because of me, but I could have done more to prevent their deaths, especially as Jade's had been directly Fury-related.

A single glance down at the diamond at the end of my necklace told me that what was happening to Alex could be Fury-related, too. Instead of its usual dove gray, the stone had turned black. . . .

No wonder I was feeling so frightened.

I had to find John, and right away. I had to tell him. Something terrible was going on back in Isla Huesos. Something so horrible, the Persephone Diamond could pick up the Fury-vibes via cell-phone video.

"This is *proof*," I turned to say to Hope, "that bringing me to the Underworld hasn't made the problem go away."

Only Hope was no longer on the back of the chair where she'd been perched for her busy feather-grooming ritual. She was huddled on the high shelf from which I'd dragged the crate containing my book bag, her head tucked under her wing.

"What's wrong with you?" I asked her, proving I was completely losing it. Like she was going to answer me.

Then I heard it: the crunch of a footfall on gravel.

There was no mistaking the sound . . . especially because the bird heard it, too. She lifted her head from her wing, and looked towards the stone arches, the ones that led out to the courtyard.

Only then did I notice the breakfast things were gone. Someone — or some*thing* — had come and taken them away, most likely while I'd been bathing. Surely I hadn't been so absorbed in watching the screen of my cell phone that he — or she. Or *it* — had done the work in front of me.

I followed the gaze of the bird. She was peering at the long white curtains, softly billowing in the breeze. That's how I happened to see, out of the corner of my eye, the same thing she had . . . a dark shadow moving beyond one of the stone arches.

I was not alone.

"Who's there?" I cried, leaping up from the couch onto which I'd sunk and desperately holding up my phone like it was a weapon.

There was no response from the courtyard.

The silence was hardly comforting. My diamond had turned black — maybe not even because my cousin was in danger, like I'd thought, but because *I* was.

You're safer, because I can protect you. John's words of warning came flooding back. *But you have a heartbeat, Pierce, and you're in the land of the dead.*

It occurred to me that the person in the courtyard could be John. Except that my necklace had never before turned black in his presence. It had always stayed the color of his eyes, a silver-gray.

And while we hadn't parted on the best of terms, wouldn't he have called out a greeting?

To be on the safe side, I switched off my phone and — keeping a careful eye on the curtains — slipped it up one of the tight sleeves of my dress.

"John?" I called. My voice came out sounding strangely high and girly. So I cleared it and said, again, "John?" That was better. I sounded more authoritative. "Is that you?"

Nothing happened. No one appeared through the curtains.

I could have sworn I saw another shadow.

"John," I said, my tone sounding more panicked. "If that's you, could you come in here? Because there's something we really need to talk about."

Of course there was no response. I was pretty sure it wasn't because John was giving me the silent treatment.

I'd always wondered why in scary movies the girl alone in the house felt like it was such a good idea to go outside to investigate the creepy noise. Why couldn't she just stay inside where it was safe until the police got there?

Now I understood a little better. I'm not particularly brave — except maybe when it comes to rescuing people or animals other than myself, and often by the time I get around to it, I'm too late. But I had to do *something*. I couldn't call the police, because there weren't any police in the Underworld. I had no idea how to get hold of John, since he hadn't given me one of those tablet things, and I certainly didn't know his number, if he even had one, to call him from my phone . . . which only seemed to play videos of my cousin trapped in a box, anyway. And I wasn't going to wait for whatever it was that was out there to come in and get *me*.

I grabbed a heavy gold candlestick from the mantel. I didn't want to hurt anyone, but if someone was going to hurt me first, I'd definitely act in self-defense.

Holding the candlestick baseball-bat style, I stepped cautiously up to the arch where I'd seen the shadow. The material of the curtain was sheer enough that I could make out some tall shrubs and even the outline of the fountain through it.

Any of those shapes could be a Fury waiting to pounce, I warned myself. Demons came in all sizes. The satyrs on the tapestries in John's bedroom proved it.

My heart in my throat, I reached out to pull back the curtain, ready to swing the candlestick at anything that moved. . . .

Nothing did, though. I saw only the courtyard, with its gloomy stone pathways and droopy-branched trees, along with the fountain, at the middle of which was a stone statue of a beautiful woman in a long dress, pouring water from an amphora that seemed never to empty.

I couldn't understand it. *Something* had been out there. I was sure of it. The bird — maybe even my diamond — had told me so.

Lowering the candlestick, I stepped through the curtain and out onto the gravel path. The moist, chilly air clung to me as if we were long-lost friends, the burbling of the fountain eclipsing all other sound.

Until a figure darted out from behind a shrub.

I screamed and whirled around in time to see him duck through the closest arch. I followed him back inside only to encounter Hope, swooping from her perch to check on me. Her wings got tangled in the gauzy curtain, causing it to balloon out over my head. This made me cry out a second time, and throw my arms over my face to protect my eyes. When I finally untangled us both, I saw that he'd gotten away.

I'd also seen that he wasn't any kind of otherworldly creature like the ones depicted on the tapestries. He wasn't a satyr or a walking skeleton or even a man. He was a child, a boy who couldn't have been more than ten or eleven years old.

He was also dressed in the strangest clothing I'd ever seen. And that was counting the dress I had on.

When I caught up to him, he was racing down the hallway . . . or at least as fast as he could race, considering he was carrying a silver tray with some of the breakfast things from John's room — or our room, I guess I should say.

That didn't seem to stop him, however, from speeding away as fast as a water bug.

Once I got over my initial shock, it occurred to me that it was highly unlikely that a ten-year-old boy who was running *away* from me intended to do me harm. Especially since he was dressed in what must have been the height of fashion in the 1840s — black pants that cut off at the knee, white stockings, huge clumpy shoes with silver buckles; an oversized blue velvet jacket covered a shirt that might once have been white, but had seen better days.

If he had shown up in that ensemble anywhere else — except possibly a Renaissance fair — he'd have gotten the snot kicked out of him. In the Underworld, he actually fit right in.

"Wait," I cried. For a child carrying about twenty pounds of silver, he seemed exceptionally mobile. He was already halfway down the hall. "Come back!"

"Sorry." He didn't even slow down to look at me. "We're not supposed to speak to you."

"What?" I had to break into a jog — and lift my long skirt — in order to catch up with him. "Who said you couldn't speak to me? Who's *we*?"

My mind was spinning. John had said nothing about additional occupants of the castle. Furies, maybe, but not people. He'd said only that he'd told his "men" that if they saw me anywhere I wasn't supposed to be, they were to bring me straight to him.

This was no man . . . and no Fury, either. When I looked down at the stone at the end of my necklace, I saw that it had gone gray again. The threat of danger had passed. Unless the only danger there'd ever been was the one threatening Alex. . . .

The boy, meanwhile, kept walk-running. The sconces up and down the hallway hardly cast enough light to see by, sending flickering shadows everywhere, including along the deep red velvet curtains that hung on either side of every door — all locked. I'd tried them earlier — that lined the corridor. I had no idea where he thought he was going.

"What were you doing out there in the courtyard?" I demanded. "How long were you there?" I had a sudden, horrifying thought. "Were you *spying* on me?"

That got to him. He paused long enough to turn a pair of huge blue eyes up at me. "No," he declared, indignantly. "I was gathering your breakfast things to return them to the kitchen. But then you came back and wouldn't stop playing with your magic mirror. So I had to hide because the captain said we weren't to talk to you. I *wasn't* spying."

"Oh," I said, flummoxed by this response. He'd reeled off a string of unfamiliar names and objects — Who was the captain? What magic mirror? — so I hardly knew how to respond.

"And the captain won't like that you were messing about with his things," he added darkly. "He's very particular about them."

I looked down in the direction of his gaze and realized I still held the candlestick in my hand.

"Oh," I said, again, embarrassed that I'd been caught arming myself against someone who, back in my world, would have been a fifth-grader. I turned and set the candlestick on a small marble table nearby. Then I turned back to him and said, because he was so small, and the silver tray so large and heavy-looking, "Here, why don't you let me help you with —"

This was a mistake.

"*No,*" he said, and took off again. "Captain Hayden told *me* to do it."

Captain *Hayden?*

"Do you mean John?" I asked, following him.

"Yes, of course," the boy said scornfully, as if my ignorance made *me* the crazy one. "Who else?"

Who *was* this little boy? And what was this "captain" business? John might be over a hundred and eighty years old in earth years, but physically he was only eighteen or nineteen. I didn't know much about things that had to do with the sea, but I did know that rank, even in olden times, was a matter of seniority.

"Can you take me to, er, Captain Hayden?" I asked the boy. "Because I need to see him, right away." I had to ask him about what I'd seen on my cell phone . . . and now I needed to ask him who else lived in this castle besides us.

"How can I take you to see him," the boy demanded, with a scowl, "when he said I'm not even supposed to be talking to you? That would be disobeying a direct order, and I never disobey orders."

I'd never strangled a child before — I'd never spent much time with young children, actually — but I seriously considered it at that moment.

"Yes," I said, from between gritted teeth. "But this is an emergency, so I'm sure he wouldn't mind. He gave me this necklace, see?" I pulled the diamond from the bodice of my dress. "It warns me whenever there's a Fury around. And it just told me there was one around a minute ago." This was a slight exaggeration of the truth, but I figured the kid didn't have to know this.

The boy glanced at the diamond, unimpressed. "I've seen that necklace before. I was ship's boy on the *Liberty.*"

The name rang a bell. Then I remembered why. I'd seen it before on the *side* of a bell. *Liberty, 1845* had been written on the brass bell on one of John's shelves.

Only what was a ship's boy? And what was the *Liberty?*

I didn't think exposing my ignorance to this child would be the smartest choice, however.

"That's very nice," I said instead, smiling in what I hoped looked like a friendly, and not completely fake, manner. "I'm Pierce Oliviera. What's your name?"

"Henry Day," he said. "And I know who you are. We all remember you from the last time you were here. It's not like we could forget, could we? Nothing was ever the same again. You know that necklace is cursed?"

"Yes," I said, keeping the smile frozen on my face. What did he mean, *We all remember you from the last time you were here?* "It's the Persephone Diamond. It's supposed to bring misfortune to all who touch it . . . unless they happen to be the chosen consort of the lord of the Underworld. As you can see," I assured him, forcing my smile to be even brighter, "I'm all right."

It felt odd to say the words *chosen consort of the lord of the Underworld* out loud. Odd and a bit pretentious. Especially since I still wasn't convinced that's who or what I actually was.

Neither, obviously, was this boy, judging by his response.

"Except you're not all right, are you, miss?" Henry's gaze never wavered from mine. "You're here."

That wiped the smile clean off my face.

"Can I go now, miss?" the boy asked. "This tray is heavy. And he said we weren't supposed to talk to you."

"Of . . . of course," I stammered. What had I been thinking? Had I really believed I could pull this off? Even this little boy didn't believe I was anyone but Pierce Oliviera, recent high-school dropout and NDE: survivor of a near-death experience. I was no queen, of the Underworld or any world. "But I really do need to see your, er, captain. So if you'll just tell me where I can find him —"

"He's down at the beach," Henry said unhelpfully. Then he turned around and used his hip to open a door to his left . . . a door I'd found locked the night before. "He's working. I wouldn't bother him if I were you . . . not even for a Fury you think you saw. Besides, you're not supposed to leave this part of the castle. It isn't safe."

Then he disappeared into the passageway.

I slipped my foot in the jamb before the door could sway all the way shut behind him. He didn't seem to notice that the lock had failed to catch.

There was a now-familiar flutter overhead. I looked up. Hope had alighted atop one of the carved stone figures affixed to the hallway wall. Like all birds in the pigeon family, she seemed to have an affinity for statues. The bird was bobbing up and down, as if bursting with a message.

"Forget it," I whispered to her. "You stay here."

I didn't regret my decision. Except the part where I didn't stay where it was safe, the way Henry had warned me to. And that I'd left my candlestick behind.

So bitter is it, death is little more;
But of the good to treat, which there I found,
Speak will I of the other things I saw there.
DANTE ALIGHIERI, *Inferno*, Canto I

The dog was on me before I'd gone two steps.

It wasn't the dog that the book on Greek mythology we'd studied in school had described, Cerberus, which had three heads and was supposed to stand guard at the gate to the Underworld.

It was close, though.

His massive front paws landed on my shoulders, drilling me back against the door I'd just slipped through, then forcefully pinning me there like a butterfly mounted to a museum display. Standing on his hind legs, his sharp white fangs hovered inches from my face as he growled down at me. His drool dripped in long white streams to the flagstone floor.

I heard someone shout "Typhon!" from behind him in a harsh tone. The dog didn't move, his red-eyed gaze on me, his stinking hot breath in my face. I was the stranger who had dared to violate his space, and so I was the one who had to face his wrath.

A moment later, a rough hand wrapped around the dog's studded collar and yanked the animal away from me. It yelped like a puppy, its long pink tongue lolling and its equally long black tail wagging, as it was shoved out a side door to what appeared to be a stable yard. There it sat and whined piteously, scratching to be let back in, apparently quite sad about not having been able to have me as a snack.

It was only then that I felt safe enough to turn my head and take in my surroundings.

I could see that I was in a kitchen that, like the rest of John's castle, was made entirely of stone, with a high, arched ceiling. It had only two points of egress, the door to the hallway from which I'd just entered, and against which I'd been pinned — and now leaned against for support — and the other to the stable yard where a man dressed all in black leather had shoved John's dog, and where I was assuming John kept his horse, Alastor, another creature from the Underworld who hated my guts.

He was going to have to get in line, though. The boy who'd pulled Typhon off me was standing a few feet away, next to the wooden plank table that ran down the center of the room, staring at me with a look that suggested he disliked me even more than the dog had. It was difficult not to notice the size of his bare biceps — not as large as John's, but still impressive — since he'd folded his arms across his chest, and this had caused the muscles to bulge. The fact that they were circled in vicious-looking rings of black tattooed thorns did even more to draw attention to them.

It was hard to figure out if that was why he was so much more noticeable than anyone else in the room, or if it was because he was what my friend Kayla would have called smokin' hot, despite a jagged scar that ran down one side of his forehead, through a dark brow, and halfway to the center of his left jaw. Whoever had wielded that knife had thankfully — for him — spared his dark eye.

Not so thankfully for me, however, since he was able to use both eyes to give me a deathlike stare.

"Um," I said, finally feeling the blood flow returning to my limbs. "You might want to think about getting that dog neutered."

The boy with the thorn tattoos sneered. "I'm guessing she'll be wanting to get us *all* neutered," he said.

"Frank!" cried an old man I hadn't noticed before. He was standing beside an enormous fireplace that took up most of the length of the far wall. Over the fire hung numerous huge black pots. From them seemed to emanate the foul smell that filled the air. Either that, or it had been the dog. "Mind your manners, please. Henry, please pour the captain's guest a cup of tea. I believe she needs it."

"She's not the captain's guest, Mr. Graves," the boy with the thorn tattoos — Frank, the old man had called him — said. "Guests aren't usually confined to quarters. Prisoners are, though. And don't prisoners usually get punished for disobeying orders?"

There was a gleam in his cold dark eyes as he said the word *punished* that suggested he enjoyed administering punishments.

I clutched the back of the chair nearest me and sank down into it. I was pretty sure it looked natural, though, and not like my knees had given out, which of course they had.

"Stop trying to frighten her, Frank," said a mountain of a man sitting across the table from me. I hadn't noticed *him* because he'd been so quiet. But he was even bigger than Frank, and like him, dressed in black leather and covered in tattoos. Unlike Frank, who looked to be about John's age, and wore his black hair in a complicated pattern of short braids close to his head, this man was older, and had shaved his skull completely bald . . . except for one long single black braid growing from the back of his head. His tattoos were of colorful birds and flowers, not thorns. "As if that dog didn't scare her half to death already."

"Her being so easy to frighten just further proves my point," Frank said, continuing a conversation I'd obviously interrupted . . . a conversation they'd been having about me. "She's not the one. So why are we bothering with niceties?"

"Only a fool is never afraid, Frank," Mr. Graves, the old man by the fire, said. "Heroes are the people who carry on despite their fear, because they know the job's got to get done."

"— and they're the only ones left to do it." Frank snorted. "Yes, yes, you've only mentioned it a thousand times. How did she even get in here, Henry? Did you forget to lock the door again?"

"It's not my fault." Henry, having set the tray of breakfast things down on the table, looked indignant. "She followed me. She said I was spying on her. She says she wants to see the captain. She says she saw a Fury."

Frank let out a harsh bark of laughter.

"Just now? That'd be quite a trick, considering none of us heard or saw anything. What kind of Fury was that, then, miss? The invisible kind?"

I felt myself flush. I'd gotten used to being the outsider in school, the one other people laughed at or simply chose to ignore because my near-death experience had made me the oddball, the misfit, the girl who didn't fit in.

It was something else entirely to be standing in the place I'd always insisted existed, and find myself being treated in the exact same way.

"Excuse me," I said, a little hotly. "It wasn't Henry's fault. I did follow him, because I was looking for John. Or the captain, as you call him. Would one of you please tell me how I could find him?" I just hoped I wouldn't have to encounter that dog again in doing so. . . .

"I apologize, my dear," old Mr. Graves said. "It's been a long time since we've had visitors, and I'm afraid we've forgotten our manners. Please don't allow anything Frank says to trouble you. He was always an able seaman, but never much of a gentleman."

I shot Frank a worried look, fearing he'd be insulted upon hearing this. He only folded both hands behind his head and put his boots up on the table, looking pleased to be referred to as *never much of a gentleman*.

"I'm Mr. Graves, ship's surgeon to the *Liberty*," the old man said, apparently not noticing his shipmate's behavior. "And this is Mr. Liu, ship bosun." The giant with the braid, who had a cup of tea in front of him, nodded at me unsmilingly.

None of this made any more sense to me than what Henry had said earlier. The *Liberty*, again. Was Mr. Graves supposed to be some kind of doctor? Because he certainly didn't look like one, in his old-fashioned black wool suit.

If he was a doctor, maybe the foul-smelling substances in the pots he was tending over the fire were special medicines he was brewing to heal wounds inflicted by Furies. I hoped so, since it would be nice to think John had someone besides me to take care of him.

On the other hand, if these four — Mr. Graves, the brutish Frank, the mysterious Mr. Liu, and rude little Henry — were the only company John had had for a hundred and sixty-odd years, it explained a lot about his brooding.

Mr. Liu and Frank looked almost exactly like the guards I'd seen working with John that day I'd died back when I was fifteen. The day John had decided to keep me, instead of sending me on to my final destination.

What was it Henry had said, back in the hallway? *We all remember you from the last time you were here.*

No wonder they looked like those guards. They probably *were* those guards.

And no wonder none of them liked me. I was the girl who'd thrown tea in their boss's face, and run away.

Now it seemed more likely that what was in the pots Mr. Graves kept stirring was poison . . . poison that was going to be used on me.

"It's very nice to meet you all," I said, deciding it was best to be diplomatic, since it looked like I was going to be stuck with these people for a while. I rose on still unsteady legs to walk over and shake Mr. Graves's hand.

The doctor simply stared over my head, seeming to notice neither my hand, nor me standing there in front of him.

This was explained when Frank said to me scornfully, a second later, "He can't see you. He's *blind*."

"Oh," I said, feeling mortified. I hadn't noticed until that point that Mr. Graves's eyes had a milky-white sheen to them, and that he'd never once looked directly at anyone who was speaking. "I'm so sorry."

"Don't be," Mr. Graves said, managing to find my hand anyway and give it a squeeze. "It's not your fault."

"Actually, it could have been," Frank said. "It was a Fury that —"

"Frank, the young lady said she'd like to see the captain. Why don't you go fetch him?" Mr. Graves snapped. To me, he said, "Miss Oliviera, I do apologize. It's been quite some time since these fellows have been in the company of a young lady."

"Speak for yourself, old man," Frank said. He came to his feet with sudden alacrity. "Why don't I just take her to the captain?"

"I hardly think *that's* a good idea," Mr. Liu muttered, into his teacup.

"His orders were if she showed up, we were to bring her straight to him," Frank said.

Mr. Graves's face expressed the exact dismay I felt upon being reminded of this. "Just go and fetch the captain, Frank. Or young Henry can do it."

"*What?*" Henry cried, looking stricken. "I don't want to go down there. All those dead people. And I'm the one who always gets stuck handing out the blankets —"

"It's not important," I said quickly. Blankets? What blankets? What on earth was Henry talking about? "I'll just wait until John comes back —"

"See?" Henry looked triumphant. "I told you. She's not the one."

"It doesn't matter," Frank said, impatiently. "Either way, we're stuck with her."

This wasn't a very nice thing to hear about yourself — that people thought of you as someone they were stuck with. Not that I hadn't been thinking the very same thing about them . . . and not that I didn't share Henry's fear that I wasn't Queen-of-the-Underworld material.

"Excuse me," I said. I felt like I had to say something, especially if I'd been chosen as consort for the reason I suspected . . . that I'd always felt a certain obligation to help wild things. They certainly qualified — though I was willing to admit that my success rates hadn't been very good thus far. "I get that some of you may not like me, which is fair, since I realize the last time I was here, I didn't make the best impression." That was an understatement. "But I do think we all have something in common."

Mr. Liu looked curious. "What would that be, Miss Oliviera?"

"Well, we'd all like to —"

— *go home*, was what I almost said. Then I remembered that for them, home no longer existed. Everyone they had known on earth, all of their families and loved ones, had died over a hundred years ago. They had no homes to go to. Maybe *this* was their family now, the Underworld their home.

"Go to Isla Huesos," I said lamely instead. Surely that was better than the Underworld, wasn't it?

When they sat and stared at me — except for Mr. Graves, who couldn't see, and wore a troubled expression instead — I began to suspect I'd made an even worse mistake than saying *home*. "You've heard of Isla Huesos, haven't you?" I asked worriedly.

The blind man spoke first, in a slightly stiff tone. "Every man who's ever sailed under the Union Jack knows Isla Huesos. It's only one of the busiest — and wickedest — ports in the Americas."

"Oh," I said. "Right."

This was not the answer I'd been expecting. I wasn't quite sure how to break it to him that while Isla Huesos might have been one of the busiest ports in the Americas nearly two hundred years ago, now it was where about a half million tourists showed up every year, generally either by cruise ship, rental car, or commercial airline, to sunbathe, rent Jet Skis, and buy T-shirts that say *My Grandma Went to Isla Huesos and All I Got Was This Crappy T-shirt*. Hardly the wickedest place in the Americas . . .

On the other hand, it was also a place that had gotten its name from the many thousands of human bones that had been found littering its shores back in the fifteen hundreds. *Isla Huesos* means "Island of Bones." How those bones had gotten there had always been a source of some speculation.

The fact that it turned out to have an underworld beneath it may have been a clue.

"I've never been to Isla Huesos," Henry said, a wistful expression on his face. "The *Liberty* was on her way there when —"

Mr. Graves suffered a coughing fit, possibly from breathing in the fumes of whatever it was he was cooking.

"Well, don't let her fill your head with dreams, kid," Frank warned Henry, his voice a rumbling growl. "Because you're not going there now, either."

"I'm not trying to fill anyone's head with anything," I said, stung. I was only trying to do what I was pretty sure was my new job. "I'm just saying maybe we aren't so different as you think. I know I behaved . . . badly towards your captain the last time I was here." I could feel myself blushing, but I plunged on, keeping my gaze on Mr. Graves, who could not, of course, even see me. "But I feel differently now. I want to help. John gave me this." I pulled the diamond by its chain out from the bodice of my gown to show them. "I was thinking that maybe, using it, and working together, we could figure out how to defeat the Furies someday —"

My words were met first with incredulous silence . . . then laughter. Everyone was laughing at me, even Mr. Graves.

"What?" I glared at them. "I don't understand why that's so funny. Think about it. Why would someone have gone to all the trouble of making a necklace that alerts its owner to the presence of evil spirits if there wasn't some way to get rid of those evil spirits? On TV people get rid of ghosts all the time just by waving some stinky burning stuff and saying an incantation. So I would think the Underworld would have an even better weapon."

"Furies are not ghosts," said Mr. Liu, wiping tears of laughter from his eyes.

"What's TV?" asked Henry.

"If bad smells worked on Furies, we'd be rid of them all by now, thanks to Mr. Graves." Frank nodded at the black pots bubbling on the fire behind Mr. Graves.

"Frank," the blind man said, his laughter dying abruptly, and his voice growing testy, "as I've explained to you before, the fire-brewing of a world-class lager is an art, not a science. You'll be thanking me once this mash is processed."

Beer? *That's* what the doctor was making? Well, I supposed it wasn't like there was a 7-Eleven they could run to. Apparently the Fates didn't serve ice-cold Buds.

"Look," I said, trying to bring the conversation back on topic. "I'm not saying you're wrong. But isn't it possible you might be? John said the Furies would leave my family alone if he brought me here. But they haven't." I pulled my cell phone from my sleeve and turned it on. "Look."

Frank was already shaking his head. "Don't bother. Yours won't work here." He fished in his pocket and brought out a flat black device that looked very much like the one John had used earlier that morning. "Only ours do."

"Hers does," Henry said, coming to stand by my chair, drawn as much by the expression on my face as I watched my cousin's struggles as by any ten-year-old boy's fascination with gadgets. "I saw her playing with it. What's it showing you, miss?"

"This," I said, tilting the screen so he could see the dark, disturbing image. It probably wasn't appropriate for a child his age . . . but then, he lived in the Underworld. "Can you tell what it is?"

"That's impossible." Frank, looking incredulous, glanced from me, to Mr. Graves, to Mr. Liu, and then back again. "It's working. How can hers be working?"

Henry took the phone from me and squinted down at it. "It's a man," he said. "No . . . a boy. He's in a box. A dark box. It doesn't look as if he's being attacked by Furies to me, though. He's just trapped. Do you know that boy?"

I took the phone back from him. "I do," I said, my heart rate beginning to speed up, as it had the last time I'd seen the video. "It's my cousin Alex."

"Does Captain Hayden know you have that?" Mr. Graves asked nervously. "I can't imagine he'd be too pleased —"

Mr. Liu held out a hand the size of a slice of country ham. "May I see it?" It wasn't a question so much as a command.

I passed him the phone, then glanced down at my necklace because of the sense of foreboding that had once again gripped me. As I'd expected, the stone had turned black.

Henry noticed it, too, and asked curiously, "Wasn't your necklace silver before?"

Before I could answer, Mr. Liu looked up from the screen.

"This boy," he said, solemnly, "isn't in a box. He's in a coffin."

The word *coffin* slammed into me like a fist.

"Oh, God," I said, the blood seeming to go cold in my veins. "Of course." I couldn't believe I hadn't realized it before. "It's a coffin. Not a real coffin . . . it's a tradition at Isla Huesos High

School. Coffin Night." I could see from their expressions that they didn't have any idea what I was talking about. I babbled on anyway, because I was so upset. "The senior class makes a coffin and hides it. . . ."

I reached across the table to take my phone from Mr. Liu's fingers. The screen remained fixed on the morbid image of Alex. Now that I knew what I was looking at, I could see plainly that it was, indeed, a coffin.

"I *knew* Alex was up to something," I said, more to myself than any of them. I was so disturbed, I wasn't thinking straight. "He was so pleased when I told him Seth Rector and those guys asked me to be part of the coffin committee. But he hates them . . . I don't know why. I'm sure he found the coffin — Seth was storing it in my mom's garage — and was going to do something awful with it, and they caught him, and nailed him into it as a prank. But this has gone way further than any prank should go. He looks as if he can't even breathe! Please, you've got to tell me what I can do. I've got to go back. I've got to help him!"

Mr. Liu, a somber expression on his face, said in his deep, slow voice, "Often the images we see in this world of the world above are not what is occurring now, but what is to come."

I glanced at the screen. "Wait . . . so this *isn't* happening?"

"It may be happening now," Mr. Liu said, soberly. "It may already have happened. Or it may happen in the future. There's no way to tell."

"That's why the captain ordered us long ago not to look up personal acquaintances on the magic mirrors," Frank chimed in.

"Though he did a good job that time I saw my mum get her purse snatched, remember that?" Henry was beaming. "He showed up in time to give that man a great big —"

"So John went," I said, my hopes suddenly soaring. "John went and helped your mother?"

"Henry," Mr. Graves said, sounding uneasy. "Please don't put ideas in Miss Oliviera's head. That was an extraordinary circumstance, miss —"

"Did you not hear me? Did you not see this?" I stood up to show them my phone. Alex was still pounding on the sides of the coffin. I hoped someone had remembered to drill air holes through the top. But knowing Seth Rector and his friends, I doubted it. "*This* is an extraordinary circumstance. And what about this?" I lifted the diamond at the end of my necklace, which was inky black. "This means there are Furies around. If they aren't here, like you keep assuring me, then they're there, around Alex. So if there's some way I can help him, I've got to go. You've got to tell me where I can find John so I can go —"

"Miss Oliviera, you haven't been here long enough to realize that our work is of vital importance," Mr. Graves said. "If the dead went unsorted because the captain was always running off to help the living, do you have any idea of the consequences, of the chaos? The souls of the dead would come spilling out onto the earth. They'd have nowhere to go, nothing to do but haunt the living. It would be a disaster. Your cousin's difficulties are heartbreaking, yes. But so is pestilence, I can assure you."

"Didn't Captain Hayden bring you here because members of

your own family are possessed by Furies and are trying to kill you?" Mr. Liu asked.

"Yes," said a quiet voice from the stable yard door. "He did. Pierce, could I have a word with you, please?"

I don't know how long he'd been standing there, or how much he'd overheard.

Judging from the expression on John's face, the answer was *enough*.

"Let us go on, for the long way impels us."
Thus he went in, and thus he made me enter
The foremost circle that surrounds the abyss.
DANTE ALIGHIERI, *Inferno*, Canto IV

Was that really necessary?" I asked as soon as I was able to catch my breath. Whenever John hurtled me through space and time to some other location (or astral plane), I always felt a little nauseous afterwards, or as if I might have left a limb or vital organ behind.

When I looked down, I saw that not only did I seem to be in one piece, I was holding my cell phone in one hand . . . the one that wasn't clutching John's arm in a grip so tight, I was sure my fingers were going to leave a mark through his leather sleeve.

"It was," he said. "We're running behind schedule, and it's clear you and I need to talk." Then he must have noticed the expression on my face, since he looked concerned and asked, "Are you all right?"

"Just give me a second," I said. It didn't help that he hadn't told me we were going to the beach. I could feel the heels of the delicate slippers I was wearing sinking in the sand.

"Take as much time as you need," he said.

But his dark eyebrows were still lowered in disapproval, the way they'd been since the moment he'd appeared in the kitchen doorway. I hadn't yet determined how much of our conversation he'd overheard. Mr. Liu saying they were stuck with me? Frank flirting (or that's what he seemed to think he'd been doing) with me?

John hadn't mentioned it. He'd simply crossed the kitchen to take my hand, I'd blinked in surprise to see him, and a moment later, it was all gone — the noisy confusion of everyone in his crew trying to make excuses at once, the smell from Mr. Graves's mash, everything except Typhon's noisy barking . . .

Because he was still doing that, only now it was beside me along the shore of the vast, cold lake on which I found myself. A large black horse stood chewing on the grassy dune nearby, pausing every so often to give me — and Typhon — the evil eye: Alastor, John's horse, who'd once tried to kick me in the head.

There was no need to ask where we were. I knew even before I heard the long, sad blare of the marina horn from the dock.

"Sorry," John said. He was apparently referring to the horn. "We've been behind schedule all day." He picked up a piece of driftwood and gave it a powerful throw. Typhon dashed after it with a joyful bark.

"The people leaving on those boats are already dead," I said. I raised my cell phone to show him the video of Alex. "My cousin

Alex is not. But he will be soon if we don't do something. Look at him."

John glanced down at the screen.

"Pierce," he said, his mouth tightening. "I'm sorrier than I can say. But —"

"That's *your* coffin, you know," I said. "The one the seniors at Isla Huesos High build for you on Coffin Night, because they think you're dead and will keep haunting the cemetery until you get a rightful burial."

"They don't bury it," he said, with a grim smile. "They burn it on the fifty-yard line."

I gasped, my heart seeming to stop in my chest. "They wouldn't! You don't think —" I looked down at my phone. "Do you think they'd really burn him alive?"

"Pierce, no." His smile turned sympathetic. "They're not going to burn your cousin alive. I'm sure they're only trying to scare him. Even so, what the men told you was right." John's gaze had gone deadly serious. "I can't let you go back there. It's too dangerous."

I released his arm. Typhon had returned, holding the drift wood in his huge, slobbery jaw, his massive tail wagging behind him. In John's presence, the dog somehow seemed more mischievous than terrifying, maybe because of the obvious adoration for his master that gleamed in his eyes.

Tears stung my own eyes . . . not only because I was so disappointed, but because of the cold. A biting wind blew in from the surface of the lake, whipping my hair around my face and flattening my skirt to my legs.

"Pierce," John said, after taking the driftwood from Typhon's mouth and tossing it away again for the dog to chase. He put out a long arm to catch me by the waist, then pull me to him. "I know you're worried about your family, and you want to go back to Isla Huesos to help them. But Mr. Liu was right. What you're seeing on that screen may not have happened yet. It may *never* happen. It's more like a glimpse, a . . . shadow of something that could happen in your cousin's life. What we have to be concerned with are the facts. We know for a *fact* that someone in your family has tried to murder you . . . twice. Did it ever occur to you that what you're seeing might be a trick by the Furies to lure you from here so they can try to kill you again? It's *you* who needs protecting, Pierce, not your cousin."

"I'm already as close to dead as I can get, living here," I pointed out. "What does it matter if they kill me?"

"They can still hurt you," he reminded me, in a voice that was every bit as cold as the wind from which his body shielded me. "In ways you can't imagine, and that I'd rather you never find out."

He didn't have to say more. The scars left over from similar attacks — not just on him, but on his shipmates, too — were testament enough.

"Oh, John," I said, with a groan, dropping my head to rest it against his chest. "I'm sorry. I didn't mean what I said this morning. Not the way it came out, anyway. I was upset."

I felt his lips brush my hair. "I know," he said.

His voice wasn't cold anymore, but when I looked up at him, I saw that he wasn't smiling, either. Nor did he smile when Typhon, struggling to return with the driftwood, tripped over it instead, then fell into the waves.

It was going to take more than an apology, I suspected, to make him smile again.

"Is this why you hid my phone from me?" I asked. "So I wouldn't be able to see what the Furies were doing to my family? Did you know something like this was going to happen? Did you know all along?"

"No," John said, his arms tightening around me. "I didn't even know you had a phone, to be honest. You dropped your bag when you crossed over yesterday, and Henry must have put it away. He was trained to wait on ship's officers. He's a little fuzzy on any aspects of the job outside those duties."

I remembered the orderliness with which John's clothes had been organized, as opposed to his books.

"Oh," I said, reaching up to wipe my streaming eyes. All I could hear was the wind and, more distantly, the sound of waves splashing against the hull of a tall boat that was pulling away from a nearby dock. Though the boat stood higher than a three-story house, and held many hundreds of people, none of them waved the way passengers on cruise ships so often do when departing from an exotic port. This wasn't that kind of boat, and they weren't leaving on that kind of trip.

I saw two large figures in black moving busily around the crowded dock. One had a long dark braid, the other a scar across his face. Mr. Liu and Frank.

"I've never seen one of those work here," John mused as he looked down at my cell phone. "And certainly not in that way.

Henry started calling the tablets we found when we arrived here 'magic mirrors' because they work like the ones in the fairy tales. Ask them a question and they tell you the answer . . . generally only to which boat the departed soul in front of you is assigned, but to him, that seemed magical enough. . . ."

I probably should have taken the fact that the Fates — or whoever — had granted my smartphone the same power as the "magic mirrors" John and his crew had as evidence of my burgeoning consort powers, or something.

But I was still too upset about Alex to think of anything else.

"Henry said sometimes your tablets tell you more." I looked up into his eyes. "Henry said he saw his mother get her purse snatched once, and you went and rescued her."

John looked skyward. Only in this case, the sky was the ceiling of the vast subterranean cavern in which the Underworld was sealed. It glowed, as always, a depressing shade of grayish pink.

"That was different," he said. "Henry's mother was being attacked by a local street thug back in his native village. It wasn't a trick of the Furies, as this very likely is. Here, put this on. I can tell you're freezing."

He didn't lend me the leather coat he was wearing in order to keep me warm, the way he had the last time I'd been in this same place. Instead, he pulled something from a polished wooden rack. Similar racks, I noticed, appeared at random intervals all along the twin docks.

After he unfolded it, I saw that it was a blanket, kind of like the ones they give out on long airplane flights. Only this one was much thicker, made to withstand the chilly dampness of the beach.

"I know you," he added, helping to arrange the blanket over my shoulders. "You won't drop the subject until I agree to check on your cousin, so I'll do it. But only under one condition."

"*John,*" I said, whirling around to clutch his arm again.

"Don't get too excited," he warned. "You haven't heard the condition."

"Oh," I said, eagerly. "Whatever it is, I'll do it. *Thank you.* Alex has never had a very good life — his mother ran away when he was a baby, and his dad spent most of his life in jail. . . . But, John, what *is* all this?" I swept my free hand out to indicate the people remaining on the dock, waiting for the boat John had said was arriving soon. I'd noticed some of them had blankets like the one he'd wrapped around me. "A new customer service initiative?"

John looked surprised at my change of topic . . . then uncomfortable. He stooped to reach for the driftwood Typhon had dashed up to drop at his feet. "I don't know what you mean," he said, stiffly.

"You're giving blankets away to keep them warm while they wait. When did this start happening?"

"You mentioned some things when you were here the last time. . . ." He avoided meeting my gaze by tossing the stick for his dog. "They stayed with me."

My eyes widened. "Things *I* said?"

"About how I should treat the people who end up here." He paused at the approach of a wave — though it was yards off —

and made quite a production of moving me, and my delicate slippers, out of its path. "So I decided to make a few changes."

It felt as if one of the kind of flowers *I* liked — a wild daisy, perhaps — had suddenly blossomed inside my heart.

"Oh, *John*," I said, and rose onto my toes to kiss his cheek.

He looked more than a little surprised by the kiss. I thought I might actually have seen some color come into his cheeks.

"What was *that* for?" he asked.

"Henry said nothing was the same after I left. I assumed he meant everything was much worse. I couldn't imagine it was the opposite, that things were *better*."

John's discomfort at having been caught doing something kind — instead of reckless or violent — was sweet.

"Henry talks too much," he muttered. "But I'm glad you like it. Not that it hasn't been a lot of added work. I'll admit it's cut down on the complaints, though, and even the fighting amongst our rowdier passengers. So you were right. Your suggestions helped."

I beamed up at him.

Keeper of the dead. That's how Mr. Smith, the cemetery sexton, had referred to John once, and that's what he was. Although the title "protector of the dead" seemed more applicable.

It was totally silly how much hope I was filled with by the fact that he'd remembered something I'd said so long ago — like maybe this whole consort thing might work out after all.

I gasped a moment later when there was a sudden rush of white feathers, and the bird he'd given me emerged from the grizzly gray fog seeming to engulf the whole beach, plopping down onto the sand beside us with a disgruntled little *humph*.

"Oh, Hope," I said, dashing tears of laughter from my eyes. Apparently I had only to feel the emotion, and she showed up. "I'm sorry. I didn't mean to leave you behind. It was his fault, you know." I pointed at John.

The bird ignored us both, poking around in the flotsam washed ashore by the waves, looking, as always, for something to eat.

"Her name is Hope?" John asked, the corners of his mouth beginning to tug upwards.

"No." I bristled, thinking he was making fun of me. Then I realized I'd been caught. "Well, all right . . . so what if it is? I'm not going to name her after some depressing aspect of the Underworld like you do all your pets. I looked up the name *Alastor.* That was the name of one of the death horses that drew Hades's chariot. And *Typhon?*" I glanced at the dog, cavorting in and out of the waves, seemingly oblivious of the cold. "I can only imagine, but I'm sure it means something equally unpleasant."

"Typhon was the father of all monsters," John said. He'd given up trying to suppress his grin. "The deadliest of all the creatures in Greek mythology."

"Nice," I said sarcastically. "Well, I prefer to name my pets something that reminds me there's —"

"Hope?" His grin broadened.

"Very funny." True, I'd admitted to him that I was inexperienced. But I didn't have to prove it by acting like I was twelve. "But you must think there's hope, too, or you wouldn't be taking me to help Alex."

The smile vanished. "I never said I was taking you to help

83

your cousin Alex. I said I was going myself, and only under one condition — that you stay here, where it's safe."

My heart fell. I couldn't hide my disappointment, so I didn't bother trying.

"John, how are you going to help Alex if I don't go with you?" I asked. "You don't even know where the coffin is hidden. I do. And supposing Alex hasn't gotten himself locked into it yet . . . how are you going to talk him out of doing whatever boneheaded thing it is he's planning on doing that's going to get him locked into it? You can't. He'll never listen to you, because he doesn't know who you are. Which is why I *have* to go with you."

"Did you not listen to a word I said?" John looked down at me like the awards for most naïve girl in the world had already been handed out, and I'd won first prize. "This whole thing could be a trap."

"All the more reason I should go with you," I said. "If there *are* Furies in the area, I can warn you." I pulled out my diamond. It was back to a silvery gray. "That's why I was looking for you in the first place —"

He knit his brow. "What are you talking about?"

"My diamond turned black when I first saw the video of Alex —"

"That's impossible," he said flatly.

I was getting a bit tired of everyone telling me how impossible everything I seemed perfectly capable of doing and observing was.

"No," I said. "It did. It does, every time the video plays —"

"It should only turn color in the presence of Furies."

"And you should show up on film," I reminded him. "But you don't, which was how I got accused of assaulting my study hall teacher last year, when you were the one who actually did it, even though there was a video of the whole thing. You just weren't on it."

He glowered as he always used to whenever the subject of Mr. Mueller came up. "That man was evil. You should never have —"

"— gotten myself into that situation, I know. But anyway, that's when I saw Henry and followed him to the kitchen, and met everyone, and we started talking —"

"I was wondering where they all disappeared to," John muttered. "I should have known *you* were the distraction. It's nothing to do with you," he added quickly, noticing how I'd raised my eyebrows at the word *distraction*. "They're good men — they've stuck by me through —" Whatever he'd been about to say he bit off suddenly, saying instead, "Well, quite a lot. But as you've probably already gathered, we don't get a lot of company around here. At least, not of the living variety. I'm sorry if they were pestering you —"

"They weren't pestering me," I said, wondering exactly what it was he and the crew of the *Liberty* had endured. "And they clearly adore you. But there's something I don't understand . . . Aren't you a little young to be a captain? Not that I'm sure you weren't wonderful at it," I added hastily, "but Frank's got to be your same age, and Mr. Graves and Mr. Liu are both older than you. How on earth did it happen?"

He shut down. It was like a curtain being pulled across a window. This was a subject he definitely did not wish to discuss.

"The title is honorary," he said, not meeting my gaze. "I can't stop them calling me that, even though I've asked them not to. I was the highest-ranking officer to survive the . . . accident."

Accident? I supposed this was another one of those things he didn't want to tell me because it would make me hate him.

Recognizing that dropping that particular topic — for now at least — would probably be best, I said, "John, I can warn you about the Furies. And I know *exactly* where the coffin is. All you have to do is take me back to Isla Huesos — just this one time, to help Alex — and I'll never mention going there again. I'll even," I said, reaching up to straighten the collar of his leather jacket, which had gone askew, "forgive you for the waffles —"

John seized me by both shoulders, pulling me towards him so abruptly that Hope gave an alarmed flap of her wings.

"Pierce," he said. *"Do you mean that?"*

When I pushed back some of the hair that had tumbled into my face and raised my dark eyes to meet his light ones, I saw that he was staring down at me with an intensity that burned.

"You'll never mention going back to Isla Huesos again if I take you there right now, this once, to talk to your cousin Alex?" he demanded. "You'll give . . . cohabitation another chance?"

His sudden fierceness was making me nervous.

"Of course, John," I said, "But it's not like I have a choice."

"What if you did?" he asked, his grip tightening.

I blinked. "But I can't. You said —"

He gave me a little shake. "Never mind what I said. What if I was wrong?"

86

I reached up to lay a hand on his cheek. It felt a little scratchy, because he hadn't shaved. I didn't care about stubble. What I cared about was the desperate need I saw in his eyes. The need for me.

"I'd come back," I said, simply, "to stay with you."

A second later, the lake — and everything around it — was gone.

"Therefore I think and judge it for thy best
Thou follow me, and I will be thy guide,
And lead thee hence through the eternal place."
DANTE ALIGHIERI, *Inferno*, Canto I

When John flung us both back to earth, it wasn't to the middle of a breezeway at Isla Huesos High School, the last place I'd been before I'd found myself in the realm of the dead, and so where I'd been expecting to next cross paths with the living.

Which was why I was surprised to find myself instead inside a small, dark room that smelled strongly of earth, ankle deep in dead leaves . . . and bloodred flower blossoms that looked strangely familiar.

"Where are we?" I asked, ducking my head. The vaulted ceiling, supported by rough-hewn wooden beams that looked at least a century old, was lower than my standing height.

"Shhh," John said. He'd been forced to kneel, and was peering out from behind the rusted metal grate that barred the single door. "There are people out there. I don't want them to hear us."

I stared around the bare room, which was windowless, save for a few tiny cross-shaped slots in the thick brick-and-plaster walls. I could see that a substantial shiny new chain had been wrapped several times around the grate and securely fastened with a padlock, to make certain that no one could get in or out of the structure.

Slowly, comprehension dawned. A metal grate, chained and locked? A dim, cramped space? Dead leaves? Red flower blossoms?

"Are we inside *your crypt*?" I hissed, rushing to John's side, the dead leaves and flowers crunching beneath my feet.

I didn't rush to John's side for fear of ghosts. I had just exited an entire realm of ghosts. I'd had a near-death experience before. I knew what being dead was like.

I'd simply never been on this *side* of death before.

"Yes," John whispered. He was still peering out through the door. "This is the crypt they assigned me."

Not where his body was buried. I noticed the subtle wording right away.

Looking around, I saw that he was right. John's crypt was empty, except for the two of us, and lots and lots of dead leaves. There was no coffin.

Wasn't that the point, after all, of Coffin Night, which Isla Huesos High School celebrated every year, even though the administration frowned on it? The senior class built John a coffin — though they'd been doing it so long, no one remembered anymore who the coffin was for, or why they even did it — and hid it.

The hiding is symbolic, Mr. Smith had told me, explaining the ritual. *The hiding represents burying.*

All so John would stop haunting the island. Because however John had died, all those years ago — *if* he had died — his body had never been found. And his anger over that was thought to have brought the hurricane in 1846 that had killed so many people, and caused the old Isla Huesos Cemetery to flood, and displace all the coffins buried there.

That's how the new Isla Huesos Cemetery — the one we were in now — had become such a famous tourist destination, because of its unusual crypts — all raised in order to keep the coffins within them above sea level, so they wouldn't be washed out to sea (or into people's yards) like they had during that devastating hurricane in October 1846.

I shivered, kneeling beside John in the leaves and dead flower blossoms that carpeted the floor of his tomb.

"Why did we come back this way instead of popping up somewhere less . . . cramped?" I asked, substituting the word *cramped* for *creepy*. I was trying not to feel weirded out that I was in my boyfriend's crypt. It was only a building, after all.

A very unpleasant one.

"This is a portal," he said, as if that explained everything.

"A what?"

"A portal," John whispered. "A direct link from here to the Underworld. That's why you don't feel dizzy this time."

I hadn't even noticed, but he was right. I didn't feel sick, for once, though we'd just jumped between astral planes.

"This is a doorway through which the souls of the departed enter the world of the dead after they pass," John explained softly.

"The doorway closes behind the dead once they enter. They can never leave again —"

"Unless they escape," I interrupted. Because this was what had happened to me.

He glanced down at me with a teasing smile. "Unless I choose to *let them* escape," he said, "because they seem to want their mothers so badly."

"That was *two years ago*," I reminded him. I shouldn't have mentioned the thing that morning about being inexperienced with men, even if it was technically true. He was never going to let me help him if he always thought of me as someone he had to protect. "And do I have to remind you that you didn't *let* me escape, I —"

"Shhh." He held up a hand. "Someone's coming."

I looked past his shoulder as a family walked down the pathway along with Mr. Smith and some other people who were dressed in business attire and carrying clipboards. It was difficult to hear what they were saying, but not hard to imagine what they were discussing . . . a crypt. The people dressed in business attire were probably from a local funeral parlor.

The family wore the somber, unhappy expressions of the newly bereaved. Someone they loved had passed away.

Not far behind them followed a man in coveralls — obviously a groundskeeper who worked in the cemetery. He was pushing a wheelbarrow, in which he was collecting the many palm fronds that littered the path. The high winds of the approaching storm must have torn them from the trees in and around the cemetery.

I remembered the hurricane for which we'd been dismissed early from school the day before. Was it still on its way? I had no way of knowing. From John's crypt, I couldn't quite see the sky, though the warm air certainly seemed oppressive enough for rain.

I tried to concentrate on staying quiet, the way John had asked me to.

This was hard to do, though, when I kept remembering the last time I'd stood amongst so many poinciana blossoms, the fiery red flowers beneath my feet. It had been the night I'd run into John in front of this very crypt, and been so convinced he was going to kiss me . . . only he hadn't. I'd thought he'd hated me, until I'd learned the next morning from my cousin Alex that poinciana blossoms had turned up all along the walk in front of my mom's house.

There was only one person who could have put them there.

Who could have guessed that less than a week later, I'd be *inside* that crypt with that person, going to search for Alex. It was incredible how much had changed. What was my mom going to say when she saw me? Would John let me introduce him? What had my grandmother told everyone about what had happened at school? Knowing her, it definitely wasn't anything good.

"What about Furies?" I whispered to John, suddenly fearful. "Can Furies use the portal?" I looked down to check my necklace — clear — and noticed for the first time that I wasn't wearing my Snow White gown or slippers. Somehow I was back in the clothes I'd worn to school the day before, a black zip-front sundress along with a pair of metallic silver flats.

Which was good, because running around Isla Huesos in a long white dress would not only have attracted too much attention, it would have been inconvenient, especially considering the temperature. Even inside the crypt, the air was as thick and as warm as soup. I could only imagine what it was like outside.

"Furies escape the Underworld by finding weak-willed people to possess," John whispered back. "Only the newly dead can use this portal. Or me. That's why Mr. Smith had to start locking the grate. Too many people have seen me coming and going, and have gotten curious."

I looked around the small dark room — its walls were so old and ill-maintained, the roots of the enormous poinciana tree growing nearby had begun to push through — and tried to imagine anyone curious (or foolhardy) enough to follow John into it.

"Can Mr. Graves and the others use it?" I asked, thinking of how Henry had said he'd never been to Isla Huesos.

John shook his head.

So it was another one of those things only death deities could do, like the ability to make birds come back to life, and create thunder at will.

It didn't seem fair.

"Do you ever take them with you?" I asked. "Like me?"

"I should have taken them this time *instead* of you," he said. "Unlike you, they're capable of grasping the meaning of the word *quiet*."

I narrowed my eyes at him.

"You've seen them," John said, with a grin. "If people notice *me* walking in and out of a crypt, what do you think they're going to say about Henry, or Mr. Liu, or *Frank*? And you've heard Mr. Graves. He refuses to entertain the idea of any of them going." He shifted into a fairly good imitation of the blind man. It wasn't unkind, but it was accurate. *"Isla Huesos is an island of sin. If the dead go unsorted, there will be nothing but pestilence."*

I got the message. Still, I was concerned.

"But wouldn't they like some time off?" I asked. "Not Mr. Graves, maybe, but the others? We could do something about their clothes, the way you did your own." I pointed to John's black jeans, T-shirt, and tactical boots, which I was fairly certain he hadn't acquired by strolling into the local menswear shop downtown with a credit card. "With so many people opting for homeschooling these days, it wouldn't be hard to explain what Henry's doing out of class. And I don't think anyone would say much about Mr. Liu or Frank. Isla Huesos is a really popular stop with motorcycle clubs, and those two could completely pass for a couple of —"

I broke off, realizing John was looking down at me with one eyebrow raised.

"What?" I asked.

"Nothing," he said, his mouth twisted into another lopsided grin. "You just never run out of suggestions for how I could do my job better, do you?"

"Well," I said, flushing. "I'm only trying to help. Isn't that what a consort is supposed —?"

He held up a hand for silence, then listened.

"I think they're gone," John said, nodding to the grate.

"But how are we going to get out of here?" I asked. "We're locked in. Do you want me to call Mr. Smith?" I pulled out my phone, which I'd been relieved to find in my book bag, hanging from my shoulder. "I'm sure he has the key —"

John turned his head to give me a cynical look. Then he reached out and grasped the chain in both hands.

"John," I cried. "What are you —?"

Then I remembered the night I'd stood in front of this very crypt and seen the shattered remains of a similar chain lying in front of it. Not severed by bolt cutters, but literally pulled apart, the way he was doing now. Because his leather coat had disappeared exactly the way my gown had, he had on only his jeans and the black T-shirt he'd thrown on that morning.

So I got to witness firsthand how those metal links got broken. The muscles in his upper arms pumped to the size of grapefruits, and the fabric of the T-shirt tightened around them almost to tearing. . . .

Then the metal gave way with a musical twang, and the chain snaked noisily from the grate, falling to the rain-softened earth with a clunk.

"By all means," John said, brushing his hands together in a self-satisfied way, "let's call Mr. Smith."

I ducked my head, hiding my blushing cheeks by pretending to be busy putting my cell phone back in my bag. Encouraging his occasional lapses into less than civilized behavior seemed like a bad idea, so I didn't let on how extremely attractive I'd found what he'd just done.

"You know," I remarked coolly, "I'm already your girlfriend. You don't have to show off your superhuman strength for me."

John looked as if he didn't for one minute believe my disinterest. He opened the grate for me with a gentlemanly bow. "Let's go find your cousin," he said. "I'd like to be home in time for supper. Where's the coffin?"

"It's at my mom's house," I said.

"*What?*" That deflated his self-satisfaction like a pin through a balloon. He stood stock-still outside the door to his crypt, the word HAYDEN carved in bold capital letters above his head. "What's it doing *there?*"

"Seth Rector and his girlfriend and their friends asked me if they could build it in my mom's garage," I said. "They said it was the last place anyone would look."

John shook his head slowly. "Rector," he said, grinding out the word. "I should have known."

I threw him a wide-eyed glance. "*You* know Seth Rector?"

"Not Seth," he said, darkly.

"Wait. You know his dad?" The Rectors were an extremely influential family in Isla Huesos. Besides having the largest and most ornate mausoleum in the cemetery — it made John's, which was fairly large, look like a kid's playhouse — Seth's father was a realtor and developer whose signs, Rector Realty, were plastered over the windows of every empty shop downtown. "What's your connection to the Rectors?"

"It's a long story," John said, the corners of his mouth tugged down as if he'd tasted something unpleasant. He turned around and started walking towards the cemetery gate. "Your mother's house is only a few streets from here. We can walk without any-one noticing us if we stick to the side roads."

"You say that about everything," I complained, trailing after him. "Everything is a long story, too long to tell me. I suppose after two hundred years, or whatever, things get a little convo-luted, but can't you paraphrase? How do you know the Rectors?"

When we rounded the corner, it became apparent there wouldn't be time for any stories at all, paraphrased or not. Not because the gray clouds that were hanging so threateningly over-head had burst open, the way I was half expecting them to, but because the family we'd seen earlier, along with Mr. Smith and the people holding the clipboards, were climbing into their vari-ous vehicles in the parking lot right in front of us.

It shouldn't have been a big deal. We were just an ordinary young couple, taking a late afternoon stroll through the cemetery.

I'd forgotten that, due to the "vandalism" that had occurred there earlier in the week, the cemetery gates (which John had kicked apart in a fit of temper) had been ordered locked twenty-four hours a day by the chief of police.

So it kind of *was* a big deal.

Still, that didn't explain why one of the women — the grand-mother, if her gray hair was any indication — took one look at my face, made the sign of the cross, cried, *"¡Dios mío!"* then passed out cold right in front of us.

And he to me: "The anguish of the people
Who are below here in my face depicts
That pity which for terror thou hast taken."
DANTE ALIGHIERI, *Inferno*, Canto IV

D ead?" I echoed. "She fainted because she thinks I'm *dead*?"

"Missing," Mr. Smith corrected me. He sank down into the creaky chair behind his large desk and began to shuffle through some papers. "Presumed dead. Mrs. Ortega fainted because she thought you were a ghost."

John, who'd been leaning against one of the cemetery sexton's many metal file cabinets, straightened upon hearing this, bristling. "Why do they think Pierce is dead?"

Mr. Smith had known John for a long time, since dealing with the local death deity was one of the unwritten job responsibilities of the Isla Huesos Cemetery sexton. He'd gotten to know me only recently, however, and I couldn't help feeling as if he didn't care for me too much . . . or maybe it was that Mr. Smith didn't approve of me, exactly.

"Well, there's already been one young woman brutally murdered in this cemetery in the past forty-eight hours," Mr. Smith said, giving me a sour look as he pushed on the center of his gold-rimmed glasses. "A young woman who happened to be Pierce's guidance counselor, Jade Ortega. Now another young woman has disappeared. It's a small community, what do you expect people are going to think?"

I was sitting in front of Mr. Smith's desk. During all the commotion after Jade's grandmother fainted, the cemetery sexton had smuggled John and me through the back door of the small cottage that served as the graveyard's administrative offices.

I was having a hard time processing the fact that it had been my former guidance counselor's family — of all people — that we'd surprised in the cemetery. They'd been arranging a place in the Ortega family crypt for her.

On the one hand, Mr. Smith was right — Isla Huesos was a small community, and Jade had died recently, so why *wouldn't* we have run into her family in the cemetery?

On the other hand, I didn't understand why anyone would want to bury their daughter in the same cemetery in which she'd been murdered.

Mr. Smith had explained that, as soon as Jade's body was released from the coroner, her family wanted to place her remains close to where they lived, so they could "visit her often." Jade had grown up in Isla Huesos, leaving it only to go away for college, after which she'd returned to work at Isla Huesos High School, so she could "give back to the community."

"She gave back to the community, all right," I'd muttered. "With her life."

"I don't suppose you can tell me where you've been." Mr. Smith lowered his glasses to peer at us over the frames. "Although if it was one of those horrible cheap motels up the Keys, I don't want to know, actually. It will destroy all my romantic illusions."

It was my turn to bristle. "Of course not!" I cried, feeling my cheeks turning red. "John took me to the Underworld, to escape the Furies."

Mr. Smith's skin turned the opposite of mine . . . not red, but a shade or two lighter. He grew very still behind his desk.

"The Underworld," he repeated. "To escape the Furies. God help me."

"What did you think?" John hadn't liked the motel remark anymore than I had, but it didn't make him blush. He looked angry, his dark eyebrows furrowed, his mouth tightening to a thin line. I saw that muscle in his jaw begin to throb dangerously. Outside, thunder rumbled . . . but this could have been an approaching rain band from the hurricane that must, judging from the darkening sky, still have been on its way. "You saw first-hand what happened to Jade. Do you think I was going to stand by and let that — or *worse* — happen to Pierce?"

Mr. Smith seemed to have trouble formulating his next sentence. "No, of course not. But I would have hoped — certainly, I can understand why, after what happened to Jade — and with Miss Oliviera's uncle getting arrested — you were both upset . . .

but *you*, John . . . I would think *you're* old enough to know better."

John glanced at me. I looked back at him, concerned. I could tell John wanted desperately to stomp out of the cemetery sexton's office, but I didn't think that was the best idea. I wasn't sure, but I thought Mr. Smith might have been close to having a stroke. He showed all the signs — incoherence of speech, staggered breath, sudden change in color.

"Mr. Smith," I said anxiously. "Could I get you a glass of water, or something?"

"It's just," the cemetery sexton burst out, "this isn't ancient *Greece*, John. You can't simply whisk a girl off to the Underworld, and not expect there to be *consequences*."

The muscle in John's jaw twitched some more. It was surprising to hear the word *consequences* from someone's lips other than John's. He used the word quite a lot, especially in reference to my behavior.

"I'm aware of that, Mr. Smith," he said.

"I don't think you are," Mr. Smith said chidingly. "Because if you were, and you *had* to do it, as you claim — which I don't believe you did, so I'm in no way condoning your behavior — you'd have shown a little more discretion, and the outcome wouldn't be *this*."

Mr. Smith had found what he was looking for on his desk. He held up a copy of that day's paper. Most of the front page was devoted to the storm, which was very definitely on its way.

Mandatory evacuation for tourists, screamed the headline. *Schools closed. Football game may be canceled.*

Underneath was a montage of color photographs of downtown business owners boarding up the plate glass windows of their restaurants and shops in preparation of the hurricane.

I couldn't see what any of that had to do with us. Probably he really was having a stroke.

"Do you see it?" Mr. Smith demanded, tapping the paper.

Farther down, in letters almost as large, was a headline about Jade's murder. There was no photo of my uncle Chris, but I knew he was the "local man" who'd been picked up for questioning, thanks to a tip. Also that the "tip" had been an anonymous phone call that my uncle had been seen in the area around the time Jade was believed to have been killed, even though he'd been home, asleep. Uncle Chris had been released, but was still considered a suspect, in spite of the fact that there was no evidence whatsoever to connect him to the crime or to the victim. Some tip.

"I'm sorry, no. I really don't see what any of this —" I started to say.

The cemetery sexton tapped the paper again, impatiently. "*Here,*" he said.

I looked where he was tapping.

Local Girl Missing, Feared Dead.

Beneath it was a photo of me — my most recent school photo.

"Oh, no." My heart filling with dread, I took the paper from Mr. Smith's hands. "Couldn't they have found a better picture?"

Mr. Smith looked at me sharply. "Miss Oliviera," he said, his gray eyebrows lowered. "I realize it's all the rage with you young people today to toss off flippant one-liners so you can get your own reality television shows. But I highly doubt MTV will be coming down to Isla Huesos to film you in the Underworld. So that can't be all you have to say about this."

He was right, of course. Though I couldn't say what I really wanted to, because John was in the room, and I didn't want to make him feel worse than he already did.

But what I wanted to do was burst into tears.

"Is that about Pierce?" John looked uneasy. Outside, thunder rumbled again. This time, it sounded even closer than before.

"Yes, of course, it is, John," Mr. Smith said. There was something strange about his voice. He sounded almost as if he were mad at John. Only why would he be? John had done the right thing. He'd explained about the Furies. "What did you expect? Have you gotten to the part about the reward your father is offering for information leading to your safe return, Miss Oliviera?"

My gaze flicked down the page. I wanted to throw up.

"One million dollars?" My dad's company, one of the largest providers in the world of products and services to the oil, gas, and military industries, was valued at several hundred times that. "That cheapskate."

This was all so very, very bad.

"One million dollars is a lot of money to most people," Mr. Smith said, with a strong emphasis on *most people*. He still had that odd note in his voice. "Though I recognize that money may mean little to a resident of *the Underworld*. So I'd caution you to use judiciousness, wherever it is that you're going, as there are many people on this island who'll be more than willing to turn you in for only a small portion of that reward money. I don't suppose I might ask where you're going? Or suggest that you pay a call on your mother, who is beside herself with worry?"

"That's a good idea," I said. Why hadn't I thought of it? I felt much better already. I could straighten out this whole thing with a single conversation. "I should call my mom —"

Both Mr. Smith's cry of alarm and the fact that John grabbed me by the wrist as I was reaching into my book bag for my cell phone stopped me from making calls of any sort.

"You can't use your phone," Mr. Smith said. "The police — and your father — are surely waiting for you to do just that. They'll triangulate on the signal from the closest cell tower, and find you." When I stared at him for his use of the word *triangulate*, Mr. Smith shook his head and said, "My partner, Patrick, is obsessed with *Law & Order* reruns."

I looked at John. He glanced down at my wrist, around which his fingers were tightly wrapped, and slowly released his hold.

"I'm sorry, Pierce," he said, his tone as apologetic as his eyes. "But Mr. Smith is right. The last thing we need right now is more people knowing we're here. In and out. That's what we agreed this visit had to be. We're only here to help your cousin Alex. Remember?"

"Of course," I murmured, lowering my gaze in the hopes that he wouldn't see the disappointment his words had brought to my eyes. I don't think I'd realized until that very moment how much I'd been counting on seeing my mother, even if it was only a glimpse.

"Unless, of course, you *want* your father to find you, Miss Oliviera." Mr. Smith's voice cut through the tension in the air like a knife blade. He'd folded his hands on his dark green desk pad . . . but he didn't sound as calm as he looked. I noticed that his fingers were shaking. "Is that newspaper article accurate? *Are* you being held against your will?"

"What?" I glanced at the paper and saw there was another photo, farther down the page from the one of me. It was a grainy screen grab from a video camera.

A video camera hanging from the ceiling of an outdoor breezeway at Isla Huesos High School.

I actually hadn't thought things could get any worse.

I was wrong.

"That's you," I said faintly to John, pointing to the large shadowy figure prominently depicted in the video still. "You *do* show up on film. Not your face so much. But the rest of you."

John looked over my shoulder at the photo.

"And you," he said in an unhappy voice. "You're even wearing the same clothes."

It was true. In the photo, though John's image was blurred, I was clearly distinguishable in my black dress. What was worse was that I appeared to be in a great deal of distress. The much larger figure of John was carrying me away. It didn't take a great deal of imagination to make it seem as if he was doing so against my will. My arms were flung out in the air, and I was screaming. For anyone who did not quite get the message, the paper had helpfully identified John in the caption beneath the photo as the *alleged kidnapper.*

What had been cropped from the photo was the image of the person at whom I'd been screaming and flinging my arms, from whom John had been dragging me away: my grandmother.

I felt a chill pass over me. It had nothing to do with the fact that the air-conditioning in Mr. Smith's office had been put on at such a high setting, condensation was forming on the windowpanes.

"This photo has been altered," I said to Mr. Smith, feeling outraged on John's behalf. "It didn't happen like that."

"It doesn't matter," Mr. Smith said. "That photo has already been on most of the twenty-four-hour news shows and plastered all over the web. Mrs. Ortega, Jade's grandmother, was only the first person to recognize you. Fortunately I convinced her that it was a case of mistaken identity, and the rest of the family was so busy dealing with her, they didn't even notice you. But I won't be around to do that for everyone. And I'm not convinced I should."

"My grandmother was standing *right there*," I said, tapping the spot on the photo where her image had clearly been removed. "She was trying to kill me. And I was trying to fight back, only John wouldn't let me, because he was afraid I'd get hurt —"

"Miss Oliviera," Mr. Smith said, in the same snippy tone he'd been using since we walked into his office. "Please. I know John is . . . special . . . to you. But if you want me to help you, it's very important that you tell the truth."

Suddenly I realized what it was in Mr. Smith's voice: disapproval. Disapproval and, of all things, fear. He was afraid. Not for me.

Of John.

Which made me feel colder than ever, and a little bit fearful myself.

"I *am* telling the truth," I said, just as John said, "What are you talking about? You can see for yourself she's not hurt —"

"Well, someone is hurt. Very hurt. Pierce's grandmother is claiming to have severe facial lacerations," Mr. Smith said. "As she tells it, it's because you struck her, John, as she was trying to keep you from abducting her beautiful, innocent young granddaughter, whom you have probably killed, or at the very least —"

"Oh, my God," I interrupted. Anger replaced fear. "She's such a liar. *I* punched her, not John, and it was because she confessed to killing me."

Mr. Smith raised his eyebrows. "I beg your pardon, but you look very much alive to me, Miss Oliviera."

"The first time I died," I said. I reached inside my book bag to pull out my jean jacket and tug it on. But my chill had nothing to do with the temperature of the room. "When I was fifteen, she sent me a scarf that tripped me while I was trying to rescue a bird, so I hit my head and fell in our pool and drowned."

Mr. Smith's eyebrows nearly hit the roof. "I think the local police are unlikely to believe that constitutes proof that the owner of Knuts for Knitting is a murderess."

"She did it because she's possessed by a Fury," I said, my voice trembling as much as my limbs. "She said she wants me to die so I'll be with John forever and then she and the other Furies can spend eternity torturing him by hurting me."

"*What?*" Mr. Smith shook his head. "No, I'm sorry. But that's too ridiculous, even for Isla Huesos."

"It's the truth," I insisted. "If *you* won't believe me, who will?"

It was only then that Mr. Smith finally did something remotely human. He lifted his glasses to pinch the bridge of his nose . . . and when he did, I saw that his fingers were shaking even more than before.

"I've known your grandmother for over twenty years, and I've never heard her mention the existence of Furies, much less that she's *one* of them," he said. "The woman organizes the church bake sale, for God's sake."

"All I know is that ever since John gave it to me, my necklace turns black every time I'm around her," I said. Mr. Smith knew all about my necklace. He was the one who'd explained its bloody provenance — Marie Antoinette had lost her head because of it. "I thought it was *my* fault we didn't get along . . . that there was something wrong with *me*, because she's always made me feel so awkward and clumsy. She's never made it a secret that I'm not good enough, because I'm not as smart or pretty as my mom, and that I need to try a lot harder if I'm going to get as far in life as she did." My voice caught. This was the first time I'd ever said any of these things out loud. It felt bad to say them in front of John. I didn't want him to know this about me.

But my grandmother was a Fury, I reminded myself. It wasn't like she knew what she was talking about. She was pure evil. Or possessed by it, anyway.

"Now I know the truth," I went on, in a less shaky voice, "which is that it wasn't me at all . . . it was her. She's a monster inside — literally — who's wanted nothing more than to hurt John — and now me — for years."

"Pierce," John said quietly, reaching down to touch my shoulder. I wondered if he could feel it trembling through the denim of my jacket. "You don't have to say another word to him. We don't have time for this, anyway. Let's go —"

"No," Mr. Smith said, dropping his glasses back into place and speaking in a tired voice. "John, you can't afford *not* to make time to listen to what I have to say. And Pierce . . . I'm ready for that water you offered me. Or make it tea, please. There's a little kitchen in the back room, right down that hallway over there. You should be able to find everything you need. Would you be a dear?"

I was startled. No one but my mother had ever asked me to make tea for them before. And no one had ever called me a dear. Especially right in the middle of a conversation about relatives of mine who were trying to kill me.

"Now?" I asked.

"Yes," Mr. Smith said, loosening his tie a little. An older gentleman who dressed with great attention to style, today favoring white linen trousers and a mint-green shirt with a pink knit tie, Mr. Smith did look a little under the weather, I had to admit. "I mentioned to you once that I, too, went through a near-death experience . . . although like most people, I was not fortunate enough to remember my trip to the Underworld. But that is, of course, what sparked my interest in all things related to the afterlife. Ever since, however, my heart hasn't been as strong as it used to be. I think some herbal tea would be just the thing. . . ."

"Yes, of course," I said, and climbed to my feet, meeting John's gaze. He shook his head sharply, indicating that he didn't want me to go. He wanted to leave.

What was I supposed to do, though, deny a sickly old man the tea he'd requested? I shrugged helplessly at John, then hurried down the hallway Mr. Smith had indicated.

"She's not a child," I heard John say in a razor-edged tone, as soon as I was out of the room. "So you can't simply send her off to the kitchen because you have something to say that you don't want her to hear. Whatever you have to say to me, you can say in front of her."

"Oh, I don't think you want her to hear what I have to say to you," Mr. Smith snapped . . . which of course made me pause before I set one foot in the kitchen and hug the shadows along the hallway wall so they couldn't see me as I eavesdropped. I knew snooping was wrong, but why was Mr. Smith so angry? I had to find out. "I've known you for a long time, John, so I'd like to think you won't strike me dead for saying this, because we're friends, and friends should be able to speak honestly to one another. But for the love of all that is holy, *what* could you have been thinking? This is the twenty-first century, and we're a civilized country. With *laws*."

"Fortunately," John said, in a calm voice, "no one asked you, since it isn't any of your business."

"Isn't any of my business? She's seventeen years old, and you're —"

"Nineteen," John said flatly.

"— one hundred and eighty-four. And you transported her . . . well, not across state lines, but to the realm of the dead, which I'm quite sure her father would find more objectionable if he knew about it."

"Would he find it so objectionable if he knew I did it to keep her from being murdered?"

"Why didn't you come to me about it, John?" Mr. Smith's tone was pleading. "I might have been able to help."

"Or you might have ended up dead, like Jade, or Mr. Cabrero, Pierce's grandfather," John said shortly. "Or do you think he didn't find out the truth about his wife, and try to stop what she was doing?"

"What?" Mr. Smith sounded shocked. "Are you saying that old woman killed her husband, too? Act your age, John. Carlos was my friend, I'd have known —"

"Would you?" John asked, his tone icily polite. "You just said you went to church with her, but you had no idea what she really was. Do you truly think if I'd had any other choice, I wouldn't have taken it?"

"Truly? No. Because I know how you feel about that girl. So when the opportunity presented itself, you were more than happy to take it. I'm sure it hasn't even been that difficult of an adjustment for her, since she's journeyed to your world before. But none of that makes what you did right, John, any more than what was done to you. I'm positive there must be a better way. I understand about the Furies. They're a problem, I grant you —"

"A *problem*?" John's voice rose in disbelief.

"Let me do some research. Perhaps there's something I missed, some way to get rid of them that no one's thought of. In the meantime, her father's wealthy, he could send her anywhere to get her away from the grandmother. . . ."

Suddenly I realized why Mr. Smith had sent me out of the room. He wasn't just angry with John for kidnapping me and taking me to the realm of the dead, like Hades had done to Persephone: He was trying to persuade John to give me up.

"Tell me you're here to do the right thing and bring her back," Mr. Smith went on, his voice low and urgent. "It's the only way. Her parents are frantic . . . like your own mother must have been when she got word of your disappearance, John, all those years ago. Are you going to do to Pierce's mother what was done to yours? I can't believe that."

I couldn't believe Mr. Smith was talking about me like I was some kind of stray kitten and didn't have a say in what *I* wanted to do, or where *I* wanted to live. Although truthfully, I didn't, since the Fates — and John — had more or less decided for me.

The truth was, however, the Furies had decided before any of them.

I was going to storm back in there and say that . . . but then, of course, they'd know I'd been eavesdropping. Also, John ended up saying it for me.

"According to that paper you showed us, the damage is already done," he pointed out coolly. "So I don't see the good of her coming back now. That being said, there's nowhere on this earth her father can send her where the Furies can't find her . . . *and* nowhere he can send her where I can't find her, either, as long as she wants me."

"As long as she wants you," Mr. Smith repeated slowly. "And how long do you think that's going to be? Does she even know the truth yet about how you ended up where you are?"

Though I strained to hear John's reply to this question, only stony silence followed.

Until I heard, "How are you coming along back there with that tea, Miss Oliviera?" from Mr. Smith.

Startled, I jumped and hurried as softly as I could down the hall, my ballet flats fortunately soundless on the industrial carpeting.

"Fine," I called when I got into the kitchen.

Only I found that I was still shaking, feeling colder than ever despite the denim jacket.

I had lied to Mr. Smith, of course. I was not fine.

I wasn't sure I'd ever be fine again.

*"To tell us in what way the soul is bound
Within these knots; and tell us, if thou canst,
If any from such members e'er is freed."*
DANTE ALIGHIERI, *Inferno*, Canto XIII

It was while I was warming my hands over the teakettle, waiting for the water to boil — trust Mr. Smith not to have a microwave or electric teakettle or modern conveniences of any kind — that I looked out the small kitchen window and saw it:

Hope appeared from nowhere — just fluttered down from the sky — and landed in the small dirt yard behind the cemetery sexton's office.

At first I thought there was no way it could be her.

Although when I saw her waddling around, lifting up dead leaves in search of food, I knew it couldn't be any other bird *but* her. How many other ravenously hungry white doves with black underwings were there in Isla Huesos? Especially following me around.

Why had she left the Underworld? And *how*?

I looked around the tiny kitchen, which was clearly only used as a place to prepare beverages for the bereaved, and perhaps to store ant traps, and was shocked to find a half-full bag of birdseed. I shouldn't have been surprised, though. The cemetery stretched across nineteen acres of land, and was probably a resting stop for a large variety of birds on their migratory path south every year. I was willing to bet Mr. Smith could give my mom a run for her money on their different orders and genera.

Taking the bag of birdseed with me, I opened the glassed-in screen door to the back steps into the yard, then sat down on the top one, reaching into the bag and sprinkling a few generous handfuls of the seeds onto the step below me.

Hope eyed me, but didn't come over right away. She was obviously insulted I'd left her behind, and was giving me the cold shoulder.

"Come on," I said. "You know you want it."

The yard was more of a fenced-in storage area for the cemetery grounds — complete with a toolshed and piles of damaged headstones and statuary in various states of repair — than it was an actual backyard.

It was late in the day, and evidence of the approaching hurricane was everywhere, from the luridly purple clouds in the sky overhead, to the Spanish limes that had been knocked by the wind from a nearby tree and now lay in pulpy messes all over the muddy yard, to the humidity that caused me to peel off my denim jacket and tie it around my waist.

So there was no one around to overhear me talking to a bird.

"We left in a hurry," I explained to Hope. "Besides, you're safer there than you are here. You shouldn't have followed us."

She gave a grudging coo and bobbed over to inspect the seeds. She made it clear, though, with her standoffish attitude, that it was about the food and not me.

A second later the glassed-in door opened behind me and a black loafer — attached to a white-trousered leg — appeared on the step beside me. The loafer had a tassel on it. Due to Mr. Mueller, I had an aversion to men's shoes with tassels on them.

But Mr. Smith's tasseled loafers, which he'd paired with pink socks, didn't bother me . . . perhaps because he'd never had an affair with my best friend, and driven her to suicide.

"Oh," Mr. Smith said, looking surprised to see a dove pecking seeds from the steps of his office's storage yard. "You've made a friend."

"John gave her to me," I said. "Her name is Hope. I know it's a dumb name, but I like it, and she already responds to it. Watch. Hope?"

The bird looked up, annoyed at being disturbed from her feast. When I waved at her, she shook herself all over like a duck flicking water off its back, then dropped her head to continue eating.

Mr. Smith looked even more surprised.

"Well," he said. "Wasn't that nice of John? You're aware, I suppose, that mourning doves received their name because of the mournful — almost funereal — sound of their cry, not because they're seen more frequently in the morning hours. That's a common misconception."

There probably weren't many cemetery sextons whose jobs were better suited to them, thanks to their obsession with the subject of death, than Mr. Smith.

"That makes her a highly appropriate companion for the consort of the Lord of the Underworld. I've also heard," Mr. Smith went on, sinking down onto the step beside me, "that mourning doves are monogamous, mating for life."

"Great," I said, looking at Hope a little sadly. I wondered what happened to her mate. I hoped she hadn't met him yet, and that she was not a grieving widow. Although she didn't look that unhappy, gorging herself on the handfuls of birdseed I'd thrown her. "I thought she was just a regular dove."

"Her coloring is unusually pale for a mourning dove. But you can tell by her markings," Mr. Smith said. "Those black feathers under her wings and tail."

"So she has a dark side," I murmured. Just like the person who'd given her to me. I ought to have known. I turned to Mr. Smith and said, "You haven't asked about your tea. I knew you only sent me to make it so you could talk to John alone. But you shouldn't blame him for what happened. None of it is his fault. Where is he, anyway?"

"He's inside. I told him I wanted to speak with you alone for a few moments. I don't think he likes the idea very much . . . in fact, he's probably plotting how to hasten my demise at this very moment. He's very . . . protective of you, isn't he?"

"Well, he and I only just got together," I pointed out, "after years of misunderstandings and fights that kept us apart. And now it turns out someone in my family is trying to kill me. I think he simply wants to keep me from getting my head bashed in, like Jade. Or worse, as he keeps saying." Only I still didn't think there could be anything worse than what had happened to Jade.

"I blame myself," Mr. Smith said glumly. "I always knew your grandmother disapproved of your grandfather's interest in death deities and the possibility that there might be an underworld beneath Isla Huesos. I just assumed it was because Angela Cabrero was so devoutly religious. She, like so many people, wants to believe there's a heaven and a hell and that's that. I didn't realize her dislike of the idea that there might be shades of gray in between was . . . *personal*."

"Allegedly it's not," I said. "It's the Fury possessing her that wants to get revenge on John, and has been forcing her to use me to do it. But I don't know if I believe that. She *allowed* the Fury to possess her, which makes me think all that hate had to have been there all along."

"Good heavens," Mr. Smith said. "Now we're talking about whether or not the average human being has the will to resist a Fury. That's the kind of thing your grandfather and I could spend an entire afternoon debating, and John told me I'm allowed a mere five minutes with you. He says you're only here to make sure your hapless cousin is all right."

He noticed my frown at the word *hapless* and continued, "Please, I met the boy. Your cousin Alexander is indeed hapless, by which I mean unhappy, not ill-fortuned. Certainly Alex has had his fair share of hard knocks, but I think we make our own luck. Don't tell me you believe that nonsense about fate. No, our parents give us life, but what we do with that life is our own responsibility."

"Actually," I said, thinking of the breakfast that had appeared that morning, piping hot and impossible to resist. "The Fates are real. I've had personal experience with them. Although I've never seen one. I'd like to, though."

"I didn't say I don't believe in *the* Fates," Mr. Smith said. "From my studies about the afterlife, I believe the Fates are spirits, just like the Furies. Like what other people might call angels, but the kind that walk on earth, not the kind with wings. When people are moved to do good by the spirit of human kindness, I believe that's the work of the Fates . . . as much as other people are moved to do evil by the Furies."

I wrinkled my nose at him. "So you think the Fates are kind of like the power of prayer?" He might have been onto something. John *had* said the things he wanted badly enough — within reason — had a tendency to appear.

"Something like that," Mr. Smith said, with a chuckle. "In any case, John wants to find your cousin and get you back before nightfall, which I can understand . . . although it's a shame, because it's Coffin Fest tonight, if it doesn't get shut down because of the rain, and that's something you really ought not to miss. . . ."

"Coffin *Fest?*" I'd heard of Coffin Night, but Coffin Fest was a new one. They certainly loved their dead on the Island of Bones.

"Oh, just something they throw together downtown this time of year," he said, waving a hand dismissively. "Quite small, you understand, because it's more of a locals-only tradition. They're careful not to put it in the calendar of events they hand out to tourists, because the authorities don't like to encourage Coffin Night. A few vendors set up stands selling street food and the inevitable Isla Huesos T-shirts, a local band plays Cuban music, people dance to celebrate the fact that they're alive, but it's nowhere near," he added, "the tens of thousands we get showing up for New Year's Eve. That isn't what I wanted to talk to you about, though. What I actually wanted to talk to you about was whether or not you're happy."

I looked at him in surprise. "Happy?"

"Yes, *happy*," Mr. Smith said, emphasizing the word as strongly as he had *hapless*. "I'm sure it all seems very romantic and thrilling, having a strapping young man like John drag you off to the Underworld. Who wouldn't love it? But his good intentions aside — wanting to save you from the Furies and all of that — you must see that what John did was wrong . . . very, very wrong."

I thought about waking up that morning in John's arms, after my horrible nightmare about losing him, and how his kisses had made me feel as if I were melting into him, almost as if we were one person. Then later how I'd determined to take care of him, the same way he'd tried over the years to take care of me, even when I'd kept pushing him away . . . and how later still, I'd seen the great pains he'd gone to in order to incorporate my suggestions on how to better serve the needs of the dead. . . .

"Being with him doesn't feel wrong," I said to him, my eyes filling with tears. "The only thing that feels wrong is when I try to imagine living in a world without him in it."

Mr. Smith's own eyes widened slightly behind the lenses of his glasses.

"I suppose it's just as well, then," he said, "that you apparently *must* remain in his world. Which I was surprised to hear, since I was quite sure you knew all about what happened to Persephone when *she* ate in the Underworld. In fact, hearing that you ate while in the realm of the dead almost made me think that you did it on purpose so you'd be forced to stay with him, since you knew full well —"

"I thought it was only pomegranates," I interrupted. "That's what they taught us in school. Persephone ate the seeds of a pomegranate, the fruit of the dead."

Mr. Smith raised his eyebrows. "Ah, yes, of course. That's the most common retelling. The safe, watered-down version one would expect . . . wouldn't want to frighten the children, or cause them actually to think too much. Poor Persephone ate the wrong thing, that's all."

I had no idea what he was talking about.

"And John, of course, didn't stop you. Well, he wouldn't, would he?" The cemetery sexton's tone was arch. "That would hardly be in *his* best interests."

"He thought I knew," I said. The tears filling my eyes began to spill over. "Why are you so against us being together? Why does it feel as if everyone wants us to break up? Not only the Furies or my grandmother, but *everyone*, even you?"

"I'm not suggesting you break up," he said, appearing startled by my tears. He reached into his pocket, then produced a neatly folded handkerchief, which he handed to me. It was pink, of course, to match his socks and tie. "But when you visited me here the other night and I said you might want to try being a little sweeter to him, I wasn't saying you should *move in with him* and then spend the rest of eternity in the Underworld. At least, not the next *day*. My God, your poor parents. Supposing they find out I had a hand in encouraging you?"

"You said what we do with our lives is our own responsibility, Mr. Smith," I reminded him as I dried my tears. "You're not responsible for what I did. *I* am, for falling in love with him. That happened way before I met you. So you can let yourself off the hook." I passed his handkerchief back to him. "As for my mother . . . well, I don't know what I'm going to do about her. Right now, I'm mostly worried about Alex."

"I am sorry for what you're going through," he said, with a sympathetic smile at me. "Tell you what, I'll do some research about this food and drink rule in the Underworld. Who knows, maybe John is wrong? It's possible it's been misinterpreted over the years. It wouldn't be the first time. There are many scholars who staunchly believe your pomegranate theory, which is why it was the one you were taught . . . though in most cultures, including Judaism, Hinduism, and ancient China, the pomegranate, because of all its seeds, has always been associated with fertility and reproduction, not death. But that's an exciting thought." He raised his eyebrows. "What if the narrative of Persephone's tale has been taken too literally, and the pomegranate is actually symbolic of —"

I held up a hand to stem the tide of his words, fearing I was about to hear a lecture on the cultural history of the pomegranate. Mr. Smith was as bad as my mom in some ways. He could go on for hours about the minutiae of death deity lore the same way she could go on for hours about roseate spoonbills.

"All I want to know is what the deal is with babies in the Underworld," I said tiredly. "Can people get pregnant there, or what?"

Mr. Smith suddenly looked as if he might be stroking out again. A sheen of sweat broke out across his forehead, and he seemed to go a little gray. I found the heat a relief after the chill of the Underworld and the air-conditioning of his office. He apparently did not. He used the handkerchief I'd passed back to him to wipe his face.

"This is exactly why Patrick and I chose not to have children," he muttered. "So we would never have to have conversations like this. And yet . . . here I am."

"If you could answer the question," I said as politely as I could, "that would be great. I really don't want to have a freaky demon baby, and I can't imagine John wants one, either."

"Yes, well," Mr. Smith said, removing his glasses and beginning to polish them, his fallback gesture whenever he felt uncomfortable, I'd noticed. "I can only imagine having a freaky demon baby would be unpleasant for all concerned. So you'll be happy to know in my study of psychopomps, I've never come across a death deity capable of siring children at all, even freaky demons . . . I suppose because life is the very opposite of death. Hades and Persephone certainly had no children together."

"Okay," I said, feeling relieved. That was one worry off my mind.

"But you see my concern, don't you, Miss Oliviera?" Mr. Smith slipped his glasses back on and looked at me with worry in his brown eyes. "I know John would kill me for pointing this out to you, but there's still so much you haven't experienced in life. And now you'll never get to. Can you honestly tell me you have no regrets at all about that?"

I sprang up, shooting down the steps to pace the small, cluttered yard, suddenly unable to keep still. The sun had finally managed to burn through some of the thick cloud cover to the west, creating a magnificent orange and yellow fireburst against the thunderheads, and burnishing all the statues atop the nearby crypts — the angels and Virgin Marys and cherubs — with gold.

"Of course I have regrets," I said, thrusting my hands into the pockets of my dress. "But how do you think John must feel? He's spent nearly *two hundred years* not . . . *experiencing* things. That's what I don't understand, Mr. Smith. When I was here before, you were on John's side. You even seemed a little disappointed in me for not liking him more. Now you seem worried I like him *too much*."

"I'm not on anyone's side," Mr. Smith insisted from the steps. "I simply don't want to see you get hurt. And I want to make sure you're fully aware of the risk that you're taking, that you know what you're doing —"

"Of *course* I don't know what I'm doing," I exclaimed, throwing my hands into the air. Hope, whom I paced too near, waddled irritably out of my way. "All I know is that a bunch of people hate my boyfriend for reasons that totally aren't his fault, and because of that, innocent people have gotten killed, including me. It's totally messed up and I hate it, but if there's something I can do to stop it, I'm not going to sit around and give lectures to people about pomegranates. I'm going to actually *do something*. So it really doesn't help for you to say things like John's going to hasten your demise for saying this or kill you for saying that. You know he's not like that. He's *keeper of the dead*, it's not his job to punish the living. So if you want to help, *help*. Otherwise, save the lectures."

Mr. Smith blinked a few times at my outburst.

"I see," he said, finally, a troubled frown on his face. "You certainly don't hold back when it comes to expressing your feelings, do you, Miss Oliviera? I beg your pardon if I've said anything to offend you. The events of this past week have been a bit . . . overwhelming for me, though I suppose they've been much more so for others — such as poor Jade Ortega." His voice dropped to a hoarse whisper. "But the truth is, ever since you showed up here, this island has been thrown into such a state of disruption, from the storm to Jade's murder to the revelation that your grandmother is a Fury, I *don't* know what John is like anymore. I've been forced to reevaluate everything I ever thought I knew . . . including my opinion of John Hayden. Like you said, he *is* keeper of the dead. But you still don't even know what he did to become that way, do you, Miss Oliviera?"

"No," I said, freezing in my tracks. A sudden breeze picked up, rustling the palm fronds over our heads, and causing the clouds to close in on the brief but dazzling display of sunlight that had broken through, darkening the sky once more. "He said it was a long story." He'd also said it would make me hate him. I tried to put that out of my mind. It couldn't be true. "I know it has to do with a boat. I met the crew — well, some of them — already. The *Liberty*."

"The *Liberty*," Mr. Smith said grimly. "Yes. Stay right where you are, Miss Oliviera." The cemetery sexton rose to his feet, his joints popping noisily in protest. "I have a book you need to read. It might help clear up a thing or two for you —"

Of course. I was on the run from evil spirits that wanted to kill me and now, according to the local paper, the law. Yet Richard Smith, cemetery sexton and death deity scholar, had a book for me to read in all my copious spare time.

He pulled open the glass door.

That noise wasn't the one that caused Hope to flutter her wings and take off. It was the scrape of the wooden gate to the storage area being thrown open that did that.

Mr. Smith turned around, as nervous as Hope, to see who was coming into the yard. When he saw it was the same grounds-keeper I'd noticed pushing a wheelbarrow behind Jade's bereaved family, he visibly relaxed.

I didn't, however.

"Oh, Mike," Mr. Smith said with a cheerful smile, as the man shoved his wheelbarrow — empty now, except for a few tools — into the yard. "I had no idea you were still here. You should have gone home hours ago. They're saying this storm looks set to hit us dead on. You must have windows to board up. . . ."

"Nope," Mike said, his gaze flicking over me. He was probably only a few years older than John, but with his scruffy beard and violently colored tattoos of busty women all up and down his arms — he'd cut the sleeves from his Isla Huesos Cemetery coveralls in order to show them off — he seemed decades older, somehow. "Not bothering. I'm betting this one's going to fizzle out over Cuba. Who's this?"

It wasn't only the way Hope had reacted to him (she hadn't flown for the security of a high branch of the nearby Spanish lime tree when Mr. Smith had come outside). There was something about Mike that set me on edge right away. He was looking at me so intently . . . almost like he recognized me.

Calm down, I told myself. He's just planning on how he's going to spend that million-dollar reward Dad's offering for your safe return.

"Oh," Mr. Smith was saying. He didn't seem to notice my unease, or the fact that Mike completely knew who I was. "This is . . . my niece, Jennifer. Jennifer, this is Mike, our new grounds-keeper here at Isla Huesos Cemetery."

Mike began to wipe the dirt from his fingers with a rag from his wheelbarrow, obviously in anticipation of shaking my hand. So I felt like I had no choice but to start walking over to him, my own hand extended.

I don't know what made me glance down at my necklace, tucked beneath the front zipper of my dress. Instinct, maybe. Or the fact that Hope had begun bobbing up and down on her branch, her feathers puffed to make herself look twice her normal size.

The diamond John had given me had turned as dark as the feathers beneath Hope's wings . . . as black as the storm clouds that had begun to tower in the sky.

With a burst of clarity, I knew it wasn't a reward Mike wanted from me. It was my life.

When I glanced back at him, I saw that he'd thrown down the rag, and reached for one of the shovels in his wheelbarrow, his gaze dead-eyed and locked on mine.

I inhaled. What came out was not the wordless scream of terror I was expecting, but a name. *"John!"*

Mike had already swung the shovel high above his head.

Where in a moment saw I swift uprisen
The three infernal Furies stained with blood,
Who had the limbs of women and their mien.
DANTE ALIGHIERI, *Inferno*, Canto IX

I turned and raced towards the steps. Mike was blocking the gate, the only other way out of the yard.

I knew I would never make it inside Mr. Smith's cottage before that shovelhead came crashing down onto my skull. A part of me could already feel the sharp metal slicing all the way down to my vertebrae. Even if I made it up the steps, it wouldn't matter. Mr. Smith was blocking the path to the doorway. He looked confused.

"Mike, what are you doing?" he asked.

The cemetery sexton was in too much shock simply to open the glassed-in door and go inside, where we both could have been relatively safe, if Mike didn't use the shovel to break the glass.

Richard Smith didn't understand that the Mike he knew was gone. He was completely and totally possessed by the Fury inside him.

Both of us, I realized, were going to die.

It's amazing what a person will do, though, in an effort to survive. As I turned to sprint for those steps, fully aware I was never going to make it without some kind of miracle, I spent my last few precious seconds of life looking around for a weapon I could use in self-defense. My gaze fell on the fractured angel statues and piles of broken headstones that lay scattered about the yard, and the vases and potted plants — the kind people left on the gravesites of their loved ones — that had been removed because they were damaged, the flowers and plants inside them spindly and dead.

I leaned down to grab a terra-cotta one, just as Mike swung that shovel . . .

. . . at the exact same moment that John burst through the door, shoving Mr. Smith aside, then came surging down the steps, moving so quickly that I had only the vaguest sense of a wood smoke–scented breeze as he passed by me. His body was a blur.

He caught the shovel in one hand, twisting it from Mike's grip just before the metal scoop sank into my skull. Then with his other hand, John shoved Mike away from me, so hard that the other man flew backwards and landed against the wooden fence.

His body hit the boards with such force it almost shook them from their pilings, before Mike bounced off the fence to land into the soft mud beneath.

"Go inside before you get hurt," John said to me, never taking his gaze from the man who was already staggering to his feet.

I recognized the dangerous, almost wild glint in John's eyes, and the way his chest was rising up and down as if he'd just run a marathon, not from the front of a small house to the back.

It was exactly like the last time I'd seen him try to kill a man. The only reason he hadn't was because I'd stopped him.

"John," I said. I felt frozen where I stood, still holding the terra-cotta planter. "Don't."

He wouldn't even look at me. His gaze was locked on the groundskeeper's.

"It's all right," John said. "Go inside."

Mike didn't look ready to give up, either. His lips curled back in a sneer as he stared down at the blood that had come away on the wrist he'd used to wipe his mouth.

"It's no use," he said to John with a smirk. "One of us is going to get to her eventually. If not her, then someone close to her. You're protector of the dead, not the living. How do you think you're going to stop us?"

"I have an idea," John said. He struck the shovel against a white marble statue of an angel, brought in for maintenance because she'd somehow come to be missing a head. The shovel splintered and broke in half, leaving John with one end that was lethally sharp. This was the end he kept. "Why don't I just kill you?"

Mike grinned. "Go ahead and try."

"John," I cried, more loudly this time. "Don't!"

But John ignored me as he stalked towards Mike with his spear. Mike, meanwhile, picked up the scoop end of the shovel and held it in a defensive stance, still grinning. He was enjoying himself.

"Boys," Mr. Smith said, finally getting over his shock and coming to life. "Stop this nonsense, the two of you. I'm going inside to call the police right now. . . ." This time when he reached for the door handle, he actually managed to make contact.

My pulse, which was already staggering, skipped a beat, because I realized Mr. Smith was still clinging to his life before — as he'd put it — the disruption of my arrival to Isla Huesos, back when his knowledge of Furies had been only theoretical and his talks with John had been pleasant tête-à-têtes when they happened to bump into each other during John's lonely rambles in the cemetery, not fights about his kidnapping girls. Mr. Smith truly did not understand what was happening. The police couldn't stop it. I was the only person who could stop it.

But how?

I figured it out a split second later when John lunged at Mike, and, in spinning to avoid the blow, Mike happened to lurch towards me. I didn't think, I just acted. I hurled the flowerpot I was still holding at Mike's head. The sound as the planter made contact with Mike's skull was sickening.

I've never knocked anyone into unconsciousness before. When I hit my grandma, I was angry. When I hit Mike, I was simply scared. It felt horrible, even if Mike completely deserved it. My heart was slamming in my chest, and I felt a little nauseous as I watched him go down. He didn't go neatly, either, the way people do in movies when they're knocked over the head. He staggered around a bit first, like he was drunk and his legs couldn't quite hold up the weight of his body.

Finally, he did sink into the mud, then lay still . . . fortunately still breathing.

Neither John nor Mr. Smith was too happy with me.

"I — I'm sure he's got a concussion. I'd better go call an ambulance," Mr. Smith stammered, before rushing inside to do so.

I wanted to point out that Mike could have had a lot worse than a concussion if I'd let John do what he wanted to him, but I was shaking too much to speak. And the iciness I felt had nothing to do with the sudden burst of cool air that came from the cemetery sexton's office after he flung open the door.

John was upset for different reasons than Mr. Smith.

"Why did you do that? Why didn't you let me handle it?" he demanded, taking me by the wrist and pulling me away from where the unconscious man lay at the bottom of the steps amidst the pieces of shattered terra-cotta and Hope's birdseed.

John was still breathing hard, his long dark hair falling in his face, his silver eyes glowing. I could see how fast his heart was drumming through the tight material of his shirt. He was almost as worked up as Hope, only he wasn't puffed to twice his size . . . but he might as well have been. Between the two of them, I didn't know who to soothe first. I chose John because I didn't think Hope was capable of still stabbing the unconscious man through the heart with a broken shovel handle.

"Mr. Smith was going to call the police," I said. "Is that what you want, to get arrested?"

The corners of his mouth twitched, despite his agitation. "Pierce, I'm flattered, but do you really think there's a jail strong enough to hold me?" Then he remembered he was mad at me, and frowned. "You should have let me handle it."

Frustrated, I shoved some of my long hair from my face. "I know how you *handle* situations," I reminded him. "Remember

Mr. Mueller? You tried to kill him, too. You said I was right to have stopped you. You told me yourself killing Furies doesn't do any good. They just move on to the next willing host . . . the next body."

I saw the frantic beat of his heart begin to slow down, even as my own was growing more steady. He was still scowling, but at least he was listening.

"And anyway," I said, "when the police do get here — after we're gone — it would be good for him to be alive, so they can take him in for questioning."

"What for?" John asked, his dark brows puckering. "So he can collect the reward money for giving them information on how to find you?"

"Not questioning about *me*," I chided him. "Think about it, John. He's a Fury, and he works as a groundskeeper in the cemetery."

Behind the Spanish lime tree, where the clouds were darkening like a bruise, lightning scissored through the sky. Then thunder rumbled. But the thunder was from the approaching hurricane, growing closer. It had nothing to do with John. He was thinking over what I'd said.

"Jade told me she was attacked by three men the night she was killed here," he said. His breathing was almost back to normal now. He'd even let go of my wrist.

"The fence isn't that hard to scale," I said, speaking from experience, "but there were police cars patrolling the streets around the cemetery that night, so they would have seen anyone trying to get in that way. Someone with a key to the gate might have let the other two in. Someone like a groundskeeper."

"Does he have a key to the gate?" John raised his voice to ask Mr. Smith, as the cemetery sexton came back outside, looking a bit more composed. He'd put his jacket back on and straightened his tie. He was also carrying my book bag, which I'd left back in his office.

I noticed John didn't say Mike's name. He said *he* and nodded disdainfully at Mike's sprawled body.

"Mike?" Mr. Smith said. "Yes, of course, he does. Not the main gate, but the one on the side. He's the head groundskeeper. How else would he get in and out to park his truck and admit the maintenance vehicles, the tree-trimming company, and pest control? I can't do everything myself." He sounded testy. Who could blame him, really?

"Was Mike questioned by the police after Jade was killed?" I asked.

"I don't believe so," Mr. Smith said, looking troubled . . . and not simply because there was a death deity, a missing girl, and an unconscious man in his storage yard. "No one even asked me if anyone else had a key. But why would they? The police have their suspect."

My uncle Chris. None of us said it, but we were all thinking it. At least, I was.

Mr. Smith shook his head, looking down at the groundskeeper. "Mike's been such an excellent worker. He does come in late sometimes, I'll admit. I've suspected the occasional hangover. But he's young, and this is Isla Huesos, it's a party town. It's hard to find good help these days . . . especially to work *here*." His gaze slid towards John, then just as quickly darted away again.

"Whoever it was that killed Jade struck her so hard from behind that the murder weapon — whatever it was — pierced her bicycle helmet," John said grimly, looking down at the shovel scoop.

I gave an involuntary shiver, remembering how close that same piece of metal had come to piercing my own skull. John noticed my reaction and reached out to pull me close. I could tell I was forgiven for having deprived him of his chance to collect another soul.

"I thought of that," Mr. Smith said worriedly. "That's why when I asked for the ambulance — it's on its way, incidentally — I also mentioned they might want to send the police. I told them there was an accident, that a groundskeeper had fallen down the steps and hit his head. We'll have to see which version of the story Mike will stick to when he wakes up, the slip-and-fall, which will earn him a nice workman's comp settlement from the city, or the one about seeing you, Miss Oliviera, which could eventually earn him one million dollars. I won't, of course, corroborate that one."

I swallowed. The groundskeeper's words echoed in my head. *One of us is going to get to her eventually. If not her, then someone close to her.* Did he mean Alex?

I had to make sure my cousin was safe. I couldn't go back to the Underworld until I had.

But with my dad's issuing the bounty on my head, and our encountering Mike, John was going to have something to say about that. . . .

I could hear a siren in the distance.

"We'd better go. Because what about *that*?" I pointed at the broken shovel. "Won't the police find John's fingerprints on it, and think *he's* the murderer? And they'll know Mike's story is true if he says we were here. Our footprints are all over the yard."

"Not if I have anything to say about it," Mr. Smith said. He was picking his way delicately through the mud — he didn't want to lose the shine on his loafers — to hand me my book bag. Then he went to unwrap a hose that was coiled against the side of the cottage. He turned the water on, aiming the nozzle everywhere we had stepped.

The footprints in the yard began to vanish. Soon all that would be left was soft mud, rotting Spanish limes, dead leaves, and Mike . . . who looked dead, but wasn't. I could see his chest rising and falling, and he'd begun to moan softly.

"You mentioned earlier that if I wanted to help, Miss Oliviera, I should save the lectures, and help," Mr. Smith said as he sprayed. "Perhaps that's exactly what Fates do."

I shook my head, bewildered. "I'm sorry?"

"Perhaps Fates are people like us . . . ordinary souls who've found themselves caught up in the battle between good and evil, and have chosen to take a stand and help do what's right." Mr. Smith was lecturing again, but this time the speech seemed to be directed at John, too. His tone was kindly, however. "Maybe that's why John's fingerprints aren't in the Isla Huesos Police Department database, and why no one will find his footsteps here. Small things that take just a moment to do, yes, but that could add up, in the end, to make an enormous difference to someone. What do you say to that, Miss Oliviera?"

"I . . . I don't know," I said. I was confused. I supposed he was right, though. This could certainly explain how John was able to drift like a ghost in and out of the Isla Huesos Cemetery — and my various schools — leaving behind no trace, except rumors and the faintest images on video, and broken padlocks and chains.

I didn't see how such tiny facts were going to help win the war against the Furies, though.

When I glanced up at John to see what he thought about all this, I found him staring at the old man with his dark eyebrows lowered, a clear sign the cemetery sexton had said something John hadn't liked. But what?

"We have to go," John said tersely. The ambulance sounded as if it were right around the corner.

"You do indeed," Mr. Smith said, hitting the steps to the back door with the spray from the hose. He needed to reinforce his story that Mike had slipped.

John took me by the arm. I knew what was going to happen next: John was taking me back to his world.

There was no use arguing, not now that I'd almost gotten killed . . . and John had almost killed someone. This muddy yard, full of broken angels and headstones, was the last I'd see of Isla Huesos, and of earth.

I looked up at the tree limb where Hope had been sitting, and was dismayed to see that she had already flown off, probably back to the Underworld. Not that it mattered. I'd see her there in a few seconds anyway.

The sight of her empty branch made me sad. Though the thought of leaving Alex alone and helpless made me even sadder.

"John," I said, turning to him in desperation. "What if we —"

"Pierce," he said, urgently. The siren had cut off. I heard the door of a vehicle being slammed outside the fence, then men's voices. "It's too late."

He was right. I turned back to Mr. Smith, my heart heavy.

"Please," I said, "will you check on Alex? And if you see my mother, will you tell her . . . will you tell her —"

I broke off. What words could you possibly choose as the last ones ever to say to your mother?

Mr. Smith was turning off the water.

"You can tell her yourself," he said, with a kind smile.

The next thing I knew, I was standing in my own backyard.

He seemed as if against me he were coming
With head uplifted, and with ravenous hunger,
So that it seemed the air was afraid of him.
DANTE ALIGHIERI, *Inferno*, Canto I

I spun around to stare at John in astonishment. "What are we doing *here*?"

John held a finger to his lips, then pointed to the French doors leading from the back porch into the living room of my mom's house.

I was so shocked at finding myself in the last spot I'd ever expected to be — which was incidentally the first place he and I ever had kissed — that for once I didn't check to see if I had arrived with all my fingers, or pay attention to my queasy stomach. Instead I just stood and looked around in wonder.

Everything in my mom's yard looked exactly as I'd last seen it. Uncle Chris had put away all the patio and porch furniture in preparation of the coming storm, but the waterfall in the pool was still going. The sound of its gentle cascade was as soothing as the fragrance of the flowers from the ylang-ylang tree that stretched from a jungle-like tangle of plants beside the path on which we stood.

"But I thought for sure we'd be going back to the Underworld," I whispered as John drew me deeper into the shadows of the tropical brush. "After everything that has happened —"

"Say you want to go back now, and I'll take you there in a heartbeat," John said, gripping me by the shoulders. "*Please* say it. Nothing would make me happier."

"But what about Alex?" I couldn't help casting a yearning glance towards my mom's French doors. She was so close . . . right behind them, probably, talking on the phone, or maybe sitting and crying on the horrible white couch her decorator had advised her to buy, which stained easily and wasn't very comfortable, either. "You heard what Mike said. If they can't get to me, they're going to get someone close to me —"

Not my mother, my heart whispered. Alex was bad enough, but *please*, not my mother.

John's shoulders slumped perceptibly. "That's what I thought you'd say. Mr. Smith was right." He sounded resigned . . . bitter, but resigned. "He told me I did this all wrong."

I knew what he was talking about without having to ask, because of course I'd overheard his conversation with the cemetery sexton back in the cottage. He was referring to how he'd taken me. Mr. Smith definitely hadn't approved of that.

I laid both my hands on the hard wall of John's chest, searching for the right words to comfort him.

"You did what you felt was right at the time," I said. "It's just . . ."

I didn't want to be pessimistic, but if what was left of the crew of the *Liberty* and what Mr. Smith referred to as the Fates were all that John had on his side, it was no wonder the Furies were winning.

I knew it wouldn't help to say this out loud, however.

"It's just that you're up against so much," I finished instead. Then I quickly amended it to "We. *We're* up against so much."

"*We're* not up against anything," John said grimly. "It's my fight, not yours. If there's danger, I don't want you getting involved again like you did back at Mr. Smith's —"

I stuck out my chin. "Oh, right, because I'm not already involved," I said sarcastically. "And I thought I was quite handy with that flowerpot, thank you."

He narrowed his eyes at me, clearly not impressed. "Yes, well," he went on, "while you and Mr. Smith were having your talk on the back steps, I had some time to think over some of the things he said to me. And I decided maybe he was right."

"Right about what, exactly?" He looked so mysterious . . . but determined at the same time, like nothing was going to stop him from doing whatever it was he was about to do.

So I was surprised when he pointed at the front of my dress.

"What?" I looked down, confused. The zipper up the front was firmly in place, so he wasn't trying to tell me that my bra was showing. I knew he liked me better in more feminine nineteenth-century garb, but I didn't see what I could do about it then. And this hardly seemed the time or place for a make-out session.

"Your necklace," he said. "Is your grandmother here? Can you tell?"

I realized he wanted to know if there were any Furies present, not get inside my top. Embarrassed, I pulled the diamond out from the bodice of my dress by its chain. It was as solidly gray as the clouds moving quickly overhead.

"No," I said. "It seems clear."

He nodded, then glanced towards the back porch of my mom's house. Denuded of furniture and the long curtains and hanging lamps that normally decorated it, it suddenly appeared ominously unwelcoming.

And all at once, I didn't care if my mom was behind those French doors. I wanted to go nowhere near them.

Because I'd seen that look on John's face before. It was the same one he'd worn just before he'd caught me up and dragged me down to his world.

"John, why are we here?" I demanded suspiciously. I realized I had overheard most of what John and Mr. Smith had discussed in his office, but not *everything*. "Is it to see if Alex is trapped in the coffin in my mom's garage? Or some other reason? Like . . ."

You can tell her yourself, the cemetery sexton had said, as I'd stood there trying to stammer out something for him to say to my mom the next time he saw her.

I reached out to grip the front of John's shirt, words suddenly failing me.

But John was already taking me by the arm and marching me towards the porch that ran along the back of my mom's house.

"This is what you said you wanted," he reminded me in a steely tone as he dragged me along.

My heart staggered and seemed to stop.

He was right. This was, of course, exactly what I'd kicked and screamed for — what I'd *begged* for — just a day ago . . . to come home.

Now that it was actually happening, however, I found myself wanting the exact opposite. Just like in my nightmare, it felt as if a hole was being ripped in my gut.

I should have been happy, of course. I should have been over the moon. But all I could think was, how was this happening?

"I thought because I ate there," I heard myself babble, "I could never leave the Underworld, like Persephone."

"*What?*" John looked back at me, his expression indicating that he thought I was nuts. He didn't slow down, though.

"John," I said. I didn't want to be one of those girls who begged her boyfriend not to leave her. This situation, however, was more serious than a typical breakup for a number of reasons. "Slow down. Maybe we should talk about this. . . ."

I was so upset, my emotions must have registered in the spirit plane, since Hope appeared in a sudden burst of white feathers, whistling her disapproval of John's actions as she fluttered over his head, beating him with the tips of her dark wings. Even in my distress, I was moved. I'd no idea she'd grown so fond of me in such a short time.

"What —" John let go of me to throw his arms defensively over his face. "What's the matter with her?"

"Maybe she's upset," I said, with a touch of astringency, "because you're listening to Mr. Smith, instead of your heart."

He spun around to face me. He still wore that look of

forbidding determination, almost as if he were daring me — someone, *anyone* — to attempt to dissuade him from the course on which he was set. Whoever tried was going to get worse than what John had attempted to give Mike, it was clear. Yet there was surprise in his gray eyes, as well. "I thought this was what you wanted. Mr. Smith told me to —"

"Well, who says Mr. Smith knows everything?"

"— give you a chance to say good-bye to your mother. That's what you said you wanted, isn't it?"

I stared at him as the blood in my veins began to move again, and comprehension dawned. "*That's* why we're here? You brought me so I could say good-bye to my mother?"

"Yes, of course," he said. I noticed the now-familiar muscle twitching in his jaw. He looked as if he wanted to punch something. If there'd been anything around besides me to throw into the pool, I'm sure it would have gone in. Fortunately, Uncle Chris had done a good job of clearing the deck of anything portable in preparation of the storm. "Why else would we be here?" he demanded. "Besides to find your infernal cousin. Mr. Smith says it's wrong to keep you from your mother, and I suppose in a normal world, he'd be right. But he doesn't seem to understand this *isn't* the normal world. . . ."

No. Because in a normal world, I could see my mother anytime I wanted. And bringing me to see her was something any normal human being would do without a second thought.

This wasn't a normal world, though. It was a world in which bringing me to see my mother was a huge, colossal step for my boyfriend, who happened to be a controlling death deity.

John, misinterpreting the reason for the tears that filled my eyes, widened his own eyes immediately in response.

"Oh, no." His deep voice had a note of warning to it. *"Don't cry.* This visit has to be quick — no long, tearful reunions, all right? You can't *really* say good-bye to her, Pierce. Your mother will never let you leave. The Furies may not be here yet, but you can be sure they know we're around, and they're on their way. We've got to get out before they arrive. Just tell your mother you're all right, find out about Alex and the coffin, and then say you have to go. And no crying." He looked almost as painfully awkward as he had the time we'd sat close to this very spot and revealed our true feelings about each other, and he hadn't seemed to know what to do with his feet. "You know what it does to me when you cry."

He didn't understand that I was so emotional because I was happy, not upset. I supposed that — again, in a normal world — I wouldn't have been standing there washed in relief because my boyfriend was bringing me to my own house to see my mother, not dropping me off because a nosy cemetery sexton had convinced him it was the "right" thing to do.

But that's what I'd feared was happening.

"I won't cry," I assured him. "I just thought . . . I . . ." Now the blood in my veins was pumping a little too quickly. A lot of it was pouring into my cheeks. I could feel myself blushing. ". . . I thought you were bringing me back. Forever."

He looked puzzled. "Why would I do that, when I waited almost two centuries to find you?"

As he spoke, he reached out to take me by the waist and pull me against him, then lowered his mouth to mine and kissed me with a thoroughness that left no doubt in my mind that he had no intention of abandoning me anywhere.

"John," I said a little breathlessly, when he let me up for air. "Maybe it would be better if you waited for me out here."

"No," he said simply, and took my hand and began walking me towards the French doors to my mother's home.

It hit me that if my mother had overheard one word of our conversation — much less have looked outside and seen us kissing — she'd have killed me before Grandma ever got another chance. My father, too. Being consort of the Lord of the Underworld of Isla Huesos was *not* what either of them had planned for me to do with my life.

Although it definitely had certain benefits.

It was somewhat ironic that as I was thinking this, one of the French doors opened, and my uncle Chris stepped out onto the back deck, staring into the yard as if he'd seen a ghost. Perhaps, in a way, he had.

In this case, however, the ghost was me.

"Piercey?" he called into the darkness that was quickly descending around us. "Is that really you?"

It was harder than I thought to keep my promise not to cry. Uncle Chris was the only person who'd ever called me Piercey . . . with good reason, because as a name, it sounded terrible. Yet I had never minded somehow when he'd said it.

I dropped John's hand and hurried up the porch steps.

"Oh, Uncle Chris," I said, throwing my arms around him. Until I felt his warm, solidly built body — he liked to joke he was one of the few ex-cons who'd come out of prison having gained more fat than muscle, a result of being overly fond of soda — I hadn't believed he was real.

"Piercey." One of his hands went to my hair, stroking it as if to test if I was real, too. "Where did you come from? Your mom's been worried sick about you."

I pulled away from him, reaching up to furtively dash the tears from my eyes, hoping John wasn't looking.

"I've been around," I said vaguely. "I know I should have called. Is Mom really upset?"

"I'll say she's upset. She hasn't slept since you disappeared."

His gaze had swept past me and now focused on John, who'd climbed the porch steps behind me and was standing a few feet away. Unfortunately, John seemed to be radiating hostility, his fingers curled loosely into fists at his sides, his expression defensive, as if he was ready to fight at any moment, if necessary.

This was how every stray animal brought in from the wild behaved, masking its fear and vulnerability with antagonistic posturing. I wasn't sure anyone else but me knew that, or that that's what John was doing . . . or that anyone else would see through it.

"Who's this guy?" Uncle Chris demanded, in a voice as tense as John's shoulders. "This better not be the guy your grandma was telling me about, the one who hit her."

John took a quick step forward, his face going dark with indignation. "I don't hit women."

"Well, you sure did something to my niece," Uncle Chris said, his own face tightening, "because she never used to disappear for days without calling until *you* came along."

I've only been gone two days and a night, I was about to say. *Let's not get carried away.*

But John moved to stand nose-to-nose with him. It was only then that I noticed that Uncle Chris was holding his body in almost the exact same position as John's. The two men had a lot in common, actually . . . both had spent many, many years imprisoned, just serving two vastly different sorts of sentences.

"If I hadn't, sir," John said, his voice dropping dangerously low, "your niece would be dead."

> *"But fix thine eyes below; for draweth near*
> *The river of blood, within which boiling is*
> *Whoe'er by violence doth injure others."*
> DANTE ALIGHIERI, *Inferno*, Canto XII

I insinuated myself between my boyfriend and uncle before things could get any uglier.

"Okay," I said, in a shaky voice. It was shocking to me how quickly otherwise reasonable men could revert back to their cave-dwelling ancestors. "Uncle Chris, we didn't come here to start a fight, we really just came to let you know I'm all right —"

He inhaled to interrupt me, but I held up a hand to signal that I wasn't finished.

"I know Grandma may have told you some things, but let's face it, we both know Grandma exaggerates a little . . . sometimes a lot." I saw Uncle Chris's face grow contemplative as he took that under consideration. It was true, and he knew it. "My friend's name is John, and you shouldn't judge him before you've gotten to know him. I think you of all people know how unfair that is, don't you, Uncle Chris?"

Uncle Chris blinked a few times at that, as I'd known he would. His frown had deepened.

But not, it turned out, over my reminder that he, too, didn't have the most sterling reputation, having spent most of his only child's life serving a prison term for a crime he resolutely refused to discuss.

He turned his attention to John.

"Why?" Uncle Chris asked. "Why would she be dead if you hadn't come along? Who'd want to hurt Pierce?"

Suddenly, I could see exactly why John had been so reluctant to bring me back, even to save the life of someone else. . . .

After I'd died and been resuscitated, everyone had wanted so badly to know what it had been like on the other side.

But the few people to whom I'd told the truth turned out to not want to hear it. They only wanted to hear about the light everyone else saw.

Uncle Chris had been one of those people.

How could you explain to someone that his mother was a Fury, and for years had been trying to kill you, and had maybe killed his own father? How could you tell someone something so horrible, something that would change his life forever?

John knew all this, had known it all along. Maybe this was not only why he hadn't wanted to bring me back, but why he wouldn't tell me the truth about himself.

Still, when my uncle Chris asked him who would want to hurt

me, John didn't lie. He said only, "Bad people. Some very bad people."

Uncle Chris's mouth flattened into a small, thin line. Then he nodded crisply. He knew all about bad people. John was speaking in a language he understood.

"Is it drugs?" Uncle Chris asked, in a hushed voice.

I looked at John, in his black jeans and T-shirt, with his long dark hair, and studded leather wristbands. I could see why Uncle Chris had asked. To someone of his generation, it would have to be either drugs, or . . . well, a rock band.

John gave me a barely perceptible shake of his head. *No*, his eyes begged me. *Don't.*

"Yes," I said, glancing back at Uncle Chris. "It's drugs."

John's gaze instantly rolled towards the sky.

"Piercey," Uncle Chris said, exhaling gustily and dragging a hand through his hair. "We talked about this. I thought you were the one I didn't have to worry about."

We had talked about something along those lines, I remembered, outside this very house, the night before Jade was killed. But it had been about Uncle Chris giving me driving lessons. I didn't recall drugs being mentioned.

"Well," I said. "Things are a little messed up right now. That's why we're here. I wanted to make sure Alex is okay."

"Alex?" Uncle Chris threw me a look of alarm. "Don't tell me *Alex* is doing drugs."

I could see now why John had been against lying about the drugs thing. I'd thought it would simplify things. But it was only making them worse.

"He's not," I said quickly. If Alex got out of all this alive, he was going to kill me. "It's just that some of the people he hangs out with —"

"Rector," Uncle Chris said, in a flat voice. "It's that Rector boy you were with the other day, the one who brought you home from school in that truck —"

"What?" I said, taken aback. Especially because John's head jerked up when he heard the name *Rector*, the same way it had in the cemetery. What was with the people on this island and the name Rector? "No, it's not Seth. . . ." Except that of course, if Alex really was trapped in the senior class coffin, it probably was. "It's . . . some kids from off the island —"

Uncle Chris shook his head. He didn't believe me. "I already know who it is. Why else would your counselor have gotten killed?"

John was shaking his head, an I-told-you-so expression on his face.

"Uncle Chris," I said, fearing I'd created a mess in which my uncle did not — *should* not — need to involve himself. "I don't think there's any evidence that Jade was killed for drug-related reasons —"

Uncle Chris, however, was off and running, speaking almost to himself. "Seth and his father were over here this morning."

"They *were*?" I could not hide my surprise. "Why?"

"They took a bunch of the 'missing' flyers your mom made up. She said they were real eager to help go around and hang them up. But I kept thinking —" Uncle Chris looked at me, then at John, then seemed to get control of himself with an effort. "Well, there's no need to go into what I thought. I only wish your father would hurry up and get here. He's on his way, you know. His jet couldn't land at the local airport because the FAA closed it due to the storm, so he's driving down from where they let him land. Or being driven, I guess, since he's hiring a car and driver from there. Fort Lauderdale, I think it was."

"Oh," I said. Unlike Uncle Chris, I wasn't too eager to see my dad. I could only imagine what he was going to think of John. I had a feeling that, compared to meeting Uncle Chris, John's meeting my dad was going to go a lot worse.

"Where is Alex now, Mr. Cabrero?" John asked my uncle, gently. I think John could sense that Uncle Chris wasn't doing so great.

"Alex? He's out with one of those New Pathways kids. That girl, Kayla."

I looked up at this, startled. I liked Kayla. She'd been one of my only friends at Isla Huesos High School. *One* of? Make that my *only* friend. . . .

"Alex is really worried about you, Piercey" — Uncle Chris's glance at me was apologetic — "but he was here all day and finally asked if he could go out for a while, and I said yes. Stupid of me, I know, but this was before I knew about the drugs —"

"And Pierce's grandmother?" John asked, before I could insist once again that Alex wasn't on drugs.

"She went home to rest," Uncle Chris said, looking at him curiously. "She had a long day. Why?"

"I'll bet," I said, unable to restrain a bitter laugh. "Her facial lacerations bothering her?"

"Hey." Uncle Chris looked stern. Or as stern as Uncle Chris could look, which wasn't very. He was better at watching TV. "That's your grandmother. You show some respect. I don't know what went on between you two back at the high school yesterday, but she was probably just trying to do the right thing. Maybe she thought your friend was the one who was on drugs." His gaze jerked towards John. "No offense, but if you want to be with my niece, you should think about getting a haircut. My mother is very conservative."

"No offense taken," John said mildly. "What about the police? Are there any police officers inside the house?"

"Hey," Uncle Chris said, narrowing his eyes. "What's with all the questions?"

"Pierce would like to see her mother," John explained. "And I wouldn't want her to run into any . . . inconveniences."

"Oh," Uncle Chris said, instantly affable again. It was easy to see how he'd gotten along in prison for as many years as he had. "There's a police car parked right outside. I don't even know how the two of you got in here without them stopping you. And there's this fancy machine hooked to the phone so if your kidnappers call, we can record it. Although I guess you weren't kidnapped, were you? We should tell your dad. He's supposed to have someone driving down from the FBI branch in Miami tomorrow —"

"The FBI?" I was surprised my dad hadn't called his buddies at the CIA, as well. "That's just great. But Mom's right inside?"

"She said she was going upstairs to take a shower," Uncle Chris said. "I swear she hasn't done a thing since she found out you were missing except worry. I was about to order Chinese when I looked out the window and saw you. Hey, do you two want to stay? We're getting moo shu."

It was so like Uncle Chris to go from wanting to beat John up one minute, to inviting him for moo shu the next.

"Uh, maybe," I said. I pointed to the French doors, looking questioningly at John. He nodded. "Let's see how it goes, okay, Uncle Chris?"

"That'd be good," Uncle Chris said. "We could talk all this out."

John followed me inside, Uncle Chris trailing behind us, his expression curious rather than suspicious.

"I hate it when families fight," Uncle Chris was saying. "It makes it so uncomfortable. . . ."

I suppose I should have counted it lucky that it had been Uncle Chris, and not some other adult, I'd run into first at home. I wasn't sure if it was because of all the years he'd spent out of mainstream society — he still had no idea how to text, or what Google was — or if his personality was really this childlike. I'd been a baby when he'd gone to prison.

There was no one but us on the lower floor. I could hear water running in the bathroom off the master bedroom, upstairs, however.

A lot had changed since I'd been gone. There were stacks of "missing" flyers everywhere, each featuring the same unflattering photo of me that had been in the paper Mr. Smith had shown us. The normally meticulously neat living room was in disarray. Mom's housekeeper would have had a fit at how smushed-in all the throw pillows on the couch were, and how many mugs and teacups had been left without coasters on the coffee table.

The biggest change of all, though, was in the garage. When I opened the door, I saw that all the pieces of four-by-eight plywood that Seth Rector and his friends had left stacked so neatly there were gone. So were the paint and other coffin-building supplies.

"This is not good," I said, looking at all the outside patio furniture that was piled up in the garage to keep it from being blown away in the coming storm, thinking maybe I'd missed something. But I hadn't.

"What's not good?" Uncle Chris asked. "Piercey, what have you gotten yourself involved in?"

There was no reason not to tell him. He and my mom had both gone to Isla Huesos High School. I'd seen all the sports trophies they'd won, still on display in the administrative wing. He knew all about Coffin Night because it was football-related, and he'd been on one of the winningest teams in Isla Huesos history.

But Uncle Chris had enough to worry about, being a suspect in Jade's murder, and all.

So I said simply, "It's nothing. Seth Rector and his friends asked if they could store some stuff in here, and now it's gone. They must have come to pick it up. That's all."

It was the wrong thing to say. Uncle Chris was immediately on the defensive, looking like a mother bear whose cubs had been teased by tourists.

"Store some stuff?" he repeated, his tone incredulous. "You let Seth Rector *store some stuff* in your mother's home? What kind of stuff?"

I swallowed. I'd never been yelled at so much by Uncle Chris in one day in my life . . . I'd actually never been yelled at by him before at all. It felt terrible.

"The senior coffin," I said, in a small voice.

I wanted to assure him that I had a very sound reason for doing something so foolish . . . that ever since the death of my good friend Hannah, I'd appointed myself a sort of watcher of people I cared about, and that included his son, Alex.

Uncle Chris didn't give me a chance to say a word in my own defense, however.

"Do you know what the juniors did when they found the coffin your mother's senior year, Pierce?" he demanded, in a heated voice. "They torched it. And the house it was in caught on fire, too. It burned to the ground."

I lowered my eyes, too ashamed to meet his gaze. Like the crime John had committed to get himself sentenced to being protector of the dead of Isla Huesos, whatever Uncle Chris had done that had gotten him a twenty-year prison sentence was never mentioned . . . at least, not in our family. But I knew it was something even more serious than burning down someone's house.

"So perhaps," John said quietly, from the doorjamb against which he leaned, his arms folded across his chest, "it's a good thing the coffin was moved."

I glanced up at him. One of his dark eyebrows was arched. I couldn't tell if he was joking or serious.

"Yeah," Uncle Chris said, not looking convinced either. He'd begun to dig around in the pockets of his jeans. "Well, I don't know about that. Tell me something, Pierce." *Pierce.* I was "Piercey" no longer. That hurt. "Is Alex involved in this? Coffin Night?"

"Um." I felt like I had no choice but to tell him the truth. "Well, he knew the coffin stuff was here. Alex doesn't really like Seth, for whatever reason." It wasn't hard to guess the reason; I just didn't want to say it out loud in front of Uncle Chris. Seth Rector, good-looking president of the senior class and son of the richest man in Isla Huesos, had everything, including a shiny new F-150 truck he'd gotten for his birthday. Alex Cabrero, newly enrolled in New Pathways and son of an ex-con, had nothing. His car was a piece of junk his Fury grandmother was always threatening to take away so she didn't have to make the payments on it anymore. "Maybe the reason it's all gone is because Alex took it to get back at Seth. In which case, Seth and those guys are going to be really mad when they find out —"

Mad enough, maybe, to stuff Alex in the class's new replacement coffin.

Before I'd even completed the sentence, my uncle was hitting a button on the cell phone he'd pulled from his pocket.

"I'm calling Alex," he said. He didn't look angry, though. He looked resigned, as if someone had told him he had only a few months to live. He was pale, and kept dragging his fingers through his hair. It stood raggedly on end, both because of its thick texture and the fact that he'd let Grandma cut it . . . big mistake.

John laid a hand on my shoulder. "Go see your mother," he whispered in my ear.

"I want to make sure Alex is all right," I whispered back, watching Uncle Chris intently. No one seemed to be picking up on Alex's end.

"I'll do that," John said. "You go."

I knew he was right. I turned and climbed the stairs to the second floor, just as my uncle's voice said, "Alex? It's Dad."

I felt my shoulders sag with relief. So, that was all right. Uncle Chris would make Alex come home, and I wouldn't have to worry about him anymore . . . just my new life as queen of the Underworld. Great.

Upstairs, I could hear the shower in my mom's bathroom still running. My dad and I had always joked that for someone who was so environmentally conscious, Mom was the biggest hot water waster in our family, taking the world's longest showers.

I went to stand in my bedroom doorway, looking at my room for what I knew was most likely the last time. This was going to be my only opportunity to pick up anything I wanted to take back with me to the Underworld.

What do you pack for eternity? My gaze roved the room. The only jewelry that held any sentimental value to me was the necklace I was already wearing around my neck. I'd never collected stuffed animals or designer clothes or shoes or anything like that. Really, my room was kind of empty, except for my laptop and the books on my bookshelves. John had already said he'd get me whatever books I needed, and it wasn't like there was a web to surf in the Underworld. The only difficulty, really, was my music. I had all the songs I liked stored on my phone. But what about when the charge ran out? And how was I going to download *new* music?

I'd never considered a life without music, although I supposed deaf people got along without it. And if Mr. Graves could get along without *seeing*, I could certainly get along without iTunes.

I shoved thoughts of music from my head and went to my closet and looked inside. There was one thing . . . the white dress I'd worn to the Welcome to Isla Huesos party Mom had thrown for me. John had liked how I looked in it so much, he'd asked me to wear it on our first date . . . a date we'd never had a chance to have because of Jade being murdered, and then my grandma trying to kill me.

I took the dress from the closet.

Then my gaze came to rest on a photo in a silver frame on my nightstand. It was of me and my mom and dad in happier times, before the divorce, before the accident, which I now knew hadn't been an accident at all.

I picked it up. The dress and the photo were all I would take, I decided. In fact . . .

I sat down on my bed, then opened my book bag. Now was a good time to divest myself of things I *didn't* need, things that were only weighing me down in my new life, like my econ textbook and school notebooks. I didn't need my pill case, either. I knew from the dozens of doctors I'd seen after my accident that I was supposed to take my pills for all the aftereffects I'd suffered from what my grandmother had done to me — pills to wake me up, and pills to put me to sleep, and pills to help with the headaches from the pills that woke me up and put me to sleep.

Since finding myself in the Underworld, however, I'd taken no pills, and had no trouble waking up or falling asleep.

Maybe what I needed — what I'd always needed — was not

pills, but to find my true place in the world . . . which was a completely different world than this one.

It was as I was digging through my leather bag that I realized someone had actually *added* to the assorted junk I'd been carrying around. Which explained why my bag had felt a little heavier when Mr. Smith had handed it to me in the yard outside his office.

I was surprised to pull out the bag of birdseed I'd found in the kitchen of the cemetery sexton's cottage. *I* hadn't put it there. Mr. Smith must have.

That wasn't all, though. Beneath the bag was a book.

It was small but thick, the brown hardcover showing its age in the flaking gold script across the front, *A History of the Isle of Bones*. When I opened it, the sepia-colored pages gave off a scent vaguely reminiscent of vanilla wafers, an odor I'd always loved, because it reminded me of being taken as a child to the children's section of the library for storytime. It was the smell of books.

Of course. This was the book Mr. Smith had said he was going to give me, about the *Liberty*. He must have put it, along with the birdseed, in my bag when he'd gone inside to call the ambulance. I suppose he thought he was being a "Fate" — doing something kind.

A History of the Isle of Bones was four hundred and fifty-six pages long.

"Seriously?" I said in disbelief, forgetting where I was. "He couldn't have given me the abridged version?"

"Pierce?"

It was my mother.

And I: "O Master, what so grievous is
To these, that maketh them lament so sore?"
He answered: "I will tell thee very briefly."
DANTE ALIGHIERI, *Inferno*, Canto III

My mother's voice was coming from across the hall.

Realizing I could no longer hear the sound of water running, I got up from the bed and hurried to the hallway. My mother's bedroom door was open just enough for me to be able to see that she was wearing the soft, fluffy bathrobe I'd given her last Mother's Day. I felt a pang when I saw it, and had to restrain myself from running towards her and flinging myself into her arms.

Because her next words stopped me cold.

"Zack, how can you even say such a thing?" my mother asked in an agitated voice as she squeezed the ends of her long, dark hair with a towel. "I refuse to believe Pierce would ever *run away*, especially with a boy."

She was on the phone. And she was talking to my father. Arguing with my father, actually. About me.

Well, what else was new? Their arguments about me, starting from the time of my accident, for which my mom had always somewhat irrationally blamed my father — though it was my own fault, not Dad's, that I'd died. Oh, and Grandma's — were what had ended their marriage.

But where had my father gotten the idea that I'd run away?

"When? When did this happen?" my mom demanded, going to sit on her bed. She looked upset. "When did Pierce call you and say she wanted to leave Isla Huesos?"

Standing in the shadows of the hallway, I felt my heart skip a beat. Oh, God, of course . . . the phone call I'd placed to my father a few nights earlier, when I'd seen the Coffin Night supplies in our garage . . . and learned the truth about my necklace.

And John.

That had been *before*, though, when I'd been unhappy and overwhelmed and — I might as well admit it — scared to death. I was still scared, of course, and a little overwhelmed, and I certainly wasn't always happy.

But I didn't want to leave Isla Huesos anymore . . . or John.

It sounded like my mother was on my side, though.

"Zack, that was her first day at a brand-new school," Mom said, into the phone. "It's natural she called and asked you if she could come home. The counselors at New Pathways said she might. Every student feels insecure and miserable their first day at a new school. That *doesn't* mean she's run away. What about that boy on the security tape? Pierce didn't look as if she was going with him willingly. And he punched my mother, you know."

My father must have made some kind of colorful remark about that — there'd never been any love lost between him and Grandma — since I heard my mother inhale, then sarcastically reply, "Yes, well, I understand *you've* always wanted to punch my mother, Zack, but that doesn't make me think that boy is someone whose company Pierce would keep. Did you *see* him? I know the photo was grainy, but he looks like one of those death metal goth heads, or whatever they're called. All dressed in black with long hair —"

I took umbrage at my mother describing my boyfriend this way. John was the Lord of the Underworld. How else was he supposed to dress?

"And why are you only telling me about this phone call from her *now*?" Mom wanted to know.

She had switched the phone on to speaker, probably because my dad's remark about her mother had agitated her so much, she needed to do something else while she listened to the rest of what he had to say . . . which in this case was stand up and rub the towel vigorously through her damp hair. Although my mom liked to think I'd inherited my attention deficit disorder and hyperactivity from my dad, she was the one who had all the track, tennis, and academic decathlon trophies from high school. A guidance counselor had once told me that there were many high achievers with ADHD. They'd just learned to hyperfocus their tremendous amounts of energy, the way my mom had.

"— because I didn't want to upset you." My father's booming voice — strong and deep and sounding slightly harassed, as always — filled the room. "I know how hard you've tried with her, Deborah. But there's been no trace of them, no sightings, no ransom request, nothing. Taking into consideration her phone call the other night to me, asking if she could come home, and the fact that there was always something a little squirrelly about the Mueller case —"

Mom looked up from her toweling, astonished. "That pathetic teacher of hers who poor Hannah Chang was having the affair with? Zack, that was ages ago. What has that got to do with anything?"

"The police never believed Mueller's story that it was Pierce who broke his hand that day at the school." My father's voice was flat . . . but I could hear in it an undertone of anxiety. "Mueller's a six-foot-tall, two-hundred-pound man. How's an average-size high-school girl like our daughter going to get the advantage over a thirty-year-old man that size, *and* walk away without a scratch on her? The cops have always thought there was a boyfriend involved, Deborah."

"A boyfriend?" My mom laughed. I was a little insulted by her incredulous tone. "Pierce doesn't have a boyfriend, Zack."

"Naturally she would never admit it," Dad said, "because she wants to protect him, but we have to face facts. There might *always* have been a boyfriend."

Hearing this, my mom let go of the towel and sank back down onto her bed, dropping her head into one hand. "Oh, God," she said with a groan.

I longed to burst into her room and cry, "It's true! I do have a boyfriend! But he's not a death metal goth head, whatever that is. He's protector of the dead, so okay, he has some issues, but who doesn't? Once you get to know him, you'll really like him."

Only how could I? Especially since I'd *already* told them about John — as soon as I'd been resuscitated from being dead — and the description hadn't been the most flattering. I'd said there'd been a boy — a horrible boy who'd tried to hold me prisoner in the Underworld. Mom and Dad had thought I was crazy, of course, and had sent me to talk to a million shrinks who had *also* thought I was crazy . . . only they'd called it something more polite, lucid dreaming.

What were they going to think if I told them I was now in love with this boy? That I was crazier than ever. Oh, why hadn't I kept my mouth shut?

"That composite sketch they've made of the face of the boy your mother claims hit her," my father went on, the skepticism in his voice evident. "My contacts say no one recognizes him. He's not from around there . . . or at least doesn't go to the high school or community college, hasn't paid any visits to the local men's detention center lately, and hasn't been seen at any of the local watering holes."

"What does that mean?" my mom asked bewilderedly.

"It means that it all fits," my dad said. "Maybe Pierce met him in Connecticut — who knows where — and he followed her down to Florida, and when things at that public school where you sent her didn't work out — I warned you about that, Deborah — she decided to run away with him. And now the two of them are hiding out in some cheap motel because they know how much trouble they're in. It's the only scenario that makes sense."

Hiding out in some cheap motel with a boy? Did my parents really think I would do something that immature and, I'm sorry, completely *skanky*?

"And I'll tell you what," my father was going on. "If it's true, the second she shows her face, I'm packing her straight off to boarding school, I don't care what you say. That one in Switzerland that I showed you, remember the brochure? None of this would be happening if you'd let me send her there like I wanted to."

"I realize that now," my mom said . . . which was a huge concession for her. She hardly ever admitted my dad was right about anything. "Where are you, anyway?"

There were sounds of muffled movement, like someone leaning to look out the window of a car . . . or a limo. Then my dad said, "Mile marker twenty-five. So I'll be there in about half an hour."

"Oh, Zack," my mother said, looking dejected. "Hurry. At this point I can only hope you're right and she *has* run off with a boy and isn't lying dead out there in the mangroves somewhere. If that's where she is . . . I just don't know how I'm going to — to —"

"I know." My dad's voice had changed. He was speaking in a tone I hadn't heard him use in a long, long time. It was almost . . . gentle. "I'd much rather have it be this than the alternative, Debbie."

I saw my mom turn her head towards the phone, startled. No one called my mom Debbie. She *hated* being called Debbie. It was always either Deb or Deborah, but never Debbie. She'd only ever allowed my father to call her that, a sort of pet name between the two of them, in their tenderer moments.

But Dad hadn't called her Debbie since . . . well, I couldn't remember the last time. Before my accident, when all the fighting between them started.

Tears glistening in her eyes, my mother picked up the phone, turned it off speaker, and cradled the receiver to her ear, all of her attention now hyperfocused on their conversation.

"Oh, Zack," she said, and then began to murmur endearments that I knew instinctively were not for me to hear. Not that any of their conversation had been for me to hear, but the words she was saying were private.

I shrank slowly back into my room, careful not to make a sound, grateful for the thickness of the carpets — hand-woven by a women's cooperative — Mom's decorator had imported all the way from Kabul.

So this was how it was. My parents were on the brink of reuniting, bonding over their combined concern over my disappearance. I could burst into my mom's room with a big, "Guess what? I'm home!" and ruin it.

Or I could just stay missing, since my parents were planning to send me off to boarding school in Switzerland anyway, and let nature take its course.

Of the two choices, I preferred the latter.

Uncle Chris had already seen me. But Uncle Chris wasn't like other adults. He hadn't demanded the kind of explanations my mother and father would, because Uncle Chris was too damaged from his years in prison to think the way normal parents did.

More than anything, I longed to go into my mother's bed-room, give her a big, reassuring hug, and tell her everything was going to be all right. Except I knew that, like John had predicted, she was only going to want me to stay, and I couldn't. I also couldn't tell her that everything was going to be all right, because I didn't know that it was.

Maybe it would be better for everyone — with my father arriving in half an hour, and he and my mom seeming to be getting along so well — if I stayed missing.

So I went over to my bed, opened one of my school notebooks, and jotted a quick letter.

Dear Mom, I wrote, *I'm sorry about everything. It's too complicated to explain, but I'm fine, and with someone I love. Please tell Dad hi, and that I'm the one who hit Grandma. He was right about her. You should listen to him, she's a liar and not as great as you think. I love and miss you both. Be happy.*

Love,

Pierce

P.S. My boyfriend's name is John, and he's very nice.

I knew it was a terrible thing to do, leaving a letter instead of personally saying good-bye. But I also felt it was kinder . . . and quicker. Long explanations — like the truth — would be useless. My mother was a scientist. She believed in things she could analyze, like the mating and migration habits of birds. Predation and competition, endangerment and extinction, those were things she could understand.

She would never understand this.

I left the note on the middle of my bed where she'd be sure to find it, and had stuffed the dress and picture in its frame into my bag and was creeping down the stairs when I ran into John, coming up to find me.

I put a finger to my lips and pointed towards my mother's bedroom. Her door was still ajar. Evening had fallen, casting the first floor of the house into shadows. My mom had switched on her bedroom light, and it threw a warm slice of yellow across the red carpets from Afghanistan.

"How did it go?" John whispered.

"I couldn't face her," I whispered back. "I left her a note instead. I think she's going to be fine." My dad would make sure of that. "Did Uncle Chris find Alex?"

He nodded and took my arm, his gentlemanly instincts kicking in as he helped guide me down the stairs. I guess he forgot I wasn't wearing a long dress with a train that I might accidentally trip over.

"Yes," he said. "He's still outside on the deck, speaking to him by phone. It looks as if we'll have to go get him. He won't come home."

I paused on the steps. "What do you mean, Alex *won't* come home?"

"Your uncle told him you're back, and that he wants him to come home." John looked down at me, his expression grimly serious. "He also mentioned it's apparently going to be very bad tonight after midnight, because of the storm." I had to suppress a smile. Uncle Chris was obsessed with the weather. "But your cousin has told his father that he doesn't *want* to come home," John went on. "And your uncle says that's fine."

"*Fine?*" I shook my head. "Why would he say that?"

John shrugged, still looking grim. "Your uncle says he doesn't want to make your cousin angry."

Comprehension dawned. "Uncle Chris was in jail for a long time," I said. "He feels guilty about missing so much of Alex's childhood. He doesn't want to be the bad guy —"

"Interesting way of showing it," John said wryly. "In any case, your cousin says he's at —"

Hope chose that moment to show up, swooping in from nowhere with a noisy patter of wings, and buzzing in front of me and John like an angry hornet.

I reached out and closed my hands gently over her body, surprised that she allowed herself to be captured at all, and even more surprised that she didn't struggle. Only the fact that I could feel her heart drumming so frantically against my fingers through her fragile ribs gave away her consternation about the situation.

Something was wrong. Very wrong. It wasn't until I heard an all-too-familiar voice from the bottom of the stairs that I knew what it was.

"Pierce," my grandmother said. Her tone was venomous.

I felt John's fingers tighten around my arm. I didn't have to look down at my necklace to know it had turned as black as the heart of the plump old woman standing by the newel post, clutching her purse in one hand and a spare set of my mom's house keys in the other.

"Grandma," I said. I felt Hope's heart give a panicked skitter in my hands. *Now* she began to struggle, frantic to get away from the evil presence she sensed all around her . . .

. . . or maybe the fear she felt radiating from me.

The front door stood wide open behind my grandmother. I had no idea how she'd managed to get in without either of us having heard her.

But I wasn't going to run.

"When I heard you were back, I thought, no, even *she* wouldn't be stupid enough to come to the most obvious place any of us would think to look for her," my grandmother said. "But you didn't disappoint. That's the one good thing about having a stupid grandchild. She's so predictable."

"You'd better get out of here," I warned her, narrowing my eyes. "My dad's on his way, and you know how *he* feels about you. There's no way he's going to believe the things you've been saying about me."

"Isn't he?" Her mouth curled into a smile that anyone else would have described as angelic . . . but I knew better. "What about your young man?" Her reptilian gaze fell on John. "She's got you wrapped around her finger, hasn't she? What did she do, cry? So of course you let her have whatever she wanted, which was . . . what? To come see her mommy." She sneered, then reached into her massive purse. "Well, this just makes everything a lot more fun."

There was a Band-Aid on her cheek covering the place where I'd hit her. It was hard to see in the semidarkness of the foyer, but the skin around the bandage looked redder than the skin on the opposite cheek, but more like she'd layered on the rouge a little too thickly than like my fist had actually damaged it that badly. I wondered if rouge wasn't the only thing Grandma was laying on a little thick.

"Stay back," John warned her in a hard voice, pulling me close.

"Pierce," my grandmother said, giving me a scandalized look. "Whatever is the matter with that young man of yours? He's so violent! All I was doing was trying to talk some sense into you . . . again. Good thing those nice police officers are sitting in that squad car out there, so when he goes after me — like he's about to — and I try to defend myself, they'll hear all the screaming, and come running in to arrest him . . . while you, Pierce — I'm afraid I'm going to misfire, and you're going to suffer the brunt of it. This is military grade. I'm told the burning sensation goes away in ten to twenty-four hours. But it's excruciating."

She pulled a canister of pepper spray from her purse, aiming it directly at my face.

Before she could press the nozzle — even before John could whisk me away to safety — my uncle Chris startled us all by stepping into the living room and calling, "Hey, did anyone see a bird? It was the darnedest thing, I opened the door to come inside, and a *bird* flew into the house." His bulky silhouette came into view. He paused when he saw us on the steps.

"Oh, there it is," he said, his gaze falling on Hope in my hands. "Good job, Piercey, you caught it." Then he noticed Grandma. "Mom, what are you doing here?" he asked curiously. "I thought you went home to rest."

"I did," my grandmother said, suddenly sounding like a weak old woman as she dropped the pepper spray back into her purse.

"But I heard Pierce was back. I can't believe you didn't call me right away. Isn't it the most joyous occasion? Alleluia."

Upstairs, I heard my mother's voice from her bedroom. "Christopher? Is that you? Who are you talking to? I'm on the phone."

The slant of yellow light spilling from my mother's bedroom widened perceptibly. She was heading down the hall towards the stairs — and us — her bare feet silent on the thick rugs.

What happened next could best be described as an explosion . . . except that there wasn't any fire or heat, so no one got hurt.

Afterwards, they probably blamed it on a power surge brought on by a lightning strike. I wasn't there, however, so I wouldn't know.

Just as my grandmother shouted, "Pierce is home!" my mother said, in a disbelieving voice, "Pierce? Where?" Mom lifted her hand to switch on the elaborate silver and wrought iron chandelier that hung in the foyer, and John's arms closed around me —

Then a brilliant burst of light filled the room, dazzling my eyes, and causing my mother to scream.

By the other mode, forgotten is that love
Which Nature makes, and what is after added,
From which there is a special faith engendered.
DANTE ALIGHIERI, *Inferno*, Canto XI

When I opened my eyes again, I was standing next to John in a dark, quiet alley.

High wooden fences rose on either side of us, blocking the view of all but the roofs of the houses behind them. Over the top of the fences hung the thickest growth of bougainvillea I'd ever seen, forming a brightly colored rainbow of yellow, red, and pink flowers all up and down the road. The smell of night-blooming jasmine was almost as heavy in the warm, humid air as the rain, which hung so low in the fast-moving purple clouds overhead, I felt as if I could taste it. Frogs chirped noisily, a cicada rasped, and farther off in the distance, I could hear music.

"What," I asked, dazed, "was *that*?"

Hope, to show she had not liked what John had done any more than I had, gave a few furious whistles and dug in with her talons, causing me to open my hands with a cry and let her go. She flew off, though not far. I saw her settle on top of a poinciana tree in someone's backyard, its branches stretching across the alley. She was easy to spot since she was so white, and the poinciana tree had lost nearly all of its blossoms. They lay scattered across the alley floor like a decaying red carpet. She furiously began to groom herself to show how indignant she was at the way she'd been mishandled.

John's dark eyebrows were raised in an expression of contrition . . . but his eyes didn't show a single hint of remorse.

"I apologize," he said smoothly. "I'll admit that was a cheap magician's trick. But I couldn't let your mother see us vanish into thin air right in front of her. I'm sure she was upset enough already."

"That would make two of us," I said, still trembling, both from the close encounter with my grandmother and John's method of rescuing me from it. The place where Hope had clawed me had begun to sting. I looked up and down the alley, wondering where we were . . . and how long it would be before the Furies found us this time.

"Pierce." John's voice changed. It softened. He reached out to cup my face in both his hands, looking down at me intently. "I'm sorry. I should never have listened to Mr. Smith's advice to take you to see your mother. He meant well, but under the circumstances, your grandmother was right . . . I should have known it was the first place the Furies would look for you, once they heard you were back."

I thought about overhearing my mother's voice as she spoke to my father on the phone, the way it had softened when she'd begged him to hurry up and get there, and the way he'd called her Debbie. I hadn't heard the two of them speak that kindly to each other in years.

"It was worth it," I said emphatically.

John dropped his hands and simply looked at me. "Well," he said. "I'm glad, then. Still, I'm sorry you didn't get to say a proper good-bye to her. You realize that your uncle is going to tell your grandmother everything about our visit . . . including that we're looking for Alex?"

I nodded, shuddering a little, and not at the lightning that lit up the clouds above the telephone wires. "Where are we?" I asked, absently raising the cut in my hand to my lips.

"Coffin Fest," he said. "It's being held on the street around the corner. It's where your uncle says your cousin is. Hopefully we'll be able to find him and convince him to give up on whatever his plans are concerning the coffin, then get him home before your grandmother has time to spread the word about where we are. But I wouldn't count on it. Let me see your hand."

"It's nothing," I said, pulling my hand from my lips. For such a small cut, it throbbed a bit. "Only a scratch." All I could think was, *Home.* That's what he'd called it. The Underworld, where I now lived . . . with *him.* My heart began to thud uncomfortably behind the zipper down the front of my dress.

It was fine, I told myself. I liked it there. There was no bougainvillea, but there were black lilies and mushrooms. It was cold, but there was always a fire to sit by. It was just . . .

A strong gust of wind stirred the bougainvillea and rustled the skirt of my dress, and for a second the music from the street fair sounded louder. It was Spanish music, pulsating with life and energy.

It was the opposite of what was waiting on the other side of his crypt.

"Pierce," he said, and tugged on my hand. "Let me see."

I surrendered. I had no idea how he could even locate the tiny pink scrape in the quickening darkness. The street lamps on either end of the alley had come on, but their glow didn't reach to where we were standing.

He found the wound, though, and passed his thumb lightly across it. A strange warmth filled me . . . not the uncomfortable, oppressive warmth from the pervasive humidity, but a tingling sensation that started in my hand, then slowly spread up my arm. The wound did not vanish, but it stopped hurting.

"How did you do that?" I breathed, in wonder.

"I keep telling you," he said, lifting my hand and then pressing it to his lips. "The job comes with certain compensations."

The tingling increased . . . but only because his lips always had that effect on me.

"John," I said. My heart was pounding, but whether it was from his touch, an electrical charge from all the lightning that was churning in the clouds overhead, or the Spanish music, I didn't know. It could have been my fear, which had kicked into a high setting from seeing my grandmother again. "What would happen if we ran away?"

"Ran away?" he repeated with a soft laugh, lowering my hand and looking down at the blue veins that ran across the back. "And where, exactly, would we go?"

"I don't care," I said recklessly. "Somewhere far away from here, where the Furies can't find us. Why do we even have to go back? We can go anywhere. I have a ton of credit cards. They're still good until my dad cuts them off. My parents think that's what we've done anyway, so why not really do it?"

He didn't raise his gaze to meet mine, just continued to play with my hand, spreading my fingers out, seeming to compare their size against his, which were much larger.

"Do you hate what I am that much?" he asked, in a voice that I noticed was merely curious, as if whatever I said in response, it didn't much matter to him . . . which meant, I knew, that it did.

"No," I said quickly. "I don't hate it all. What you do is important, I understand that. I just don't understand why *you* have to do it. It doesn't seem fair. Why can't Frank do it? Honestly, I think he'd enjoy it."

"You said you'd stay," John reminded me. I noticed that as usual, he'd ignored my question about why *he* had to be the ruler of the Underworld of Isla Huesos.

"I said I'd stay with *you*," I pointed out.

"What about Alex?" he asked.

"He'll be fine, too," I said. "If he's old enough to think he doesn't have to come home when his father asks him to, isn't he old enough to take care of himself?"

"I don't think you really believe that," John said. His fingers folded over mine. "Any more than you believe in anything you're suggesting. Do you?"

"No," I admitted softly. Still, wild desperation seized me. "But John, don't you *want* to run away sometimes, forget all the things you have to do, and only do things you *want* for a change? And if we did, what's the worst that could happen? Besides the pestilence Mr. Graves was talking about?" The idea of Isla Huesos swarming with walking dead didn't bother me that much now that I knew my dad was on his way. He'd take care of my mom, and Alex and Uncle Chris, too . . . I didn't care what happened to Grandma.

I didn't want to think about people who'd been kind to me since my arrival on Isla Huesos and probably didn't deserve to be destroyed by pestilence, like Mr. Smith and my friend Kayla. I pushed thoughts of them out of my mind.

John looked up from my hand, his eyes narrowing as he examined my face. "You haven't eaten since breakfast," he said, pulling me in the direction from which the music was flowing. "Let's go. There's no reason we can't look for your cousin and get you something to eat at the same time, if we hurry."

I *was* hungry, I realized. I was also feeling a little light-headed. Wait a minute . . .

"You're trying to change the subject," I accused him.

"I told you there were compensations for the job," he said, putting an arm around my shoulders, since I apparently wasn't moving quickly enough for him. Soon my feet were practically flying across the pavement. "Well, there are punishments, too, for those who break the rules."

He'd spoken of punishments before. Of consequences.

"But if we went somewhere the Furies couldn't find us," I persisted, "how could they punish us?"

"Whenever someone leaves the Underworld who isn't supposed to," he said, "it leaves an imbalance in the realm. The Furies may not punish the person who left, but they'll happily take out their wrath on those left behind."

Turning my head, I caught a glimpse of the hand he'd wrapped around my shoulder. There they were . . . the scars that had been inflicted because of what I'd done when I was fifteen. The consequences of my thoughtless action.

Horrified, I stopped walking, just at the edge of the alley. The music was loud and festive, and I could see the bright lights and crowds of the street fair. I could even smell the dizzyingly intoxicating scent of grilled meat.

None of that mattered anymore, however.

"You mean they'd make poor Mr. Graves and Henry suffer for things *we* did?" I asked, my voice breaking.

John had dropped his arm from around my shoulder. Now he stood looking down at me with an odd expression on his face . . . it seemed almost like pity.

"Yes," he said. "So the sooner we get back, the safer all of us will be."

Beginning to realize the enormity of the sacrifice he was making for Alex — and for me — I nodded, speeding up my pace . . . only to slow down again when I noticed the towering structure of the Isla Huesos lighthouse as soon as we left the shelter of the alley. Looming a hundred feet into the air, it was one of the tallest structures on the island . . . and one that I had refused to go inside when my mom had brought me for the requisite tour, remaining at the bottom to read instead all the plaques about the brave residents who, in the nineteenth century, risked their lives sailing out to save the stranded crews and cargoes of ships that wrecked while traveling through the shallow waters between Isla Huesos and the coral reef that surrounded it.

Now the Isla Huesos lighthouse sat empty, decommissioned after the hurricane of October 1846 almost completely destroyed it, even rearranging the physical shape of the island, so that the lighthouse sat almost a half mile inland.

That's how someone was able to hang a sign from one side of the lighthouse, then string it all the way across the street along which Coffin Fest was being held. In bloodred letters, the sign read:

Welcome to Coffin Fest!
Brought to you by Captain Rob's Rum
Island of Bones Radio Station 95.5
And Rector Realty
Party 'til You're Wrecked!

John must have noticed my expression when I saw the sign, since he asked, "What's wrong?"

"Nothing," I said. "Just . . . at school, they held a special convocation to announce that Coffin Night was canceled."

Not only that, but Chief of Police Santos had put in an appearance to stress the seriousness of his department's efforts to quell the community's enthusiasm for the tradition, forbidding local hardware stores from selling large quantities of wood to minors to discourage bonfires and coffin-making.

Yet here was a perfectly public event celebrating it — off school grounds, of course — with corporate sponsorship, no less.

"The police do that every year," John said. "It never works."

Apparently not. Underneath the sign streamed hordes of people, most of them dressed normally, but some wearing costumes, many of them pirates, others dressed as zombies or ghosts or undertakers or sexy skeletons. Almost all of them were carrying red plastic drink cups, despite the fact that there was a police cruiser parked next to the crosswalk. Two very bored-looking police officers leaned against it, flirting with a couple of sexy girl pirates in tight bustiers and high heels.

Everyone I saw was smiling, despite the thunder rumbling overhead, and the fact that already I had felt a few drops of light rain fall.

I glanced back at John. Since I was pretty sure by now that he had died in a shipwreck, the event seemed . . . well, tasteless. Though of course the festival organizers hadn't had any way of knowing that the reason for Coffin Night himself was going to show up.

"It's horrible," I said to him emotionally, nodding at the sign. I found the fact that drops of fake blood were dripping from the letters particularly offensive. That was my *boyfriend's* fake blood they were using to promote their businesses and products.

"Oh, I don't know," he said with a crooked smile. "If there's going to be a coffin hidden anywhere on Isla Huesos — outside the cemetery, of course — it's kind of them to let us know this is the place."

I didn't share his confidence. He hadn't heard Seth Rector's elaborate plans for how they were going to hide the coffin. The plans had referenced an airplane hangar. None of them had included Coffin Fest.

"Well, I still think it's *horrible*," I said again. "And now not only does my grandmother know we're here, so does the entire Fury population of the island, I'm sure. *And* we were both on the front page of the paper this morning. How are we going to walk in there without people recognizing us?"

"Like this," he said, his smile turning enigmatic, and took my hand.

A second later, he was guiding me across the street, dodging laughing couples and some people dressed as vampires and even young parents pushing babies in strollers, until we were standing in front of a booth selling frozen fruit slices on a stick. We'd passed directly in front of the police officers, but they never looked away from the two girls in the pirate costumes.

I glanced up at John in astonishment. "How did you do that?"

"Sometimes people see only what they want to see," he said, with a shrug.

I realized this was coming from the phantom of the Isla Huesos Cemetery. Mr. Smith had told me sightings of John Hayden going in and out of his crypt were so common, and had been happening for so long, he'd developed a reputation . . . so much so that they'd never needed to install security cameras in the cemetery. No one ever ventured into the cemetery after dark, except for me and, unfortunately, Jade . . . and her killers.

Still, just to be safe, I opened my bag, reaching inside for a hairband. I had my other dress to change into, if necessary. In the meantime, a quick braid and my jean jacket would have to do as a disguise.

"It's still hard to imagine," I muttered as I braided, holding my hairband in my mouth, "what you ever did to create all this." By *all this* I was referring to the craziness of the street fair, the loud music, and the people and the costumes.

I never expected him actually to answer me, because I'd been asking the same question, in similar variations, for so long, and he'd never told me before.

To my utter astonishment, this time he did, so swiftly and in such a low voice I might have missed it if he hadn't been standing so close by.

"I killed a man," he said.

We ceased not to advance because he spake,
But still were passing onward through the forest,
The forest, say I, of thick-crowded ghosts.
DANTE ALIGHIERI, *Inferno*, Canto IV

My hairband fell to the sidewalk. I knew I would never find it again. Too many people were passing by, drinking from the red cups that they were buying from a Captain Rob's Rum stand nearby.

Of course I didn't think I'd heard him correctly. Why would he have told me something so important now, so casually, in the middle of a *street fair*?

Before I could stop myself, I blurted out the first thing I thought.

"Just *one*?"

The look he gave me was shattering.

Given everything I knew about him, though, I'd *expected* him to have killed a man.

It was the fact that his having taken a single life had resulted in his banishment to the Underworld for all eternity that I found so astonishing.

"I had no idea," he said, with a dry smile, "that you were so bloodthirsty, Pierce. Should we try to find you one of those pirate costumes?"

"It's . . . it's not that one man isn't enough," I stammered. I could hardly hear myself think with all the music. The Latin rhythms seemed to pulsate along with my heartbeat, which had quickened at the realization of my callous blunder. "It's just that I've had to stop you from killing quite a few men before, in my presence. So I'm surprised —"

He saw that I was being jostled by the crowd in the street, and taking my hand, drew me towards the sidewalk until we stood beneath the low-hanging branches of a gumbo-limbo tree, away from the masses and the lights, where it was a bit darker and quieter. Hope had followed us, of course, and she sat in the gutter, contentedly pecking at an abandoned grilled corn on the cob.

"The man I killed was a ship captain," John said. His voice had lost its hard edge, but his expression was remote, as if he were telling someone else's story. "He was captain of the *Liberty*. I was his first mate."

This was a little bit of a shock, but I said nothing, keeping my gaze on an orange tabby cat that had slunk out from behind the fence in front of which we were standing. The cat's eyes glowed as it caught sight of Hope . . . then it caught my warning gaze, and slunk quickly off.

"We were sailing from Havana to Isla Huesos," John went on. "From there we were to head back to England. Not far from Isla Huesos I discovered something . . . unsatisfactory with the course the captain had charted. I tried to discuss it with him privately, but he wouldn't listen. Word about his plan got out, and some of the crew agreed with me. There was a mutiny. I'm sure you know what a mutiny is."

"Yes," I said. I'd seen a movie about a mutiny once. The crew of the ship had ganged up on the captain and taken command away from him, because they hadn't liked the harsh and unfair way he was running things.

"Then you probably know that a mutiny is considered a serious offense," John said. The festive music and screams of laughter in the background were at odds with the serious expression on his face. "On ships, when tried and found guilty, mutineers are dealt with swiftly . . . generally hanged, but sometimes set adrift."

Just like that, I was back on board the creaking deck of the ship from my dream, watching John being cast about on those massive waves, unable to do a thing to help him, as the rain poured down upon us both.

My heart felt as if it were frozen inside my chest. My hands had gone suddenly cold as well, despite the warm temperature around us.

"When the men approached the captain and said they disagreed with his plan, things turned ugly, especially when I took their side. The captain . . . well, he was furious. He was the one who struck the first blow, though, Pierce, you've got to believe me." His gaze was pleading. "I never meant to kill him."

"Of course," I murmured. "You were only protecting yourself."

His gaze grew bitter. "Well, not everyone saw it that way," he said. "It turned out there were more men on board who supported the captain's plan — dangerous as it was — than didn't. I insisted that since I'd been the main instigator, I was the only one deserving of punishment —"

"So they set you adrift," I said, in a small voice, even though I already knew the answer.

He shrugged as if it were no big deal. Except I'd seen for myself, in my dream, how terrifying it had been.

"Mutineers — especially ones who murder their captain — don't deserve a coffin, let alone a proper burial," he said lightly. "But for some reason, people here on Isla Huesos seem to think that's what I need in order to rest. So every year, this is what they do." He raised a hand to indicate the festival.

I gazed up at his face, longing to be able to provide some kind of balm to soothe the wounds I saw there. Not literal wounds, but emotional wounds, ones he tried hard to hide.

"So you drowned to death," I said softly. "Like me. That's another thing we have in common, besides horrible family members."

His lips twitched. "Technically, you froze to death before you drowned," he pointed out. "And don't forget your head wound. But yes, we do have that in common."

I reached out to take his hand. It felt wonderfully warm and strong in mine.

"And after you drowned, when you woke up?" I asked.

"I was in the Underworld," he said. "The one with which you're familiar. Only I was alone. There was no manual, no guidebook telling me what to do. I had to learn it all by experience. Fortunately Mr. Graves, Mr. Liu, Frank, and Henry showed up a short time later. They've been a great help."

"They were part of the . . . mutiny?" I asked carefully.

He nodded. "I wish to God they'd never gotten involved. But Henry overheard me trying to reason with the captain. He went running to Graves, and Graves enlisted Mr. Liu and Frank without my knowledge. So there was nothing to be done for it. They're good men. They deserve a better fate than this."

Even as he spoke the words, I saw a cloud as dark as any of the ones in the sky overhead pass across his face. I thought I knew what was troubling him, and took his hand in both of mine.

"The captain of the *Liberty*," I said, thinking of what he'd said to my uncle about Bad People. "He must have been very bad."

"He was the worst person I have ever known," he said, without the slightest hesitation in his voice. His gaze had grown cold as his tone . . . but I knew that had nothing to do with me. It was from the memory of the man he'd killed.

Another chill swept over me.

"That's what I thought," I said. "Because otherwise someone like Mr. Graves wouldn't have committed a crime as bad as mutiny. And when you died, you would have ended up being sent by someone like yourself to a place like where the Furies go . . . which is why they come back, because they hate it there so much. But instead, you ended up ruler of an underworld. So someone must think that what you did was pretty brave, and wanted to reward you."

Slowly, I saw him come back to me from whatever dark place he'd been.

"It's seemed more like a punishment than a reward most days . . ." he said, his tone one of bitter resignation. Then his gaze lifted to meet mine, and his voice changed. ". . . at least until I found you."

The crackling heat in his eyes was nothing compared to the warmth that washed over me after he lowered his lips to mine. I didn't resist, closing my eyes and allowing myself to relax for what seemed like the first time in days.

Killed a man. That's all he'd done.

It wasn't nothing, of course. Killing a man was still an appalling thing to do.

Yet it was hardly as deplorable a crime as he'd been leading me to believe he'd committed, with all his insistence that I'd hate him if I ever found out the truth. He hadn't lit a bag full of kittens on fire, and then callously stood back and watched them burn alive. He'd merely led a mutiny at sea, and in doing so had killed his own captain . . . in self-defense.

Of course I only had John's word to go on about this. What I ought to have done, I realized, was read the book Mr. Smith had given me. Not that I didn't believe John, but it was always good to —

I opened my eyes, realizing something was wrong. He'd stopped kissing me.

"Here, miss. You dropped this," said a surprisingly familiar, high-pitched voice at my elbow, and a second later, the hairband I'd let fall to the sidewalk was presented to me on an open palm.

When I looked down to see who was speaking, I was astonished to see it was Henry. Little Henry Day from the Underworld.

I stared at him in confusion, not understanding for a full five seconds or so what I was seeing. He was standing right next to me, wearing the exact same clothes in which I'd last seen him.

Except at Coffin Fest in Isla Huesos, he did not actually look out of place. He looked like every other boy there dressed as a nineteenth-century pirate . . . and there were quite a few of them. Their costumes were only not quite as authentic as Henry's.

"What . . . ?" I exclaimed, wonderingly. "How . . . ?"

Frank, whose presence I somehow hadn't noticed until that moment, spoke up behind him.

"Now *this*," he said, tipping the red cup he held towards me, "is very good stuff. We've got to get Mr. Graves to learn how to make *this*."

Mr. Liu, standing beside him, did not look so convinced. He wasn't drinking. He was scanning the crowd with a critical gaze.

"Too many pirates," he said disapprovingly. "I do not see the appeal in dressing like a pirate. And what have they done to the lighthouse?"

I whirled back towards John. "What are they doing here?" I asked, stunned. "I thought —"

"Hello," John said to his crew, one of his dark eyebrows quirked up. "Kind of you to give us a moment to ourselves."

"Didn't want to disturb you," Frank said. He'd purchased a deep-fried turkey leg to go with his beverage, and was gnawing on it. "You looked otherwise occupied."

"Henry had other ideas," Mr. Liu said, in his deep voice.

"This is yours, isn't it?" Henry asked, shoving my hairband at me. "I saw you drop it."

"Yes, it is, Henry, thank you so much," I said, taking it from him. I turned my wondering eyes back to John.

"I thought," John said quietly, "that after what happened at the cemetery sexton's, it might be a good idea to seek backup. Isn't that what they call it these days?"

"Yes," I said. "Only I thought they can't come here —"

"Not on their own, no," John said. "While you were upstairs with your mother, and your uncle was on the telephone with your cousin, I went and got them, and brought them back here. Not that I wasn't impressed by your bravery with Mike," he added, with a sly smile. "But next time there may not be a flowerpot so handy. And Mr. Liu can be a very intimidating presence, when he chooses."

Mr. Liu looked modest, though Frank objected, "What about me? I can be intimidating, too. Tell him, Miss Oliviera. I intimidated you, when you first saw me, didn't I?"

"You didn't," Henry said. "Typhon did."

I shook my head, too stunned to speak.

"They've been looking for your cousin," John said, ignoring them. "Unsuccessfully so far, I'm sorry to report. Alex was in some duress in the video they saw on your phone, so it's possible he is here, and they've walked right by him. He may look quite different."

Remembering Alex's dirt-and-tear-smeared face, I fervently hoped he *did* look quite different . . . and that we found him in time to make sure he stayed that way.

Realizing suddenly that a member of John's crew was missing, I asked, "Where's Mr. Graves?"

"Someone had to stay behind," John said, in what I noted was a careful tone. "Mr. Graves volunteered. He's never been fond of Isla Huesos."

What John left unspoken was that Mr. Graves had *had* to stay behind — not because of his dislike of the island, or even because of his blindness (which hadn't seemed to me to hamper his activities one bit), but because someone had to tend to the souls of the departed in John's absence . . . and face the consequences if we did not return in a timely fashion.

I swallowed, remembering what Mr. Graves had said about pestilence.

"Thank you," I murmured gratefully, slipping a hand into John's.

"It's too soon to thank me," he said. "We haven't found him. Mr. Liu, any sign of a coffin?"

"Not yet," Mr. Liu replied, in his stoic manner. "But the farther down the street you go, the more people there are. That's where the music is."

"And the food," Frank said, raising his turkey leg.

John glanced questioningly at me.

After bending to separate Hope from her ear of corn — she was vocal in her protest, but it was for her own good. The orange tabby had returned — I scooped my hair back into the elastic band, and said, "Let's go." I sounded much braver than I felt.

I needn't have worried about anyone noticing John and me, however. Even though, as Mr. Liu had pointed out, there was a startling number of people dressed as pirates, all eyes seemed drawn to him, Henry, and Frank. Especially Frank. With his authentic tattoos and scars, all he was missing, really, to complete his ensemble was a parrot and an eye patch.

Maybe this was why the first person who actually did know me walked straight by before she finally noticed me . . . because she was busy staring at Frank.

"Kayla?" I asked cautiously, because I almost hadn't recognized her, either. At school, we had a dress code. What Kayla had on definitely defied it. She was wearing a long white dress that flattered her dark skin tone, her waist cinched to an impossibly small size with a black velvet bustier that was pushing her sizeable breasts to gravity-defying heights. Over her bare shoulders she'd thrown a purple velvet cape that matched the purple streaks in her wildly curling black hair, and she'd glued rhinestone stars to the corners of her dramatically made-up dark eyes.

"Wait . . ." The girl stopped in her tracks as she blinked back at me. "No way. *Pierce?* Oh, my God, *chickie!* Gimme a hug!"

I pushed her arms down before she could throw them around me, not wanting to attract even more attention than she already had with her screams, then dragged her from the center of the street to an empty space between two booths, one selling more frozen fruit slices on a stick, the other selling T-shirts that said *I Survived Coffin Fest on the Island of Bones.*

"Oh, my God, chickie," Kayla said, grabbing my arms. "Where have you been? Do you have any idea how freaked out I was when you didn't show up at two in the parking lot the other day like you said you would? You told me to call the police if you didn't show, so I did. And then the next thing I knew, your grandma was running around, saying some boy *kidnapped* you."

Her dark eyes sparkling — the fake gemstones actually paled in comparison — she looked over at John, who'd paused in front of the frozen-fruit stand to wait for me. It must have been as obvious from the surreptitious looks he was throwing in my direction as it was from the way my cheeks heated up in response to those looks that we knew each other.

"Wait, that's *him*?" Kayla cried, delighted. "*That's* the guy? Oh, my God, he could kidnap me any day of the week. You . . . are . . . so . . . lucky."

She emphasized each word with a punch to my shoulder, then stood there grinning at John, twirling a strand of her dark curly hair around one finger, each nail of which she'd painted white with black zebra stripes.

"Kayla," I said, reaching up to massage my shoulder. She punched pretty hard. "He didn't kidnap me. He —"

"Duh. Who's his friend?" she wanted to know, referring to Frank, who was pretending not to notice that she was looking at him by negotiating a purchase of frozen fruit on a stick for Henry.

"I saw him from way off and was like, 'What's with the smokin' hottie with the scar?' Seriously, I would not mind having a hunk like him kidnap me, either."

"Kayla," I said. I didn't want to rain on her good time — from the look of the sky, that was going to happen any minute regardless — but I needed her to hold off on the boy talk for two minutes so I could clear up some family business. "As you have clearly figured out by now, I'm experiencing some . . . personal problems at the moment. And I really need your help."

"Yeah?" Kayla hadn't taken her gaze off Frank. "Well, introduce me to your pirate friend over there, and I'll help you out."

"I thought you liked Alex," I said, a little disappointed.

She dropped her finger from her hair and gave up playing sexy eyes with Frank, turning towards me instead. "Seriously, you think *you* have personal problems? Your cousin is turning into a freak and a half. He asked me to meet him here at this thing, which I did, but will he dance with me, or even buy me a drink? No. He didn't even dress up, which is traditional at this soirée. It's like all he wanted was someone to sit with so he wouldn't look like such a loser being all by himself. It's lunch at school every day all over again, basically. He's just sitting there —"

My eyes widened. "Wait. *You know where Alex is right now?*"

"Of course I know where he is," Kayla said. "I just ditched him. Not that he's even noticed I'm gone, I'll bet. If this was supposed to be a date, your cousin Alex is sadly delusional —"

I reached out and grabbed her wrist. "Kayla," I said. "If you take us to Alex, I'll introduce you to Frank. Please, it's very important. I think Alex is in a lot of trouble. More trouble than me, even."

Kayla looked me up and down. "Now that's a lot of trouble," she said. "Because according to the paper, you're in one million dollars' worth of trouble. Do you know what I could do with one million dollars? Not that I would ever turn you in, but I could open my own hair and nail salon . . . no, with that kind of money, *ten* salons —"

"*Please,*" I said, giving her wrist a desperate squeeze.

"All right," Kayla said, with a shrug. "Jeez, calm down, I'll do it. Why not? I don't let the girls out very often" — she was referring to her breasts, which she was planning to have surgically reduced when she turned eighteen because, she said, her knees hit her nipples when she rode her bike — "so when I do, someone ought to appreciate them. Lord knows your cousin doesn't." She looked back over at Frank. For money to purchase the frozen fruit slices on a stick for Henry, I saw that Frank was using a silver Spanish dollar dug from the pocket of his leather trousers.

"Of course it's real, you bloody git," Frank said to the young man behind the fruit cart, who had apparently questioned the legitimacy of this form of currency. "That's a genuine piece of eight. I could buy your whole cart with it."

Great, I thought, sarcastically. John and his crew were doing an excellent job of blending in.

Kayla appeared to be thinking along similar lines, since she asked, "Where are those guys from, anyway?"

"Here," I assured her.

"Really?" She looked skeptical. The fruit vendor had apparently decided the piece of eight was authentic, and was surrendering more fruit on a stick than Henry could carry. "Because I'd have remembered seeing him around here. And I don't want to get into some whole long-distance thing. Those never work out."

I smiled, meeting John's gaze.

"Oh," I said, "you never know."

And with the greenest hydras were begirt;
Small serpents and cerastes were their tresses,
Wherewith their horrid temples were entwined.
DANTE ALIGHIERI, *Inferno*, Canto IX

Kayla, her hand resting on the crook of Frank's elbow, led us down the crowded street.

"I'm not sure if this is the best idea," John said, watching as Frank lifted Kayla's hand and pressed it to his lips.

"You are enchanting, fair damsel," Frank said.

"I bet you pirates say that to all us fair damsels," I heard Kayla say with a giggle in response.

"It's okay," I reassured John. "I think Kayla can handle herself around guys. Even guys like Frank."

"But what about Furies?" John asked, his gaze serious. "Will she be able to handle herself around them?"

"Oh." I hadn't thought of that. "Knowing her, she probably can, actually."

"Well, keep an eye on your necklace," he said. "I don't like that we've been out in the open for so long and there hasn't been a single sign of them. They must know by now that we're here. So where are they?"

I glanced around. Everywhere I looked were happy revelers, enjoying themselves, while overhead, lightning continued to illuminate the clouds, and thunder grumbled.

"Maybe that's it," I ventured. "We're out in the open. The Furies don't want to risk attracting too much attention."

"Maybe," John conceded. "Or maybe it's the quiet before the storm."

I looked up at the night sky, then down at my necklace. The diamond around my throat was the same purplish dark gray as the heavy clouds. He may have been right.

"Pierce?"

An attractive young couple was standing in front of us, their arms around each other. He had smeared ghoulish gray pancake makeup all over his face, and was dressed in an Isla Huesos High School Wreckers football uniform, complete with shoulder pads. She was wearing an IHHS Wreckers cheerleading uniform, carrying red and white pom-poms, and had a vampire bite painted on her neck, oozing fake blood.

"Oh, my God, Pierce!" the girl cried. "It's me, Farah, Farah Endicott, and Seth Rector." She pointed to her boyfriend, laughing. "I can't believe our costumes are that good! Can you believe it, babe?" She grinned up at Seth. "Pierce didn't even recognize us. And *she's* the one who's supposed to have gone missing!"

Farah and Seth had a good laugh over that one. They were

both grasping red cups in their hands, and while I didn't know for sure what was in them, I had a feeling from the near-hysterical tone of their laughter that the drinks were stronger than soda. John and I stood there while ahead of us, Kayla and Frank paused in the street, glancing back at us curiously. Mr. Liu, also observing the encounter, steered Henry off to the side of the street. The two of them pretended to be examining a stand hawking personally engraved shells. But really, they were watching Farah and Seth.

"Yeah," I said, acting as if I found the situation as hilarious as Farah did. "That whole missing thing turns out to have been a big misunderstanding. Obviously. Since I'm standing right here in front of you."

"Oh," Farah cried, laughing even harder. "That's so funny! Of course you're not missing anymore. So, who's your friend?"

"This is John," I said, purposefully leaving off his last name. For all I knew, Farah and Seth were going to run off after this to call my dad and try to collect the million-dollar reward he was offering for my safe return. The less information I gave them, the better. "John, these are some friends of mine, Farah Endicott and Seth Rector."

John's face, as it always did, shut down when he heard the name *Rector*. He stood and glared at the two of them unsmilingly. "How do you do?" he asked stiffly, not extending his right hand. It was full of extra frozen fruit on a stick he'd offered to hold for Henry, which I'd thought was sweet. His other arm was wrapped around my waist.

"Well, I do very well, thank you," Seth said, in a snooty British accent that I guess was supposed to be some kind of imitation of John and that I didn't find particularly funny. John didn't even have an accent to me, either because I was used to the way he talked or because he'd spent so much time around dead Americans it had faded to be barely noticeable.

But Seth managed to crack Farah up, and the two of them snickered for about thirty seconds before Seth regained control of himself, then said to John, "No, seriously, dude, it's cool. Nice to meet you. You don't look like a serial killer or whatever it is they're trying to make you out to be on the news."

Farah smacked him playfully on the chest and said, "Babe! Kidnapper. He's a kidnapper!"

"My bad," Seth said.

"Oh, my *God*," Farah said, her blue eyes going wide. "Dude, I *love* your necklace. Where did you get that?" She was about to lift the diamond that hung from my neck when I felt the muscles in the arm John had around my waist tense. He pulled me back a step before she could touch it.

Which was a good thing, since the stone really was cursed, exactly as Henry had said. The last living person who'd touched it was Mr. Curry, a jeweler who'd accused me of stealing it and tried to have me arrested.

This hadn't worked out too well for him, thanks to John, who'd objected to his rough treatment of me and caused his heart to stop.

"Oh, I don't know," I said quickly. "I got it at the mall, I guess. It's fake."

"Well, duh," Farah said, laughing. "If it were real it would be worth, like, as much money as your dad was offering as a reward for finding you —"

According to Mr. Curry, the Persephone Diamond was worth about seventy-five times that, actually. I didn't say so out loud, however.

"It's so funny, because a bunch of us were just joking that if we saw you, we would, like, totally turn you in for all that cash," Farah went on, with a giggle. "But then we found out your dad canceled the reward."

"That *is* funny," I said, but not because I actually found it amusing. "When did you hear that?"

"Oh, my God," Farah said, "it's been, like, all over the Internet."

I guess my mom had gotten my note, and told my dad. He'd moved fast. But then, he always did.

"Right," John said. "Well, we're actually looking for someone, so we have to be going. . . ."

"Wait —" Seth stepped in front of us. John removed his arm from around me and dropped Henry's frozen fruit, keeping his fists loose and ready at his sides.

But Seth didn't appear to want to keep us from finding Alex.

"Farah was kidding about the reward," he said. "We'd never do that. And I hope there's no hard feelings about our coming over and moving the coffin stuff out of your house," he added, slurring his words a little. "But, like, we didn't know when you were coming back, and your mom . . . it seemed like she was kind of flipping out. And you know, even though it looks like they're probably going to cancel the game on account of this storm that's coming, we still have to make the coffin. It's a tradition, or whatever."

I stared at him in astonishment. "Wait," I said. "*You* moved the wood and stuff out of my mom's garage?" All this time, I'd been sure it was Alex and that as soon as these guys found out he'd done it, his punishment for it was getting locked in the coffin afterwards.

But Seth's next words proved me wrong. "Yeah," Seth said. "Well, me and my dad. We came over and did it this morning. Your mom totally understood."

Of course. Uncle Chris had mentioned Seth and his dad had been over earlier in the day. . . .

"Oh, my God." Farah wiggled up to Seth and put her arms around him again. "Tell Pierce about your dad and her mom. Wait, Pierce, you have to hear this. Tell her, babe."

"Babe, not now," Seth said, glancing at Farah in annoyance. He seemed to be growing uncomfortable under John's stare. Seth was a big guy, especially in his shoulder pads.

But he wasn't as big as John.

"Fine," Farah said, making a little moue of disappointment. "I'll tell her. Your mom and Seth's dad used to go out, back when they were in high school. They were senior prom king and queen, and everything. Everyone thought they were going to get married. Did you know that?"

I looked quickly from her to Seth and then back again. The sounds of the festival seemed to fade. I barely felt John's hand close over mine, strong and supportive.

Instead all I could think about was a conversation I'd over-heard between my mother and father — not the most recent one, outside my mom's bedroom, but one they'd had after my last court-mandated visit with my dad before I'd moved to Florida. Dad had been giving Mom a hard time about her decision to relo-cate to her old hometown, teasing her that it was because "he" was available again.

"I would think you'd have better things to do right now than look up the marital status of my ex-boyfriends on the Internet," Mom had said to him, scathingly.

"I like to keep track of their mating habits," Dad had smirked.

I hadn't understood who they were talking about at the time.

Suddenly, it was all too clear: Seth's dad.

Farah, noting my stunned expression, smacked her boyfriend in the chest again.

"See, babe?" she said. "I *told* you she didn't know. Isn't that *insane*? It turns out all of our parents used to hang out. Your mom and Seth's dad and my dad and your uncle Chris, too. My mom — she went to IHHS, too, but she was a few grades younger — says they were like the four musketeers, or something. Isn't that the cut-est thing you've ever heard? Well, I guess it was cute up until . . ." She paused, then held up a hand, trying to show how tactful she was. "Well, *you* know. What happened with your uncle."

I didn't want to admit that I had only the vaguest idea what had happened with my uncle, aside from the fact that the charges had been drug related, and that he'd been in jail for Alex's entire life, practically.

207

Farah shrugged. "I guess that's when your mom stopped coming back to Isla Huesos from college, and she and Seth's dad broke up. But, hey, it's cool, because she met your dad and had you, right? Although I was kind of hoping your mom and Seth's dad would get back together now that they're both divorced."

Apparently, this was what my dad had assumed my mom was hoping, too.

A group of people, similarly attired in the Isla Huesos High School colors of red and white, walked by, noticed Seth and Farah, and shouted, "Wreckers rule!" Several of them pumped their fists in Seth's direction. He pumped his fist back at them and yelled, *Yeah!* Then they all began bumping their chests together and talking enthusiastically about some party that was going to be off the hook.

Suddenly I understood the reason why Uncle Chris had expressed relief that my dad was coming to town. He'd never shown any particular fondness for my dad before, but he'd liked the fact that Mr. Rector had started hanging around my mom's house even less.

Now my mom's weird reaction when I'd been making fun of how ostentatious the Rector mausoleum was that day we rode past it on our bikes made sense. My mom had almost *been* a Rector — well, married to one, anyway. I'd been standing there making jokes about how some people had money to burn.

Sure. Like her *ex-boyfriend from high school.*

Why hadn't she said anything? It wouldn't have been weird for her to tell me, "Pierce, back when I was in high school and had terribly poor judgment, I used to go out with an extreme douche."

Was she hiding something? Or was it that she wanted to put as much distance as she could between her high-school self and her new self?

"Are you all right?" John asked, his voice penetrating the swirling cloud of confusion in my mind.

"Yes," I said. "It's just . . . some things are starting to make sense that never did before."

"What kind of things?" he asked curiously.

"Nothing that really matters, I guess," I said, shaking my head. "Just some stuff about my mom." I reached out and wrapped both my arms around one of John's. "Promise me we'll never be like them, okay?" I asked, with a shudder, nodding at Seth and Farah. "Calling each other *babe* in that annoying way?"

"We could never be like those two," John said, leading me away after giving Seth one last stony-eyed glare.

"Why do you hate him so much?" I asked, amused.

"Hate him?" John looked surprised. "I only just met him. And you don't seem particularly fond of him yourself."

"I'm not, but every time anyone says the word *Rector* around you, you get this look on your face." I illustrated, lowering my eyebrows into a deep scowl and frowning.

He laughed. "Do I? I had no idea."

"Alex does the same thing whenever he sees Seth," I said, thinking back.

"Well, then I think I'll like your cousin," John said, "if we ever find him."

"I think you will, too," I said. "But why —?"

Light footsteps sounded behind us, interrupting me. We turned to see Farah racing breathlessly up, her cheeks flushed.

"I'm such a ditz," she said. "I almost forgot. We're having a Coffin Night party tomorrow night. And you guys are totally invited."

"Wow," I said. "Thanks, Farah. That is so nice. But we probably won't be able —"

"Oh, come on," Farah said, looking disappointed. "Try to come. Everyone in the senior class is invited . . . but don't tell any juniors. We're going to try to have the coffin done so it can be there. We want everyone to sign it. You know, as like a memento to remember the year by."

"The coffin's going to be there?" Suddenly the invitation sounded a lot more tempting. "Where's the party going to be?"

"At the new development our dads are building, out on Reef Key. You remember, Pierce, we took you to see it."

I did remember. Mr. Rector and Mr. Endicott had basically taken a beautiful island paradise and bulldozed it into an ugly subdivision, complete with tennis courts and a tiki bar.

"You can't miss it," Farah said. "It'll be in the only spec house that's done. I really hope this hurricane doesn't come like they keep saying it's going to, or of course we'll have to cancel the whole thing. This afternoon they downgraded it to a Category Two but I just heard it's back up to a Three. So even if it only brushes us, for sure no one is going to —"

Someone yelled *Farah!* and she looked back towards the group from which she'd disentangled herself in order to come over and issue her invitation.

"Oh," she said, biting her cherry-red lip. "I gotta go. But try to come, will you? It's gonna be *epic*."

Then she ran back to Seth with an excited wave to us.

I stood there for a moment, feeling dazed. Not too long ago, someone else had said *It's gonna be epic* to me.

It had been Jade.

The uneasy feeling inside me suddenly got a little worse . . . and not only because of what I'd learned about my mom and Mr. Rector's high-school relationship. A drop of rain hit me squarely on the cheek. I held out one of my hands. Another drop hit me in the center of my palm.

The groups of people around us began to move more quickly, searching for shelter. Henry started taking extra-large bites from his cotton candy, fearful the rain would melt it before he had the opportunity to enjoy it.

"It's not as bad as all that," John said, grinning as he noticed my expression. "It's only rain. And at least now we know where the coffin is."

"Where it's going to be *tomorrow*," I said. I couldn't keep the anxiety I felt out of my voice. "It isn't even built yet. What if you're right about that image I saw on my phone? What if it's of the future . . . the distant future? We can't keep chasing after Alex like this every night."

I remembered asking John that morning if I could have a tablet like the one he kept in his pocket, and his response — *Definitely not*. Now I knew why he had been so curt.

"If all your magic mirror thing ever shows is people suffering, but there's nothing you can do to help, what's the point in even having one?" I asked him bitterly.

"That's not all they ever show," John said. "They show your heart's desire . . . what you most want to see — or who — at the time you're looking."

"Then mine must be broken," I said. It made sense. Why wouldn't mine be broken? I was broken, too. Or at least I hadn't felt normal in a long time.

"Yours isn't broken," John said. "Considering it's a mobile device from earth, and no mobile device from earth has ever functioned in the Underworld before, I don't quite understand . . . yet." He was looking at me speculatively. "But it did exactly what ours do. You were worried about your family, so what you were shown was your heart's desire: the one member of your family who's in immediate danger, and needs your —"

"Wait a minute," I interrupted. Something dawned on me. "Was that how you always knew when *I* was in trouble and needed help? Like that day at school, with Mr. Mueller? And at the jeweler's that time? Because *I* was the one you most wanted to see when you looked down into your —"

"Oh, look," John said, seeming infinitely relieved by the interruption. "Here comes Frank."

Frank was sauntering over. "Found him," he said, with casual nonchalance.

My heart gave a swoop. Only something as monumental as my cousin finally being located could distract me from the discovery that all those times my boyfriend had rescued me from mortal peril, it had been because he'd been spying on me from the

Underworld via a handheld device seemingly operated by the Fates. "*Where?*"

"Exactly where Miss Kayla left him." Frank led us a few booths down, to a dark passageway set back from the street. Over the passageway was an arch made of wrought iron, covered in twinkling fairy lights, through which vines of bright yellow bougainvillea twisted.

On top of the archway sat Hope, cooing to herself. When she noticed me, she lifted her wings and took off, ducking inside the arch.

The archway led to the large outdoor courtyard, thickly canopied by tree branches through which more fairy lights had been strung, and colored lanterns had been hung to give the place a deeply romantic air.

It was from this courtyard, I realized, that the lively Spanish music we'd been hearing all night had been playing. I could see a small stage lit with floodlights, with several musicians standing on it, including a few guitar players and a beautiful singer in a tight red dress, a hibiscus flower in her hair. In front of the stage, couples of all ages were dancing. Small tables were scattered throughout the yard, many of them empty. That was probably because most people preferred the vibrant activity on the street.

There was food available, however. A long table on one side of the courtyard offered up a buffet. Hope had planted herself in front of this table, pecking the ground for any morsel that might have dropped from diners' plates. I didn't blame her. I could smell the delicious aromas of marinated chicken and seafood, and realized once again how ravenous I was. The frozen fruit I'd eaten hadn't been enough to satisfy my appetite.

"Madame." Kayla startled me by stepping out of the deep shadows of the archway and giving a dramatic sweep of her purple velvet cape. "Your cousin Alex awaits." She pointed at one of the white plastic tables sheltered by the branches of a large tree.

There was no mistaking the figure sitting slumped in the glow of his cell phone. It was Alex, all right. His thumbs were moving rapidly over his keypad.

"Thanks, Kayla," I said. To John, I said, ignoring the hunger pangs from my stomach, "I'll be right back," and started walking over to my cousin's table.

"I'll accompany you," John said, falling into step beside me. "If you don't mind."

I stopped. "John," I said. I felt flustered because of the aroma of the food and the fact that I'd come so far only to find Alex texting — *texting* — in such a beautiful courtyard while everyone else was having a good time at the festival, even if what they were celebrating was something macabre . . . the death and burial of my boyfriend. At least underneath the thick canopy of leaves I couldn't feel the hard intermittent drops of rain. "I know your magic mirror probably doesn't work up here on earth, but you can see with your own eyes that I'm not in danger right now."

His dark eyebrows lifted. "I beg your pardon?"

"I don't need your help right now," I explained. "You'll actually only get in the way. You don't know Alex. And he doesn't know you. All he knows is whatever my grandmother told him about you . . . and I highly doubt that was anything good. He isn't going to talk in front of you."

"Perhaps not." John's smile was polite. "But you're wrong about not being in danger right now." He nodded at my chest.

I looked down. In the rosy glow of the party lanterns, I saw what he meant. The diamond dangling from my necklace had gone the same color as the storm clouds that had been gathering all night.

Somewhere close by lurked a Fury.

And I began: "O Poet, willingly
Speak would I to those two, who go together,
And seem upon the wind to be so light."
DANTE ALIGHIERI, *Inferno*, Canto V

Don't worry," John said. "We'll take care of it . . . *without* getting in your way."

Already, Mr. Liu and Frank had split up, Mr. Liu taking the outer edges of the courtyard, scanning the few people at the tables, and Frank whirling Kayla out onto the dance floor so he'd have a reason to be in the middle of all the couples gathered there. Even Henry left his cotton candy and drink on an empty table, and scrambled up one of the trees for a better lookout position.

"What will you do if you find a Fury?" I blurted. "Kill it?"

Even before the words came out of my mouth, I regretted them. A cloud as dark as the ones blackening my diamond came over his face, and John looked away, saying, "No. As you reminded me earlier, killing doesn't stop Furies . . . unfortunately. But pain can be a remarkably effective deterrent sometimes."

I bit my lip. His tone was flippant, but I'd heard the wounded pride behind it.

I put a hand on his arm and said, "John, I'm sorry. Surely we can find another way to defeat them."

He shook his head, looking vaguely amused.

"Go and talk to your cousin," he said. "I'll keep watch."

Pressing my lips together, I walked to where Alex was sitting. I guess I could understand it. John had been doing this for nearly two hundred years, after all. Who was I to think I was such an expert, after less than a week?

"Alex," I said, sliding into a chair next to him.

He didn't acknowledge me, still entirely focused on his phone. It took me a few seconds to realize it was because he was wearing earbuds. Sitting in a courtyard where fantastic live music was playing, and he was wearing earbuds. Unbelievable.

I reached over and yanked one out. *"Alex."*

He jerked his face from the screen, and turned to look at me. When he realized who I was, he didn't smile. He frowned.

"Oh, hey, Pierce," he said. "My dad said you were back. He just called, actually, and said all hell has broken loose because you went to the house with your new boyfriend and left some kind of note saying that you're running off with him to get married or something. Congratulations. So what are you doing *here*?"

Married? I hadn't said anything about getting married. Why was everyone in my family so dramatic?

"What are *you* doing here?" I shot back. "Didn't Uncle Chris tell you to come home?"

"What are you now, the parental police?" Alex asked, with a laugh. "You're one to talk. Where have you been for the past two days? Off with this guy? Who is he, anyway? Did you know the cops are looking for you? Your dad is on the way into town, and I hear he isn't too happy with you. Better watch out, or he might cut off that thousand-dollars-a-week allowance."

"It isn't a thousand dollars a week," I said, even more annoyed. "Who are you texting?"

He showed me his screen. "*World of Warcraft.*"

"Well, Alex, put it down," I said. "I need to talk to you."

"What about?" He didn't put down the phone. "How your new boyfriend punched Grandma in the face? That was classic, by the way." He snickered. "Wish I could meet him."

A second later, his phone disappeared. Not because he'd decided to put it away and have an adult conversation with me, but because John had removed it from his grasp.

"Looks like you're getting your wish," he said, sliding into an empty chair beside Alex.

"Dude," Alex said, looking outraged and a little stunned at the same time. "That's my personal property. What did you do with it?"

The mobile had disappeared into thin air. It wasn't in either of John's hands.

"Your cousin asked you to put it down," John explained, pleasantly enough. "And my name isn't *dude*, it's John. Pierce has gone to a lot of time and trouble to find you tonight. The least you can do is give her the courtesy of your full attention."

Alex glared at him. Even in the pink glow of the party lanterns, I could see that his face was red, but whether it was from anger or embarrassment, I didn't know.

Perhaps it was from astonishment. Because a second later, a wide, low bowl, laden with steaming lobster tails, shrimp, chicken, chorizo, vegetables, and Spanish rice appeared in the middle of the table, along with a pitcher of ice-cold water, a plate piled high with warm Cuban bread, and enough plates, glasses, and cutlery for everyone.

No waitperson was seen delivering these things. They were simply not there one moment, and there the next.

"Now," John said, leaning forward to reach for a napkin, "we're going to enjoy this food. You're welcome to join us. When we're through, you'll get your phone back. Do you understand, Alexander?"

Now Alex wasn't glaring. He was staring, his eyes nearly popping out of his head.

I could relate to the feeling. How had John done all this? I thought the Fates worked only in the Underworld.

Then I remembered the bird John had brought back to life that day in the cemetery, and the burst of light he'd created in my mom's house. A cheap magician's trick, he'd called it. . . .

There's nothing cheap about this, I thought.

Deciding that I was so hungry, I didn't care how he'd done it, I reached for my own napkin, spreading it onto my lap, then accepting the heaping helping of paella John served onto my plate from the bowl in the center of the table.

"How . . . how are you doing this?" Alex demanded, his gaze darting suspiciously between John and me. He sounded nervous. His voice shook a little. "What do you want from me? Is this some kind of reality TV show?" He looked around the court-yard, seemingly scanning for hidden cameras. "I know my rights, you know. You can't show my face unless I've signed a waiver. And since I'm still under eighteen, my dad has to fill out a consent form."

"Alex," I said to him. "This isn't a TV show. I just want to talk."

"Why?" His eyes narrowed distrustfully. "I didn't do anything. Whatever you're messed up in with this guy, Pierce, I don't want to get involved." He glanced down at the food. It was clear he thought it was all stolen . . . or possibly bewitched. For all I knew, it might have been. "I've got my own problems to deal with."

"That's what I want to talk to you about, Alex," I said. I was feeling better already from the few mouthfuls of rice and shrimp I'd swallowed. For food that might have been conjured up from the realm of darkness, it certainly tasted heavenly. "I know how upset you are about your dad, and him getting dragged in for questioning about Jade's murder —"

Alex's expression grew defensive. "He was home with me during the time she was killed," he said. "This whole thing is completely bogus. You know who they should be asking about Jade? *This guy.*" He stabbed a nail-bitten finger at John. "Who the hell is he? I've never even seen him around here before."

"Okay," I said, in a soothing voice. Alex wouldn't have liked hearing it, but he had a lot in common with John. When Alex felt cornered, he too lashed out at the people who were only trying to help him, because for so many years the only kind of treatment he'd experienced was indifference and cruelty It was my grandmother who'd raised him, after all.

"But John was with me when Jade was murdered," I explained. "So he didn't do it, either. Someone else on this island did. We don't know who yet. So taking out your frustrations about your dad on Seth Rector and the entire A-wing isn't —"

Now instead of red, Alex's cheeks went pale. He appeared startled . . . and maybe even a little guilt-stricken. *"What?"*

"That's right, I know," I said, giving him my best disapproving older cousin look. I was older than he was only by several months, but it still counted. "I know you're going to try to do something to the coffin."

Alex's shock only increased. "The *coffin?"*

"Don't act like you don't know what I'm talking about, Alex," I said. The water John had poured into my glass was refreshingly cool, especially after the spicy paella. "You told me yourself it was kind of perfect that I was on the coffin committee. That way you'd know where they were at all times. That's what you said. It's obvious you're planning on ruining the senior coffin to get back at Seth Rector for something he did to you."

Alex shook his head. Some of the shock must have worn off. "Yeah, Pierce," he said, his voice dripping in sarcasm. "That's it. The reason I was so excited you were on this year's coffin committee was so I could destroy all of Seth Rector's dreams, the way he destroyed all mine by bullying me in kindergarten. Are you serious with this? Come on."

I glanced uncertainly at John. His attention was focused on Alex. But his fingers, I noticed, were moving restlessly, even as they held his fork. He was ready in case of any kind of attack.

I looked over my shoulder. Frank was still spinning Kayla around on the dance floor. She looked as if she was in heaven, a huge smile on her face, her head thrown back, her wildly curling hair a brown and purple aurora. She was completely unaware that as they were dancing, Frank, like John, was watching the rest of the courtyard, especially the dark corner where our table was located. Not that it mattered that Kayla hadn't noticed this . . . or that I was looking her way. She'd never been able to give me any insight as to why Alex hated Seth Rector so much, either.

I looked back at Alex.

"Actually," I said, "I *am* serious about this, Alex. I know you're planning on doing something that's going to get you in big trouble with Seth Rector. And I'm not going to let you."

Alex's face contorted into an ugly sneer. "Oh, why?" he demanded. "Because you're so concerned the popular crowd won't like you anymore? You don't want to be associated with us lowly Cabreros? Well, let me tell you something, Pierce. You kind of shot your opportunity to hang with A-wingers when you took off to go slutting around with this muscle-bound freak —"

To emphasize his words, Alex reached out and flipped the table over, sending paella flying everywhere, then lunged at John.

I don't know what Alex could have been thinking. John was almost a foot taller than he was, and quite a bit heavier, all of it lean muscle. Then there was the small fact that John was keeper of the dead and ruler of the Underworld . . . though Alex had no way of knowing this.

In a heartbeat, Alex was thrown back into his plastic chair. John stood over him, holding him down with one hand as Alex panted and struggled, looking like a bait worm on a hook.

"Are you insane?" I asked Alex in disbelief as I flicked bits of rice from the skirt of my dress. "What is *wrong* with you?"

John looked over at me and asked, "Are you all right?"

"Of course I'm all right," I said. "But your beautiful dinner . . ." I stared at the mess on the courtyard floor. "It's ruined."

"Never mind about that," John said, turning his attention back to Alex.

How was I supposed to not mind about that? I could feel everyone's gaze on us — though mercifully the music hadn't stopped. Pieces of broken plate littered the bricks, along with glass from the smashed water pitcher. Rice and lobster tails were scattered everywhere.

Mr. Liu strode over, as boldly as if he were running the place. "Everything is all right here," he said in an authoritative voice, standing in front of John and Alex and blocking the view of them from onlookers with his bulk. "Everything is fine."

The curious drifted away, though Henry scrambled down from his tree, and Frank and Kayla were making their way from across the dance floor.

"We're only trying to help you," I said to Alex. "I don't care about being popular, or the stupid coffin. I care about *you*. I'm trying to keep you from getting hurt."

"If you really cared about me," Alex said in an angry voice, still straining against the hand holding him into the chair, "you'd leave me alone. You have no idea what I'm going through."

"No," John leaned down and said to him in a low, dangerous voice I knew he hadn't intended for me to overhear. "You have no idea what *she's* been through to get here to talk to you. The only reason you're still breathing right now is because she doesn't like it when I hurt people."

Alex threw him a rebellious look, but seemed to believe him, since he pressed his lips together.

Kayla rushed over, clutching a handful of napkins.

"Oh, my God," she said, beginning to dab at the front of my dress. "Chickie, you're a mess! Alex, what is wrong with you? I saw the whole thing, don't even try to deny you started it. Whatever happened to letting it go, like they taught us in the program?"

Alex scowled at her. Apparently he didn't care to listen to New Pathways rhetoric just then.

"Kayla is right," I said. "I don't know why you hate Seth Rector so much, or what he ever did to you, but you've got to let it go. It's only going to get you in trouble."

"Show 'im, miss," Henry said, gravely, pointing at my bag. "Show 'im how much trouble, on your magic mirror. Then he'll believe you."

I saw John's eyes flash silver at me, catching the light from the nearby hanging lanterns. I wasn't certain if it was with approval or disapproval of Henry's idea, but I figured I had nothing to lose, now that my parents knew I was not being held against my will. How fast could the FBI triangulate a signal, if they were even tracing it anymore?

I reached into my bag for my cell, then turned on the power. Disappointingly, my phone behaved exactly the way it was supposed to, showing me my messages — over a hundred of them, mostly from my mother — instead of the creepy video of Alex. That was nowhere to be found.

"My, er, magic mirror doesn't work the same way here as it does back home, Henry," I said.

Henry looked disappointed. "Well, you really want to do as she says, anyway," he told Alex. "Trust me."

Alex seemed unable to sit in silence anymore. Looking from Henry, in his strange clothes, to me, he burst out, "Jesus, Pierce, what is going on? Who *are* these guys? I get that your dad is the richest guy in America, but what did you do, go out and buy your own circus?"

I glanced at John and Mr. Liu, who were, it was true, standing over him somewhat menacingly. But Alex had attacked John first. *He* was the one being the most offensive.

"These are my friends," I said indignantly. "And they came with me to help find you because I was so worried about you."

Alex's voice cracked. "You disappear without a word to anyone, then come back because you're worried about *me*? Why?"

"You're my cousin," I said, hurt by his incredulous tone. "You're someone I care about a lot. I get the sense that you're in trouble. Your dad told you I was home, and that he'd like *you* to come home, but you sat here in the dark and kept playing *World of Warcraft* by yourself. Don't you think that's a little worrying, Alex? Don't you think *that's* a sign that something weird is going on?"

"God, you are so self-centered," Alex said with a laugh. John's eyes weren't the only ones flashing. Alex's looked unusually bright, too. But his eyes were brown. "So you disappear for a while, and then come back, and I'm supposed to drop everything to rush home to see you? And because I don't, you gather this search party of freaks to come looking for me, because *I'm* in some kind of trouble?"

"That doesn't make her self-centered," John said, in a cool voice. "It makes her probably one of the few people in your life who actually cares about you."

"None of this has anything to do with her," Alex said with a scowl. "It happened over twenty years ago, and my *dad* is the one paying the price for it — continues to pay the price for it, every day. It's nice that you want to help all of a sudden, Pierce — your mom, too, moving back here to play house like everything's hunky-dory. But you're both a little late to the party."

It wasn't until the end of this speech that I figured out why Alex's eyes looked so bright: They were filled with tears.

He was crying.

> *"Nothing has been discovered by thine eyes*
> *So notable as is the present river,*
> *Which all the little flames above it quenches."*
> DANTE ALIGHIERI, *Inferno*, Canto XIV

Shocked, John released his hold on Alex.

Instead of trying to get away, however, Alex slumped forward in his chair, burying his face in his hands, weeping soundlessly.

I exchanged astonished glances with Kayla, uncertain what to do. I'd hoped that since she'd spent more time with him than I had, she could give me some insight into how to deal with him.

I could tell from her wide-eyed expression, though, that she had no idea either . . . nor, judging from the looks they gave me, did anyone else.

Except John, who said, in a considerably kinder voice than he'd used before when speaking to or about Alex, "He's had enough. Someone ought to take him home now." I think he could tell that Alex was wounded, far more deeply than I'd ever realized, because Alex had always acted as if he didn't care about anything — or anyone.

But evidently he did care, since he groaned at John's suggestion. "No. Please." He didn't lift his face from his hands. "I don't want to go home."

"Wait," I said to John, and righted one of the chairs that had been tipped over when Alex had flipped the table. Then I sat down in it, and laid a hand on Alex's back. "Why don't you want to go home, Alex?"

"Would *you*?" he asked, his voice muffled because he was still speaking into his fingers. "If you had to live with *her*?"

I knew exactly who he meant, picturing the way she'd stood at the bottom of the stairs by the newel post, reaching into her purse for the pepper spray. She'd never pepper-sprayed Alex, to my knowledge, but she liked to lecture him on what she considered his faults.

"No," I said. "But your dad is there now. And when he gets a job, you two can move out —"

"He's not going to get a job," Alex groaned. "No one will hire him, because of his prison record —"

I'd actually walked in on my mother having a similar discussion with Uncle Chris. Mom had offered him a loan — she'd even offered to buy him a boat, so he could start his own charter fishing company — but he'd refused. He appreciated it, he'd said, but he didn't want any handouts. He was going to make good on his own.

"— and he's probably going to get charged with Jade's murder."

I realized with a sense of frustration that Alex was right.

"We're working on that," I assured him.

"Working on that?" He was still speaking into his hands. "How are you *working* on that? You're a spoiled rich girl from Connecticut who died and came back to life a mental case. Everyone knows it. Now you've run off with your roid-head boyfriend. You're not exactly Nancy freaking Drew, all right?"

That stung. Not that I'd ever wanted to be Nancy Drew, except maybe when I was ten. And John wasn't a roid-head.

"Pierce." John's face was hard. "Let's go. He doesn't want our help."

John was right, I knew. You couldn't help someone who wouldn't accept that help or even help himself. But still . . .

It wasn't until Hope fluttered over and landed by Alex's feet, peering questioningly up at him, that he finally tore his hands away from his eyes.

"Oh, my God," he said, sounding disgusted. "Why is there a *bird* looking at me?"

"That's Miss Oliviera's bird," Henry volunteered cheerfully. "The captain gave it to her as a present."

Kayla punched me in the arm. "John's got his captain's license?" she whispered. "You are so lucky. Frank says he just loads cargo."

I glanced at Frank. I wondered if Kayla would like him as much if she knew the "cargo" he loaded was human souls.

To Alex, I said, "What did you mean just now when you said something happened over twenty years ago that Uncle Chris is still paying the price for? You mean his arrest? What does that have to do with any of this?"

"Nothing," he said, sullenly. "I changed my mind. I *do* want to go home."

I didn't believe in his sudden change of heart. I knew he was trying to avoid the discussion. I had never seen Alex so emotional, although I suppose I should have always known that he was. That's why he, like me, had been in New Pathways.

"I know," I said. "And we'll make sure you get home. But tell me something first. Tonight I found out that my mom and Seth Rector's dad used to go out when they were in high school . . . that they were going to get married. And your dad and Farah Endicott's dad and my mom and Seth's dad all used to hang out . . . up until your dad got arrested. Then my mom and Seth's dad had some kind of falling-out and broke up. Did you know about all of that?"

Alex gave me a sarcastic look, despite his red-rimmed eyes.

"Pierce," he said. "You must be the last person on this entire island not to know about that."

"I didn't," Kayla volunteered. When everyone looked at her, she said, sheepishly, "Well, my mom and I haven't lived here that long."

I smiled at her briefly, then glanced back at Alex. "I know Mr. Rector and Mr. Endicott are still friends. They're building that new private housing development out on Reef Key together. They asked if my dad wanted to invest in it."

Alex regarded me coldly. "Wow," he said, his voice as sarcastic as before. "I had no idea I was related to such an accomplished detective. Is that where you were the past couple of days? Doing undercover work? Tell me, Detective Oliviera, what else did you and your CSI team learn during your amazing investigation?"

"She learned," Mr. Liu said, taking a menacing step forward, "that boys who smart off to ladies often get slapped."

I blinked up at Mr. Liu in surprise. I would have expected that kind of response from John, but from his crew it was quite surprising. Even John was looking at his bosun with gratitude.

Alex, cowed, said, in a more normal tone, "Twenty years ago, before there was such a thing as Homeland Security, the Island of Bones was a major entry point for smugglers . . . not only for illegals, but for drugs. They still come across the gulf from Mexico and Colombia by submarine, because the Coasties can't spot those. But someone's always had to meet them at the shore to pick up the goods, then hide them until they can be transported safely to Miami."

"Is that what your dad did?" I asked Alex gently. "He picked up some . . . illegal cargo?"

"He was just a kid," Alex said fiercely. "*Our* age, Pierce. But because it was the new war on drugs, and Dad was a local football hero, and only a Cabrero, not a rich Rector, or a fancy Endicott, and what he got caught doing was an embarrassment to the community, they wanted to make an example out of him. So he was given twenty years for possession with intent to sell on a first offense . . . no previous record, no weapons or violence or anything like that. But he wouldn't rat anyone else out, because *some* people are loyal to their friends." He shook his head, the tears still in his eyes bright, even in the fairy lights. "This is how he's been rewarded. Some *friends* they turned out to be, right?"

The music had grown quieter. They were playing a Spanish ballad. The woman in the red dress was singing, her voice as liquid as the rain coming down outside the archway, and in between breaks in the canopy of leaves. But because the rain was light, and the leaves overhead so thick, it was dry inside the courtyard. Thunder rumbled overhead, sounding farther out to the sea than before. The storm appeared to be breaking up. Or at least, this particular band of rain was passing by.

The real storm, as John had said, was yet to come.

"So," I said softly. "It's not Seth Rector you hate at all. It's Seth's dad . . . and also Farah's dad, and everyone else who knew Uncle Chris around the time he was arrested . . . maybe even my mom" — it hurt me to add this part, but I couldn't blame Alex for feeling this way. My mom had abandoned him when he'd most needed us. Though she, like me, was trying to make things right now — "because you think they were involved in what he was doing, and they let him take the fall alone. Is that how it is?"

"Yes, Pierce," Alex said bitterly, running his fingers through his dark hair. "That's how it is. That money Rector is spending building Reef Key, and helping to put on this stupid festival tonight . . . even that hideous *mausoleum* their family has in the cemetery . . . some of that money rightfully belongs to my dad. He *earned* it, all that time he spent in prison, not saying who else was involved, the way a friend is supposed to. But have they offered him one cent since he got out? Have they offered him a job on their new development? Have they so much as asked my dad out to *dinner* since he got out of prison? Of course not."

I found myself glancing, for some reason, at Kayla, the only outsider standing nearby who did not reside in the Underworld. It wasn't that I didn't trust her with this highly sensitive information. In fact, when I was around her, the diamond at the end of my necklace turned purple, which it didn't with anyone else . . . not that it was doing so now. It remained a dark, sludgy black, indicating that somewhere, evil lurked.

Still, finding out the empire of one of the most influential men in your town had possibly been built on drug money — that was pretty explosive stuff. I wouldn't have been able to keep it to myself, if I were her.

What I couldn't understand was how my mom had, for so long.

"Alex," I said. "How do you know all this? Did . . . did Uncle Chris tell you it was true for a *fact* that Mr. Rector and Mr. Endicott were involved?"

He made a face. "Of course not," he said. "He won't talk about anything to do with his time in jail. But I've done my research. I *know* it's true. Everyone thinks the Rectors are this great, respectable family, just like they think Isla Huesos is this beautiful island paradise. But I know the truth about the dark side that lies beneath this place."

I couldn't help glancing at John. He looked back at me, his gaze troubled. Alex wasn't wrong about the dark side that lay beneath Isla Huesos.

He just didn't know how deep it went.

"— all the lies and the greed and the murder. Yes, *murder*." Alex's own eyes glittered feverishly. "You can't tell me Jade's murder isn't connected to all this somehow. It's too much of a coincidence. If you don't think she died because she stumbled onto something in that cemetery that she wasn't supposed to see, you're crazy. Or someone killed her to set up my dad so he'd have to go back to jail, where they think he'll continue to keep quiet —"

"Oh, Alex," I heard myself saying, my heart swelling with fear for him. "I'm sure that wasn't what —"

"Yes, it *is*, Pierce," he said. "And I'm going to find the proof. And when I do, I'm going to blow Seth and his dad — and this whole place — sky high."

"And what good will that do anyone?" Mr. Liu asked unexpectedly.

"What *good* will that do?" Alex's voice cracked again. "People will know the truth —"

"Sometimes it's better to shield people from the truth," John said, a faraway look in his eyes.

Wait . . . were we talking about exposing the truth about Isla Huesos's *true* underworld, or the seedy criminal underworld Alex was insisting existed? Or were we talking about shielding *me* from the truth about John's past? I could no longer tell.

In some ways, though, I could see John's point. It might be better not to know. Look at all the people out on that dance floor. Would they still gather there as happily if they knew that beneath their feet loomed a cavernous waystation for the souls of the recently departed?

"Alex," John said, before I could figure out a way to ask, "has your father ever said he wanted anything from the Rectors?"

"No," Alex said, shaking his head. "That's just it. He's never said a single word about it, he just goes and fills out applications for jobs he never gets and visits his parole officer and attends his meetings." He meant his dad's Alcoholics Anonymous meetings. "But it's not fair. I know that's where all Seth's dad's money came from. He *owes* my dad. But Dad's too proud to ask."

John shook his head. "No," he said. "No, your father hasn't asked because he doesn't want it. Rector money is dirty money, tainted . . . not to mention, illegally gained. He knows that if he takes it, no good will come from it. *That's* why he hasn't asked, not because he's too proud. Believe me."

I wasn't the only one who looked up at John curiously. Alex and Kayla did, too. He was speaking with such vehemence . . . almost as if from experience.

What did *John* know about the Rectors and their money?

"Money is money," Alex said firmly. "Especially when someone owes it to you."

"You're wrong, boy." Now Frank was chiming in. "Miss Kayla is right. You need to let this go."

Miss Kayla looked delighted to hear Frank say she was right about something. She flipped back the edges of her cape and practically preened, the way Hope liked to do.

"It's true," she said to Alex.

Alex climbed from his chair, causing Hope to give an indignant flap of her wings and hop a few feet away. "None of you knows what you're talking about," he said bitterly. "Especially you, Pierce. You've always had money. And you don't have to live with Grandma."

He was right about that. But now I was living in the Underworld, with dead people. I wasn't quite sure yet which was worse.

"If money is all he wants . . ."

I saw Frank dig into his pocket. In a flash, I saw what was going to happen next: He was going to hand Alex a fistful of Spanish coins that hadn't been in circulation for over a hundred and fifty years . . . and from their pristine condition, clearly hadn't been lying around some shipwreck Alex might have come across at the reef.

"No, Frank," I said, stepping swiftly in front of him. "It's very kind of you. But no."

Frank's gaze went to Kayla, who was looking at him curiously. "Why not?" he asked. He'd wanted to show off how wealthy he was in front of her.

"Because people will ask too many questions about where he got it," John said, perfectly understanding the situation. "And his family is under enough scrutiny."

With a shrug, Frank let the coins fall back into his pocket.

"Wait." Kayla had been watching the entire interlude with great interest, her dark eyes again glittering even more brightly than the jewels she'd glued beside them. "Are you guys really pirates?"

"No," I said to her quickly. "They're not. Did you drive here?"

She looked confused by the change of topic, then nodded. "My mom let me borrow her car for the night."

"Good," I said. "Will you drive him home?" I nodded at Alex.

"What?" Alex looked surprised. "I have my own car."

"Get the keys from him," I said to John, who nodded and, with Mr. Liu's help, began to frisk a protesting Alex.

"Will you make sure Kayla gets Alex home all right, then gets to her own place safely?" I asked Frank.

"Nothing would give me greater pleasure," Frank said, grinning at Kayla, who smiled flirtatiously back.

That made me a bit nervous, but I didn't suppose I had any other choice, unless I had John transport him. And that might tip Alex's mind, already on edge because of the magically appearing paella, even closer to madness.

"This is totally unfair," Alex was saying as John found his keys, then pocketed them. "Pierce, if you do this, I'm calling the cops. I'll tell them everything about you and your little gang, and then I'm going to collect that reward money your dad is offering —"

"Good luck with that," I said flatly. "Dad canceled the reward. I don't think anyone is looking for me anymore. If you did more than play *World of Warcraft*, you might know this."

"And I have your phone," John said, holding his face just inches from Alex's. "Remember? You're not calling anyone."

Alex went pale, then looked back at me. "Pierce," he said, his voice pleading. "Seriously. I'll let the thing with Seth Rector's dad go. I swear I will. Just make him give back my keys. And my phone. Please."

"I'll think about it," I said. "I'm still pretty worried about you, though." I looked at him imploringly. "I don't want anything bad to happen to you. So promise you'll drop this whole scheme of yours to get revenge on the Rectors for what they did to your dad. It's not worth dying over. It really isn't. I'm sure your dad would agree. He loves you. So do I, you know."

He appeared surprised. Our family wasn't particularly warm, or effusive with the *I love you*'s. Except for Uncle Chris, who'd come out of prison bursting with them. He'd even told the mail carrier that he loved him.

"I . . . I promise," Alex said, looking uncomfortable. He looked even *more* uncomfortable — and held his body stiff as a post — when I walked up and hugged him a second later. But part of that could have been because of how wet and smelly I was, in my paella-covered dress, and not because Alex hadn't been hugged very many times before in his life.

"Oh," I said, laughing as I released him. "Yeah, sorry about that. I smell a little fishy. Is there a ladies' room around here?"

"Sure," Kayla said, smiling. "This is actually the back courtyard to a hotel. You can get into the ladies' room through the back porch, over this way. I went in there earlier. It's not bad. There's only one stall, though, so you have to wait if there's a line. At least there are chairs in the lobby, you can sit while you wait —"

"Pierce." I felt a hand wrap around the arm Kayla wasn't holding. I turned to find John staring down at me, a mystified expression on his face. *"Where are you going?"*

Suddenly I remembered that I wasn't just a normal high-school girl out with a friend, gossiping about normal high-school boys. Not that I'd *ever* been that. There was only one boy who'd ever held any interest for me. He was the protector of the dead.

His eyes, as he stared down at me, were full of unspoken questions . . . and fire.

Kayla didn't notice the fire.

"Dude," she said with a laugh that sounded unnaturally loud in the courtyard. The musicians were gone from the stage, though they hadn't packed up their instruments for the night. They were seemingly taking a break. "Chill out. We're going into the hotel over there so she can clean up in the ladies' room."

Kayla pointed at the wide veranda towards which we'd been headed. Hope, who'd apparently understood the situation better than John, had already found a perch out of the rain amidst the quaint gingerbread trim.

"Do you want to come along to check out the lobby to make sure Mr. Oliviera isn't waiting there with a shotgun to kidnap her back?" Kayla asked, an amused lilt in her voice.

The laugh John gave probably seemed natural and easy enough to Kayla. But I could tell it was forced.

"Excellent idea," he said, putting an arm around my neck.

I glanced in the direction his gaze seemed to be directed . . . not the back of the hotel, but the diamond around my neck. It had turned ebony. In fact, in the red glow of the party lanterns overhead, it was almost indistinguishable from the color of the fabric of my dress, aside from the food stains.

"Don't worry," Kayla was saying with her usual self-assurance as we walked. "I know how to take care of people, *Capitán*. I've been taking care of my mom for years now, ever since my dad walked out. It's been just her and me . . . well, and my brother, but he's a dirtbag. I'll get Alex home safe and sound for you, chickie. No worries."

This didn't do much to dampen the flames in John's eyes, but I saw him grin at her addressing him as "*capitán*."

Before either of us had a chance to say anything, however, a blinding white light came from out of nowhere, filling my vision.

When it disappeared again, I could see nothing at all . . . nothing but huge purple splotches. For a split second I didn't know what happened, if it had been the muzzle flash from a gunshot or lightning or John teleporting me somewhere or what . . . all I knew was that John's arm tightened around me reflexively.

It wasn't until I heard a man's voice whisper my name — like most whispers, it carried much farther than the person who'd uttered it had intended — that I knew.

"What? One picture. What can it hurt? Look how cute they are."

A camera flash. That's all it had been, a camera flash. No wonder I couldn't see.

"Put that damned thing away," I heard another man say, in a shocked voice.

John's arm left my shoulders. Then I felt his hand in the center of my back.

"Go," he said urgently, and pushed me, stumbling, towards the darkness.

"These have no longer any hope of death;
And this blind life of theirs is so debased,
They envious are of every other fate."
DANTE ALIGHIERI, *Inferno*, Canto III

Oh, my God," Kayla said as she collapsed into one of the over-stuffed chairs in the hotel lobby into which she had pulled — and John had pushed — me. "Could your boyfriend be any more overprotective? That guy out there only wanted to take your picture because you're a totally famous kidnapping victim. Well, not anymore, I guess. But you were up until a few hours ago."

"John doesn't want some random guy posting my photo all over the Internet," I said defensively.

"Yeah, well, he seems to have made that *pretty* clear," Kayla replied, nodding towards the veranda doors, through which we could hear the camera's owner apologizing to John so profusely, it was a little embarrassing.

Fortunately, there wasn't anyone else around to overhear us, except the nerdy-looking night clerk, and he'd only raised his gaze from his computer screen once, when Kayla pushed me around the corner past his desk, towards a door marked *Damas*. It was locked. Someone was inside.

"Kayla," I said to her, as she pulled me down onto a couch across from the ladies' room door. "I'm pretty sure the bathroom is for guests of the hotel only."

"Well, there aren't any guests because of the mandatory tourist evacuation on account of the storm, so what does that guy care? We're not bothering anyone." She took a compact mirror from the small bag she wore dangling from one shoulder, then checked her eyeliner. "So what's the deal with Frank? Does he have a girlfriend?"

I hesitated. Even though the clerk was around the corner and out of sight, and the place seemed like the last one in the world a Fury might show up — amateur beachscapes, apparently painted by guests, lined the walls, and the lobby stank of too-perfumey potpourri — I couldn't shake the feeling that we were being watched.

This could have been because the large French doors to the back porch stood open to let in the night air, stirred by the blades of the large ceiling fans overhead. It was hard to see what was happening out in the courtyard, thanks to the fact that every light inside the hotel was burning. Everything beyond the veranda appeared to be a sea of darkness, despite the party lanterns.

Though I strained to catch a glimpse of John, all I could see was the occasional flash of what I could only assume was Henry's once-white shirt. Every so often, however, a snatch of the boy's laughter floated towards us.

This made me relax a little. If Henry was laughing, it was doubtful John was killing anyone. My diamond now glowed a vibrant purple, the color of the streaks in Kayla's hair.

"Dude," Kayla said, and punched me in the shoulder. *"Frank?"*

"Ow." I rubbed my arm. "That hurt."

"Sorry," Kayla said. But she didn't look sorry. "Impulse control issues. What do you think I'm in New Pathways for, anyway? Be happy I didn't hit you in the head with a fire extinguisher. So does he have a girlfriend, or not? I can't imagine he doesn't, a hottie like that."

"Frank most definitely does not have a girlfriend," I said. "Why should I be happy you didn't hit me in the head with a fire extinguisher? You didn't actually do that to someone, did you?"

Kayla, looking pleased to hear the information about Frank, reached into her bag for her lip gloss. "Yeah, I did," she said, casually. "My older brother. He's an addict."

"Kayla," I said, my eyes widening.

She shrugged at her own reflection. "He used to beat my mom up when she wouldn't give him money for drugs. That's why I understand all that stuff Alex was saying back there . . . his anger, anyway, about what the Rectors are doing, if it's true. My mom tried everything with Julian. Rehab, wilderness camps, therapy. Sometimes I *wished* he'd get arrested, just so he'd leave Mom alone. The only thing that worked, in the end, was when I went at him with the fire extinguisher, because I came home one night and found him choking her on the kitchen floor." Her grin was lopsided. "Now *I'm* the one stuck with the impulse control label. Go figure."

"Oh, my God," I said, my heart wrenching with pity for her. "Kayla, I had no idea."

"It's cool," she said airily, but I could tell that it wasn't . . . not really. "Julian moved out to Wyoming to find himself. And Mom's engaged to one of the EMTs who was on the scene that night. He's a good guy." Kayla looked at me very seriously. "But I just want you to know, that stuff Alex said about Seth's dad? I think it could be true. Not just twenty years ago, either, but *now*. My mom's an emergency room nurse here — that's why we moved to the Keys in the first place, she goes where the jobs are — and she is raking in the overtime, which should tell you something. Why are so many people on an island this small having to go to the ER all the time? There's something wrong with this place — really, really wrong with it. And I'm not talking about this Coffin Night stuff. My mom says Police Chief Santos tries to keep it out of the papers so the tourists don't see it, because that would be a major blow to the island's primary source of income. But that doesn't mean it isn't happening."

I knew Kayla was right.

I also knew what was wrong with Isla Huesos had nothing to do with Seth Rector's father possibly running a major crime operation. It had to do with the place being overrun with Furies and sitting on top of a big, fat underworld.

I couldn't admit that out loud, though, because no one — not even Kayla — would believe me.

Instead I said, "Thank you for telling me all that, Kayla. It means a lot. Alex is lucky to have a friend like you, even if it seems like he doesn't appreciate you."

"Well, I wouldn't want him to do anything stupid, either, that might get himself into trouble, like . . ." She looked down at me. "Well, no offense, chickie, but like you."

"Thanks," I said, with a dry smile.

"Because Seth and his friends . . . they're no angels, Pierce." Kayla's voice roughened. "Do you have any idea the kind of stuff they call me in the halls because of these?" She pointed at her chest.

Kayla's air of self-confidence, I realized in that moment, was just that . . . an air, an act she put on like the costume she'd worn to Coffin Fest. But she had more reason to believe in herself than any of those stupid A-wingers.

"Kayla," I said. "I hope you know you're beautiful, inside and out. Anyone who can't see that isn't worth your time."

"I hope you're not referring to Frank," she said. She held up her compact to give her hair one last finger-comb. "He better see how beautiful I am. And not just on the inside." Then she looked at me and grinned. "I'm kidding. But I'm serious about the fact that if something bad were to happen to Seth and those guys, I wouldn't mind. Any more than I'd mind if something bad were to happen to Seth's dad, if it turns out what Alex is saying is true about him." Her expression grew solemn. "But I don't want to see Alex get hurt. So whatever you need me to do, chickie, just ask. He's a dork, but he's cute. Adorable, I guess, is what he is."

I smiled at her. "I agree," I said. "Thanks, Kay —"

The door to the ladies' room finally opened, and the person who'd been inside for so long came out. It was the singer who had been performing with the musicians on the stage outside. She was even more glamorous up close than she'd looked from far away. . . .

"Hello, darlings," she said, giving us both a gracious smile. "So sorry." Then she glided past, her hips swinging provocatively beneath her tight dress, her perfume wafting in a soft cloud before her and after her.

"Wow," Kayla said, when the singer was gone.

"That's an understatement," I said with a smile. I snatched up my book bag. "I'll be right back."

I hurried into the ladies' room, locking the door behind me. As in the lobby, the décor was old-fashioned, with an emphasis on antique wood. There was even a small stained-glass window — in the design of a leaping dolphin — towards the top of the eight-foot ceiling that had been left partly opened.

I stuffed my soiled dress into the pedestal sink as soon as I'd stepped out of it, then turned on the tap. That's how anxious I was to get the smell of paella off me.

Then I realized this made no sense. I was in such a rush to get back to John, however, I hadn't really thought through what I was doing.

Oh, well. I had the white dress I'd taken from my closet with me in my bag. It had better not be too wrinkled.

I knelt down on the cool tiled floor, beginning to rifle through the things in my bag, so quickly that some of them spilled out. The dress *was* wrinkled, but not too badly. I put it on then reached for my hairbrush.

That's when I saw it . . . the book Mr. Smith had loaned me on the history of Isla Huesos. It had fallen out of my bag and onto the tiles, open to a page of illustrations. One of them was a portrait of a man in a high collar and side whiskers whose name, according to the bold print underneath, was William Rector.

Rector? Was there no escaping this family?

I laid aside the hairbrush and lifted the book, scanning the page opposite the illustration for the name Rector.

There it was. William Rector — surely Seth's great-great-great-grandfather, as the resemblance was startling — had, according to *A History of the Isle of Bones*, run the most successful shipwreck salvage business on the island in the 1830s, all the way up until October 11, 1846, when he'd died in the Great Hurricane.

The importance of shipwreck salvage as an economic industry in Isla Huesos's early history (which was why the high school's mascot was a wrecker, not a coffin) could not be emphasized enough, the book explained.

The first captain of a salvage operation to reach a stranded vessel after it wrecked was awarded, by maritime law, half the value of whatever he and his crew were able to save of the ship's cargo. This made salvaging an extremely profitable business to go into, especially since the strait between Isla Huesos and Cuba had been so highly trafficked back in the eighteen hundreds — thanks in part to the discovery of the Gulf Stream, a strong current from the tip of Florida that kicked whatever sailed on it all the way to Spain, like a slingshot — and the fact that the waters were so treacherously difficult to navigate due to the coral reef and unpredictable storms. There was often as many as a shipwreck a week off the shores of Isla Huesos . . . though some captains from those stranded ships complained they'd been run aground on purpose *by* salvagers (also known as wreckers), using all manner of tricks.

Of course no such thing was ever proven in the Isla Huesos courts. I imagined this was probably because all the judges and juries were related to the wreckers, while the captains and the companies they worked for were from the mainland. They were never going to get a fair trial, especially in a place sitting on top of an underworld.

It was just that the date, October 11, 1846. William Rector had died on October 11, 1846, in the same hurricane that had wiped out most of Isla Huesos. October 11, 1846, was also, according to Mr. Smith, the day of the last known sighting of the necklace I was wearing around my neck, on the cargo list of a merchant ship that had docked in Isla Huesos . . . but all of her cargo and crew went missing in the hurricane.

Including John.

My fingers shaking, I flipped to the back of the book Mr. Smith had given me . . . given me because, I now remembered, I'd mentioned the name of the ship on which John had been working at the time of his death: the *Liberty*.

There it was, listed in the book's index. The *Liberty*. I flipped to the page on which the notation said the reference could be found.

The Liberty *was one of over two dozen boats sunk in the port of Isla Huesos by the raging winds and floodwaters of the October hurricane of 1846, in which over a thousand lives were lost. Carrying a cargo of precious goods, tobacco, coffee, sugar, and cotton from Havana, the* Liberty *was bound for Portsmouth. The vessel was declared a total loss. No sign of it was ever recovered. Captain: Robert Hayden, Hayden and Sons.*

It took me several seconds to make sense of what I was seeing . . . at least the part that said *Captain: Robert Hayden.* I didn't much care about the rest.

Robert *Hayden?* The captain of the ship — the man John had said he'd killed — had the same last name as he did?

And the company they'd worked for . . . *Hayden and Sons?* What did that mean?

I tried to think of several different scenarios — anything except what I was fairly sure it had to mean.

"The captain of the *Liberty,*" I remembered saying to John. "He must have been very bad."

"He was the worst person I've ever known," John had replied, his voice like ice.

Oh, God. I closed the book, feeling suddenly so dizzy, I thought I might pass out. How could I have been so stupid? I'd been relieved — *relieved* — that all John had done was kill a man. I'd thought it could have been something so much worse.

But what was worse than killing your own father?

Killing your own granddaughter, I supposed. That was about it.

I felt shaky and sick, though I told myself I was being ridiculous. Nothing had changed. John was still the same person.

He was a person who had maybe — probably — killed his father. That's all.

There was a knock on the door. "Pierce?" It was Kayla's voice.

"Sorry," I said, my own voice trembling. "I need another minute."

"It's all right," Kayla said. "Take your time. I just wanted you to know that Frank and I are leaving to take Alex home. But John's out here waiting for you."

Great.

"Okay, thanks," I said. "Bye."

I probably should have opened the door and given her a hug. Who knew when — or if — I'd see her again.

I was in no condition to think rationally, though. I certainly wasn't in any condition to see John.

He must have had a good reason. He'd said he'd a good reason. What was it? Oh, yes. He hadn't agreed with the course the captain had set.

"He was the one who struck the first blow, Pierce," he'd said. "You've got to believe me. I never meant to kill him."

"Of course," I'd murmured. "You were only protecting yourself."

From his own father, it turned out.

I stared at my reflection in the mirror above the sink. Speaking of wrecks, I looked like one, circles under my eyes and my lips the color of sand. The hairband I'd been trying to use as a disguise really wasn't doing me much good, either.

I splashed some water on my face, then dug inside my bag for my cosmetic kit, which I'd always carried in case my father showed up at school to sweep me off to a fancy restaurant. This had actually happened once or twice.

What I couldn't understand was why Robert Hayden had been listed as captain of the *Liberty* in the book if he'd been dead, as John had maintained, before the ship arrived in Isla Huesos. There'd obviously been no record of the murder . . . or the mutiny. Maybe the historian who'd written the book was going by what had been listed on the ship's log. It was possible the *Liberty* hadn't been at port long enough before the hurricane struck for anyone to find out her captain had been murdered at sea . . . by his own son.

Through the window, I heard a woman's voice rise in indignation, and then a slap, and a faint scuffle. The ordinary sounds of a street festival at which there'd been way too much alcohol served, I supposed, dully.

After some lip gloss and eyeliner, I began to look more human . . . and feel that way, too. It was amazing how a little makeup could boost your confidence. Kayla was totally right about that. I took out the elastic band and finger-brushed my hair, the way I'd seen her do it.

I looked a thousand times better. Maybe John was right about the white dress.

Of course, he'd also killed his father, so possibly his judgment wasn't the best.

Except that it *was*. I knew it was. Why else had he been given the job of keeper of the dead? Why else when he was around did I always — well, almost always — feel so safe and secure?

He'd told me I was lucky my grandmother was possessed by a Fury. At least that way I knew why she was so hateful. There was no explanation, he'd said, for why the people in his family were such monsters.

Finding out your father was a monster was a good reason to kill him. Perhaps, given the opportunity, I might kill my grandmother.

I was going to go out there and ask him, I decided. *Why did you kill your father?*

It was then that I heard a familiar *coo, coo*, and looked up. Hope was sitting on the sill of the stained-glass window, fluttering her wings impatiently enough to reveal the dark feathers beneath the creamy white ones.

"I'm coming," I said to her, distracted. "All right?"

I looked to see if I'd left anything behind. The black dress. I didn't want it anymore. I knew it was wasteful to throw away a dress, but it was the dress my grandmother had tried first to kill, then pepper-spray me in. It was also the dress I'd been wearing when John had fudged the truth about the identity of the man he'd killed.

I decided it was an unlucky dress, and that I never wanted to see it again.

I pulled it from the sink, wrung it out, then stuffed it into the garbage can. Then I threw some paper towels over it so no one would notice it right away, for good measure.

I turned to unlock the door, catching a glimpse of myself in the mirror as I did so.

The diamond on the end of my necklace was jet-black.

Blacker than the uniform belonging to the female police offi-cer who kicked open the door a second later, sending it crashing against the sink, and making Hope vanish in a puff of white and black feathers.

"When the exasperated soul abandons
The body whence it rent itself away,
Minos consigns it to the seventh abyss."
DANTE ALIGHIERI, *Inferno*, Canto XIII

The police officer didn't have her gun drawn. Instead, she'd pulled out her Taser. I could see the electric blue spark leaping from one deadly looking metal prong to the other at the tip, so I knew it was charged . . . and on.

"Pierce Oliviera," the policewoman said. "Right?"

Without even thinking about it, I shook my head, denying who I was. No. I wasn't Pierce Oliviera.

In a way, I wasn't even lying. I didn't know who Pierce Oliviera was anymore. I didn't think I'd been that girl for some time . . . not since becoming an NDE, anyway. And certainly not since I'd become a resident of the Underworld.

Somehow spending so much time amongst the dead hadn't given me *less* of a sense of self. If anything, it had shown me how much better suited I was to their world, and how little welcome I was — like now, for instance — in my own.

The crazy thing was, I knew the policewoman's name. She'd been with Police Chief Santos a few days earlier when he'd questioned me at school about Jade's death, because they'd found my bike chained to the cemetery fence. Her name was Officer Hernandez. She was a diminutive brunette who'd looked then as if she'd wanted to tase me simply for being alive.

And now here she was about to tase me for . . . for *what*, exactly?

She looked down at a piece of paper she was holding crumpled in one hand. I was horrified to see that it was one of the "missing" flyers my mom had had stacks of all over her living room, with my photo emblazoned on it.

"Yeah," Officer Hernandez said. "It's you, all right."

Then she held up the Taser like it was a knife she intended to embed in my chest.

I was too scared to think. I saw what she was right away — not a member of Isla Huesos's finest, doing her job (although I doubted Police Chief Santos told any of his officers to tase me), but a Fury.

I should have screamed. If I had, I'm sure John — wherever he'd disappeared to — would have come right away.

Instead I did the stupidest thing possible. I stood there and asked, *"Why?"*

"My father," she said, shaking her head as if I were simpleminded. "He told me what your boyfriend did to him —"

What? I was too confused even to think of screaming after that. My eyes were transfixed by the dancing blue flame I saw coming closer and closer to me. Realizing what was going to happen if that flame actually touched me, I kicked her as hard as I could — blindly, because I couldn't bear to look into that leaping electric spark.

The soles of my ballet flats made contact with something soft. I heard a pained grunt, and then a crash.

When I opened my eyes, I saw that my kick hadn't sent Officer Hernandez far. She'd dropped the Taser, though. It had skidded beneath a chair a few feet away.

"Resisting arrest," she said, from between gritted teeth. "Not smart."

Then she tackled me. She was in better shape than I was, and stronger, too. We hit the carpeted lobby floor with a thud that knocked all the wind from me. As I lay beneath her, stunned, I saw the face of the hotel desk clerk peek around the corner, then just as quickly dart away. He wasn't going to get involved in an altercation between an officer of the law and someone who hadn't even paid for a room.

Not that I needed my boyfriend to fight my battles for me, but in this case a little help might have been nice. *Where was John?*

This became an especially urgent thought when one of her hands closed around the diamond dangling from my necklace.

"Still don't get it, do you?" she asked, almost pityingly, as she began twisting the chain around my neck. "Maybe this will jog your memory. My father once tried to take this necklace away from you, knowing it was much too valuable — and dangerous — for little girls like you to play with. But your boyfriend didn't like that very much, did he?"

That's all it took to make me remember.

"Mr. Curry," I gasped. The links tightening around my throat reminded me instantly of the time I'd foolishly shown the Persephone Diamond to a jeweler back in Connecticut. He too had pulled it uncomfortably close around my neck. Fortunately John had shown up just in time and objected.

Unfortunately, John's objection had been in the form of stopping the jeweler's heart.

"Wait," I begged the woman, trying to slip my fingers between the links and my skin . . . anything to ease the pressure on my windpipe. "I *saved* your father. I stopped John from killing him. He recovered . . . . The salesgirl in the shop next door . . . said he retired to move in with . . . his daughter in . . . Florida. . . ."

The chain turned out to be much sturdier than it looked. Hades must have forged the links out of some kind of indestructible gold alloy, because my neck was closer to breaking than the chain.

I couldn't believe I was being choked to death with something John had given me so long ago out of love.

"That's me," Officer Hernandez said coldly. "I'm the one he moved in with. Now I've got a message for your boyfriend. . . . Tell him it's no use. There's no safe place for you, not even the Underworld. We'll always find you —"

The amateur sunsets on the walls were beginning to swim as my vision faded. I heard a strange noise, a sort of drumming in my ears. I assumed that was the blood leaving my head. Pretty soon, my air supply would be completely cut off, and I'd be brain-dead. I reached out blindly to try to gouge my fingers into the police officer's eyes while I still had control of my limbs.

And then a miracle happened . . . several miracles, all at once, actually.

The first was that I heard John's voice snarl, "Why don't you give me that message yourself?"

Then Officer Hernandez cried out in pain. I couldn't understand why, since my fingers had barely made contact with her face, but she let go of my necklace anyway, and the pressure on my throat suddenly eased. I clawed at the links, pulling them away from my neck, then gratefully gulped in one lungful of oxygen, then another, thankful for the first time in my life for the cloying odor of potpourri, because the fact that I could smell it again meant that I was alive.

By that time my vision had returned enough for me to see John standing over me, his expression tender and livid by turns.

"Pierce." His voice sounded far away. He was lifting me gently by the shoulders. "Are you all right? My God, your throat . . . *are you all right?*"

"I'm fine," I said. I turned my head and noticed that Officer Hernandez was slumped to the hotel floor beside me. Her eyes were closed. She looked dead. "What did you do to her?"

John barely spared her a glance. "I didn't do anything to her," he said. "Yet. Pierce, I'm so sorry. I was out here waiting for you the whole time, until there was a disturbance in the courtyard . . . that singer, the one from the stage. She was flirting with Mr. Liu. Then she attacked him."

This, more than anything, brought me to my senses. I remembered the sound of the woman's voice I'd heard from the window while I'd been in the ladies' room, and the scuffle afterwards. I'd thought it nothing but noises of the street festival. "Mr. Liu?" I echoed in alarm. "Is he all right?"

"He's fine," John said, his tone grim. "Embarrassed, more than anything. I should have known it was all just to distract me from you. I didn't have any idea the danger you were in until Hope appeared from out of nowhere in front of me, screaming. I didn't even know doves *could* scream."

Hope. I turned my head and saw her perched on the mantel of the faux fireplace, peering down at me worriedly.

"Is she all right?" I heard a familiar voice thunder. "Is she —?"

"She's alive," John said to Mr. Liu, who'd come crashing into the lobby through one of the French doors to the veranda, heedless of the patio furniture in his way. There was a fresh set of bloody fingernail marks — feminine, from the look of them — down the side of his face, but Mr. Liu did not appear to be aware of them. "Barely." To me, John said, "Can you stand up?"

"Of course I can stand up —"

But I couldn't. My hands were shaking, and I felt as if my legs had turned to liquid. If it hadn't been for his steadying arms around my waist and shoulders, half-lifting me to one of the nearby overstuffed chairs, I'd never have made it.

It was only then that I began to notice other things. . . .

The hotel desk clerk peering around the corner from his desk, looking more than a little upset over the disturbance in his lobby. Henry having come in through the veranda doors with Mr. Liu to peer down at me, and Mr. Liu pushing Henry back with a murmur, "Careful!" Henry protesting, crying, "But I want to see the Fury!" The fact that the drumming sound I thought had been the blood rushing from my brain was actually coming from outside . . .

It had begun to pour heavily. The storm that had been threatening for hours had finally arrived.

Perhaps most surprising of all, however, was the sight of Mr. Smith, the cemetery sexton, standing beneath one of the sunset paintings, with his hands on his cheeks.

"Oh, thank heaven, she's all right," he said. "Is there anything I can do to be useful?"

John set his jaw. "Yes," he said, a curious note of resentment in his voice. "You can go. You've been enough trouble for one —"

"John," I said softly.

I had no idea why John was so angry with the cemetery sexton, but at that particular moment, I didn't care, because I had noticed something odd about Officer Hernandez's body:

It was smoking.

The policewoman hadn't sat up and lit a cigarette, but there was definitely steam of some kind exiting a wound I saw in the middle of her palm . . . exactly where she'd wrapped her hand around my diamond as she'd tried to choke me with its chain. It resembled a stream of black smoke, almost as if Officer Hernandez had been shot . . .

. . . or her soul was departing her body.

Except that I was fairly certain she hadn't been shot — not by any of the people gathered in that room, anyway — and I was close enough to see that as she lay on the old-fashioned carpet, she was still breathing. So she wasn't dead.

Then, over the steady stream of the rain outside the veranda, I heard what sounded like a shriek, so high-pitched it was barely audible . . . an angry, hate-filled cry that seemed to be coming from the black vapor streaming from the woman's hand.

Neither smoke nor a soul, to the best of my knowledge, was capable of screaming.

Hope heard it as well, since she tilted her head at the sound and moved, startled, out of the way of the pale apparition as it began to travel towards the wide-open French doors.

I laid my hand on John's arm, still around my waist as he knelt beside me, and pointed.

"John, do you see that?" I asked. "Do you think it's the —?"

Instead of answering, he leaped to his feet. For a second I thought he was going to try to catch it, which made no sense to me — how can you catch pure evil, especially when it's made of something as intangible as smoke?

But then I saw him hurl a ball of light and energy from his fingertips — exactly as he'd done at my mom's house — at the black thing I saw trying to escape through the doors to the back porch. Only this time, the power was directed at a single target: the Fury that had been possessing Officer Hernandez.

There was an explosive display of sparks, and a much louder scream than the one I'd heard before — and then the voice was abruptly cut off. When I lowered the arms I'd thrown over my eyes to shield them from the brilliant burst of light, all that was left of the black vapor trail I'd seen was a dark smudge on the wood-paneled wall.

The Fury was gone.

The water was more sombre far than perse;
And we, in company with the dusky waves,
Made entrance downward by a path uncouth.
DANTE ALIGHIERI, *Inferno*, Canto VII

I turned my disbelieving eyes to look up at John.

He was out of breath, his chest rising and falling rapidly as if he'd run a great distance, his dark hair sticking to his forehead, his fingers curled into fists . . . but when his gaze met mine, I saw his face break into one of the broadest grins I'd ever seen him wear.

I couldn't blame him. I was fairly certain we'd just destroyed a Fury together.

"Do it again," Henry said, bursting into delighted applause.

"Not tonight, please," Mr. Smith said. He'd sagged onto the carpet, making it look as if he'd knelt there merely to lift Officer Hernandez's wrist to take her pulse. But I could tell the fireworks display from John's fingertips had caused him to lose some muscle control. "Keep in mind there are civilians present. Between Mike and now this, I've had about all the excitement I can take for one day. I'm assuming *that* was the Fury." He nodded at the dark smudge on the wall.

"That was the Fury," John confirmed. He turned back towards me. "How did you make it leave her body?"

I shook my head. "I didn't," I said. "The necklace did, I think, when she touched it. Look at her hand."

Mr. Smith unfolded the unconscious woman's fingers. There, in the middle of her palm, was the burn mark I'd seen. It was in the exact shape of my diamond.

"Well, that's it, then, Captain," Mr. Liu said, reverentially. "After nearly two hundred years, we finally know how to get rid of them."

"Fascinating," Mr. Smith murmured. "The diamond not only detects when Furies are present, it forces them out of their human hosts when put in contact with them."

"Right," Henry said, looking at me. "We just let her get choked by them. Then you zap 'em, Captain."

"No, Henry," John said dryly. "I don't think that's how we'll do it. But a variation along those lines might do."

"Um, excuse me," called a tremulous voice from the hotel's front desk. The clerk waved nervously when we all turned to look at him. "But does that police officer need help? Like an ambulance or something? Because I could call for one. Otherwise, my boss doesn't like it when people sleep in the lobby."

Mr. Smith raised his eyebrows. "What a good idea, young man," he said to the clerk. "By all means, telephone for an ambulance immediately."

"Okay," the clerk said, and his face disappeared once more around the corner.

Officer Hernandez had begun to stir. She appeared confused, patting her belt for something, and then, not finding it, searching the ground around her.

"What's going on?" she asked blearily, of no one in particular. There wasn't a hint of any of the hostility I'd heard before in her voice. She actually sounded like quite a pleasant person. When her gaze passed over me, there was no recognition in it whatsoever. "What happened?"

Mr. Smith, his eyes widening behind the lenses of his glasses, asked, "You mean, you don't remember?"

"No," Officer Hernandez said, reaching up to touch her forehead, then seeing the wound on her hand. "Did I burn myself?"

"Yes," Mr. Smith said gently. "I believe you did. If you wait here, Officer Hernandez, an ambulance is on its way."

"Oh," she said, smiling. "Well, aren't you sweet? Call me Deanna."

"We most certainly will," he said.

I was reminded, for some reason, of what Mr. Smith had said earlier in the day, about how when people were moved to do good by the spirit of human kindness, that was the work of the Fates, but when they did evil, it was the work of the Furies.

"I thought you might be interested to know, Miss Oliviera," he said, in a lower voice, so that the officer couldn't overhear him, "that my head groundskeeper, Mike, has filed for workman's compensation after injuring himself in the cemetery today."

"Really?" I widened my eyes. This was one of the options Mr. Smith had suggested Mike would take.

"He was treated and discharged at the hospital," Mr. Smith went on, "for a concussion after what he's telling everyone was a fall down the back steps. I don't think you need to have hit him quite so hard, Pierce. He's called in sick for the rest of the week, poor man."

"Pardon me if I can't summon any more pity for him than for her grandmother," John said flatly. "Pierce, do you feel up to going?"

I nodded. Henry, meanwhile, had found the Taser that had fallen beneath the chairs. It had gotten shut off during my mêlée with Deanna Hernandez, but it took Henry only a few seconds to figure out how to switch it back on. The blue spark brought a gigantic smile to his face.

"Brilliant," he said. "Can I keep it, Captain?"

"No," John said firmly. "You may not. Mr. Liu?"

Mr. Liu quickly disarmed Henry, while John helped me back to my feet. I felt steadier now . . . especially when he slipped a hand beneath my hair and across the back of my neck as he guided me towards the door. Suddenly I felt the same waves of warmth I had when he'd soothed the place where Hope had scratched my hand. Only now that soothing warmth was spreading along my neck and radiating to the front of my throat, where the links from my necklace had pinched my skin.

He looked down at me, his eyebrows still furrowed with worry for me. "Better?" he asked.

"Better," I said, summoning up a smile.

But in spite of everything, I still heard a small voice inside my head. *Hayden and Sons, Hayden and Sons*, it whispered.

"Pierce, if anything had happened to you —" He broke off, unable to meet my gaze.

Tell him it's no use, Officer Hernandez had said. *There's no safe place for you, not even the Underworld. We'll always find you.* I gave a little shudder.

"It's all right," I said to John.

He raised his gaze to mine. "It isn't," he said, as if he'd read my thoughts.

"It's my fault, I'm afraid." Mr. Smith's voice, sounding strangely hollow, startled me. I realized he'd followed us out through the veranda doors.

I stared at him. "*Your* fault? How so?"

I was surprised to see that out in the courtyard, everyone was gone. The canopy of leaves couldn't offer protection from this sort of rain, which fell in a steady curtain from the sky. Even the band had fled, seeking shelter elsewhere . . . probably spurred to do so by what had occurred between their lead singer and John and his crew.

So I was especially surprised when a familiar-sounding voice from the shadows of the back porch said, "No, *I* was the distraction."

I'd thought we were all alone, but a man I'd never seen before stepped out from the corner where he'd been huddling.

"Patrick," Mr. Smith said, sounding irritated. "I told you to wait in the car."

"I know," the man said, sounding — and looking — strangely sheepish. He was wearing a pink short-sleeved shirt, khaki shorts, yellow socks, and a yellow bow tie, all drenched from having been caught in the rain. "But I only wanted to say again how sorry I am." To me, he said, "Hi, we've never met before, but I'm Richard's friend, Patrick Reynolds. I'm the one who took your picture, and I'm *so* sorry, I realize how uncool that was."

"Oh," I said, realizing why his voice sounded familiar. He'd been the man I'd heard apologizing to John through the veranda doors. "Hello."

I remembered Mr. Smith having mentioned his partner, Patrick. The only thing I really knew about him was that he didn't understand Mr. Smith's fascination with the dead, and that he liked to knit. He looked younger than the cemetery sexton by about ten years or so. I wondered if he had the slightest idea what his partner was tangled up in.

Apparently not, since his next words were, "I was just so excited, because I've been following your case in the paper and on the news. It's so dull in this town, you can't imagine. I never thought I'd actually get to see you in the flesh, so when you walked by, I couldn't help it, even though Richard told me not to —"

Slowly, realization dawned. Now I knew not only who'd taken the picture of me, but why John's jaw was suddenly so dangerously set, and why there were twin fires raging in his eyes.

Considering John's history, it was a miracle Patrick Reynolds was simply soaking wet and not physically maimed or suffering a cardiac blockage or something. I thought that showed real progress on John's part. Although of course I could feel his fingers tightening on the back of my neck.

"I mean, to literally bump into Zack Oliviera's daughter while watching the Busty Bayamos — they're completely our favorite local band, and we just love Angelica, the lead singer" — Patrick had not stopped talking, even for a second, he was so intent on getting his apology out, even though the rain was beginning to slant past the porch roof and onto us — "I was like, well, it can't hurt to get a photo, even though Richard was mortified, and I don't know what came over Angelica, she's normally —"

"Everyone is forgiven," John said unsmilingly. "We have to go now."

Mr. Smith's friend said, looking uneasy, "Oh, my God, I've done it again, haven't I? I'm sorry. Richard says I talk too much. But I think it's all so romantic, the corporate magnate's daughter and the —" He looked at John and smiled toothily. "Well, whatever, I just hope everything works out. Richard, did you tell them the good news?"

Mr. Liu and Henry had followed us out, and now stood on the back porch, as well. Henry, I saw, had found my book bag, and shouldered it.

"What good news?" I asked. I couldn't imagine what *good* news there could possibly be, except that we had figured out a way to drive Furies from the human hosts they were possessing, then destroy them. Although it wasn't a very practical solution to the problem, unless I was going to touch every Fury I encountered with my necklace, which meant that I had to get way more up close and personal to them than I thought was advisable.

"I already told John, Patrick," Mr. Smith said. "Honestly, they have to go now, the poor girl —"

"Told John what?" I asked. "Is Alex all right?" After my recent scare — or series of them — I felt hypervigilant.

John's hand went to my arm. "He's fine," he said gently. "You don't need to worry about anything. Frank's going to watch to make sure Alex gets home safely. I gave him your cousin's phone and keys, and told him only when Alex gets safely to his door is he allowed to have them back. Frank is to find your cousin's car — Kayla will tell him where it is — and disable it, so Alex can't go anywhere. Then I'll fetch Frank and bring him home."

I blinked at him. "That . . . that's perfect. Thank you."

He smiled at me. "Take Henry's hand."

"What?" I did as he asked. "All right. But why?"

Then I realized what John was about to do, and dropped Henry's hand, which was still sticky from all the cotton candy he'd consumed anyway.

"John," I said, narrowing my eyes at him. *"No."* Then I turned to Patrick. "What were you saying about good news?"

"Oh," Patrick said, looking confused. He'd been following our conversation intently, almost as if he'd been taking mental notes. I hoped it wasn't for a blog or anything. "I don't remember now. What was it? Something about pomegranates?" He looked at Mr. Smith, who appeared to be wishing for death. "I swear, I don't know what Richard is talking about half the time, but this afternoon, he got on the phone with some professor in California, and afterwards, he would not stop going on about pomegranates, and how they are purely symbolic, and you can eat whatever you want and not worry. Is there some new pomegranate diet where you can eat what you want and not get fat or something? Because I could totally —"

"Henry," John said curtly. "Take Miss Oliviera's hand." Henry reached up to take my fingers in one hand, then grabbed Mr. Liu's arm with his other.

"Good-bye," John said to Mr. Smith.

Then he stepped off the porch and out into the courtyard, pulling me with him, into the pouring rain.

"But I —" I began to say, turning my head to look back at the cemetery sexton and his partner. The latter seemed extremely surprised by our abrupt departure. Mr. Smith, however, appeared relieved to see us go. I saw him raise a hand to wave as the needle-like drops of rain began to stab me, quickly dampening my dress and hair.

Then I blinked to keep the water out of my eyes, and all of it — Mr. Smith, Patrick, the hotel, the courtyard, the rain, the entire island of Isla Huesos — disappeared.

*"Being by such a noble lover kissed,
This one, who ne'er from me shall be divided,
Kissed me upon the mouth all palpitating."*
DANTE ALIGHIERI, *Inferno*, Canto V

When I opened my eyes again, we were in a different courtyard . . . the one where I'd found Henry hiding, what
seemed like a lifetime ago.

Though hours and hours had passed on earth since we'd been
gone, little seemed to have changed in the realm of the dead. Time
appeared not to move at the same pace in the Underworld as it did
on earth. The grayish pink light in which John's world was con-
tinuously bathed might have grown slightly more lavender, but not
by much. The features of the marble woman in the courtyard's
center fountain were still easily discernible. The fire burning brightly
in the enormous hearth in John's bedroom continued to cast the
same warm yellow glow against the white curtains in the interior
archways as it had when we'd left. Nothing seemed different at all.

Until a bit of movement caught my eye, and I looked up, and saw the birds.

There were dozens of them — maybe hundreds — wheeling around and around in the air, their wings a pitiless black against the roof of the cavern. They weren't flying in any sort of formation, they were just circling, the way vultures do when they've spotted dying prey.

But these birds weren't making any sound. They appeared to be hovering over the island across the lake, down by the beach where the dead got sorted.

I gasped when I saw them, even though I was still reeling from having been ripped so suddenly from my world and thrust back to John's. I forgot my indignation at John's having done so in the middle of what I'd considered a pretty interesting conversation.

"Look!" I cried, pointing at the birds. Hope was the only bird I'd ever seen in the Underworld.

But to my relief, I saw that she wasn't paying the slightest bit of attention to those ominous birds. She'd swooped to a perch on top of the fountain and was already busy grooming herself after her long journey.

"Why are they doing that?" I asked about the circling birds. "What does it mean?"

"That we've been away too long," said Mr. Liu, and strode off in the opposite direction of the archways, towards a large wooden gate, his expression forbidding. "Henry, come. There's work to be done."

"Blankets," Henry said, with a sigh. "I'll have to tell Mr. Graves about the Fury and the cotton candy later." Apparently to him, tasting cotton candy for the first time and seeing a Fury torn from its human host and destroyed were equally exciting. He dumped my book bag unceremoniously at my feet, then ran after Mr. Liu, calling, "Can we at least take Typhon with us? I swear I'll keep him from biting anyone this time."

Then the gate banged shut, and John and I were alone for the first time in . . . well, what seemed like ages.

That was the only explanation I could think of for why, in the silence between us, the sound of Hope's contented cooing and the water bubbling in the fountain both suddenly sounded so absurdly loud . . . and why there appeared to be an electrical charge in the air, so strong that I felt the hairs on my arms rising.

I tried to think of something to say to break the silence, because clearly *he* wasn't going to do it. He was just standing there staring at me with an odd expression on his face, an expression I thought I recognized: It looked like the same one from that night by my mother's pool, when he knew I'd learned something terrible about him from Mr. Smith, and was sure I must hate him.

He was partly right . . . I *had* learned something terrible about him. What I couldn't figure out was how *he* knew. Had Mr. Smith told him that he'd loaned me the book? I doubted it, or Mr. Smith would have been soaking wet, along with his partner.

Yet there John stood, looking defensive and ashamed all at

once, his jaw thrust out and that muscle twitching in his cheek . . . but his eyes shining bright as stars.

The problem with eyes that shined as bright as stars was that stars were unreadable. You couldn't look into the sun and tell what it was thinking.

There were so many questions I wanted to ask him — *needed* to ask him. But I hardly knew where to start. I could tell from the way he was staring at me — *studying* me, like he was waiting for something, some signal or sign from me — that he knew questions of some kind were coming, and dreaded them.

Obviously, I couldn't come straight out and ask, *Why did you kill your father?* Or *What was Patrick talking about, I can eat whatever I want and not worry? Why did you tell me that I couldn't, then?*

Stalling for time, I reached up to push back some of my hair, expecting to find it wet — I had, after all, just been pulled through a downpour to get here — but instead discovered it was dry as bone.

I looked down. Every other time John had dragged me to his world, he'd seen fit to give me a nineteenth-century fashion makeover.

But not this time. I was surprised to find myself in my own clothes, the white dress I'd taken from my closet at home. It looked fresh and newly pressed, despite the fact that I'd been recently wrestling in it on a hotel lobby floor with a member of Isla Huesos's finest.

Pleased, I lifted my gaze back up to his, and smiled.

"Now *this*," I said, fingering the skirt of the dress, "is more my style. If I had a closetful of clothes like this, I could deal with life down here a whole lot bet —"

In three long strides he was on me, seizing me around the waist and pulling me roughly to him, so that my soft body met his hard frame with a jolt I felt all the way down to my toes.

"John." I looked up at him in surprise. This was not the response I'd been expecting to my fairly innocuous statement. Something inside of him had seemed to break. I had no idea what, or why. He didn't make a sound, or even change expression. "What's the matter with —?"

I never got to finish the question. Instead, his lips came down over mine, his mouth and tongue so commanding that any token resistance I might have considered putting up was quickly forgotten . . . not only because there didn't seem to be any point, but because I realized the truth:

I wanted him every bit as much as he wanted me.

When his lips slid from my mouth to my throat to kiss each place the links from my necklace had left red marks, I knew I was lost. I had to cling to his shoulders just to remain upright. I could feel his heart racing through the walls of his solidly muscled chest.

My own heart was like a wild thing, urging me to do things I knew perfectly well that I shouldn't. But who was going to stop me? Certainly not him. Something had come over him, a kind of desperate need that I could feel in every kiss, every look, every caress. I wasn't sure where it was coming from, or what had sparked it so suddenly. There was a sense of urgency to his movements, even though I hadn't heard the marina horn, so I didn't know why he was in such a rush.

This time, however, when I found his fingers on the buttons on the front of my dress, I didn't push his hand away. My own fingers tangled in his thick dark hair, and I murmured his name.

I don't know why this caused him suddenly to lift me off my feet, carrying me through one of the archways to his room after impatiently kicking aside the gauzy white curtain. The next thing I knew, I was sinking into the impossibly soft, downy comforter on the big white bed. I couldn't help thinking, *Oh, this is probably a mistake.*

But I couldn't see *how* it could be a mistake, or how it could be wrong, especially when, a second later, he was on top of me, the masculine weight of him so deliciously heavy, and his big callused hands slipping inside my dress. Soon his fingers were touching me in places no one had ever touched me before, each caress leaving my nerve endings feeling as tingly as if they'd just been kissed by a shooting star, landing on my skin and leaving it as glistening as a newly formed galaxy.

Surely *that* couldn't be wrong, could it?

At one point, though, he too seemed to experience a moment's doubt. His body, in the firelight, was beautiful, even with the scars. I would have traced every one with my fingers, then kissed it, if he had let me.

When I tried, however, he took both my wrists and pressed them back against the comforter, saying, "Stop," in a voice that sounded choked with emotion. He looked down at me with eyes that were no longer shining, but filled with a darkness I couldn't read.

"You said you wanted to take things slow," he reminded me gruffly.

Had I? My mind was moving so sluggishly from all the mini-explosions his fingers had been setting off along my skin that it took a moment to recall the conversation he was referring to. It seemed to have taken place a million years ago.

"Oh, *that*," I said. "No, it's okay."

"Is it?" he asked, strangely anxious. "Are you sure? Despite the . . . consequences?"

Consequences? I couldn't bear hearing the word *consequences* again. And certainly not *now*.

"Yes," I said. "It's quite all righ —"

His mouth came down over mine before I could finish what I was saying, kissing me with so much passion that I felt as if he and I were one already. Apparently the only thing he'd been waiting for was my permission. Once he received it, he took decidedly emphatic action. It wasn't long before the shooting stars returned, only now they were entire galaxies of sparkling suns and planets that seemed to expand and expand until finally they collapsed, showering us both with little bits of stars and moons and cosmos.

Afterwards, he fell asleep . . . *his* head on *my* shoulder, for a change. I marveled at how untroubled he looked . . . the first time I'd ever seen him that way. It must, I decided, have been how he'd looked as a little boy.

Then I remembered *Hayden and Sons*, and decided it was probably best not to think about his childhood.

Still, he and I were obviously always meant to be together. Of course we had a few things to work out, like any couple. Well, maybe more difficult things than most couples.

But the storm was finally over.

I should have known it was only beginning.

I followed him, and little had we gone,
Before the sound of water was so near us,
That speaking we should hardly have been heard.
DANTE ALIGHIERI, *Inferno*, Canto XVI

I opened my eyes. Just like before, it took me a few seconds to remember why the light filtering through my bedroom curtains looked so unfamiliar. It was because I wasn't in my bedroom.

This time when I turned my head and saw the boy in bed next to me, I didn't freak out . . . at least until I saw the book he was reading.

I sat up . . . too fast. I sank back down against the pillows, putting a hand over my eyes.

"Headache?" John asked. His tone was solicitous, but also a little . . . something else. I couldn't tell what.

I nodded. I didn't really have a headache. I had actually slept dreamlessly and amazingly well.

But I thought I might *get* a headache soon if we had to discuss the book in his hands.

"Here," he said, and I looked between my fingers to see what he was offering me.

A cup and saucer, I sat up, more slowly this time.

The cup contained hot tea with milk. I took it from him and sipped, keeping a careful eye on him.

"How are you?" he asked.

"I'm fine," I said. I noticed that he'd already showered. His hair was damp. He had on a fresh new shirt and pair of jeans. He'd even put on his boots.

I, on the other hand, was still wearing my white dress. It had never been intended for use as a nightgown, and was scandalously wrinkled. He had the distinct advantage over me, lookswise.

Hoping to change the subject from the book, which I feared he wasn't going to let go — it was a conversation I knew we had to have. I just wasn't prepared to have it before breakfast — I asked in a too-bright voice, "Off to sort the dead?"

"To get Frank," he said.

"Oh," I said. I'd forgotten all about Frank. "Well, tell him hi from me. I hope he had fun with Kayla."

He held up the book. Rats.

"Where did you get this?" he asked, his voice hard as stone.

"Where did *you* get it?" I countered. It was always better to go on the offensive than be on the defensive. "I believe that was in my bag, my personal property, and you removed it. You should know better than to —"

"I believe part of *cohabitation* means that what is mine is yours and what is yours is mine, as you proved yesterday when you went through every single one of my personal belongings while I was at work. Or is that not how you found your bag in the first place?" he asked.

I took another sip of tea while I considered how to reply. He completely had me.

"Mr. Smith gave it to me," I said, finally deciding it was best to go with the truth.

"Mr. Smith," he said, scowling. "I should have known."

"Yes," I said. "You should have. What was that about last night, with Patrick and the pomegranates?"

Some of the color left his face. "I thought you knew," he said.

"Of course not," I said. "You made us leave before I got to find out."

"You said last night" — he took the teacup from me and swiftly downed its contents, as if he needed quick sustenance, then set the cup aside — "that you understood the consequences."

"There won't *be* any consequences from last night," I said. "Life can't grow in a place of death. I checked with Mr. Smith."

"*That's* what you meant?" He looked even paler.

"Well, of course. What did *you* mean?"

He opened his mouth, but no sound came out. He kept his gaze glued to the book in his hands. He looked as if he'd been punched in the gut.

"John." Anxiety gripping me, as much due to his expression as his silence, I rose to my knees. "What sort of consequences did *you* mean? And what did Patrick mean when he said it was all right to eat whatever I wanted? When I told you the exact same thing yesterday, you said I was —"

I saw that some color had come back into his cheeks, and I realized something amazing: He was blushing. "I know," he interrupted. "I know what I said yesterday. But I didn't want you to think you could leave if . . . well, if things didn't turn out well between us. All I wanted was for you to give me a chance. I thought if you felt you *had* to stay because the Fates had decreed it, then you would. That's how badly I wanted you to stay. I lied." He stared down at the book in his hands. "I realize now it was the wrong thing to do. But you hadn't even given it twenty-four hours, and you already wanted to go —"

"I wanted to take things at my own pace," I reminded him. "Not *leave*. Those aren't the same thing, John."

"I understand that," he said. He lifted his tortured gaze. "*Now*. And I'm sorry. If it means anything, I honestly *did* think you knew. And I felt sick for lying to you. I wanted to tell you, lots of times. But I just . . . couldn't. And when we got to your mother's house, and I could see how much you missed her and wanted to stay there, I almost . . . I . . . but when it came down to it, I couldn't let you go. I was almost glad when your grandmother showed up," he added, with some of his old wild ferocity. "It gave me a good excuse to take you away again."

I knew I should have been horribly angry with him . . . and a part of me was.

But there was another part of me that wanted to laugh at his masculine bullheadedness, though I restrained myself, not feeling laughter would be the appropriate response.

"I forgive you," I said gravely. "This time. But I can't believe you did something so awful. You'd better never do it again.

Honestly, I expected better behavior from a lord of the dead. Especially when I've told you so many times that it's you I want, no matter where you are."

His expression of a dog that had been beaten too many times by its owner began to fade. Now a hopeful look dawned upon his face.

"John," I said, reaching out to caress his cheek. "I don't need some silly rule to make me stay and try to work things out with you. I'll always do that, because I love you."

It was sad that this was something that seemed to be news to him.

"Do you mean it?" he asked, reaching up to grasp my hand, an eager light glowing in his eyes.

"Of course I do," I said, smiling.

"Good." He held up *A History of the Isle of Bones.* "So did you read this?"

I lowered my hand from his face. We may have just shared an important moment in our relationship, but I apparently wasn't going to be let off the hook about that stupid book.

"Parts of it," I confessed. "The parts about the *Liberty.*"

He flinched as if I'd struck him. The light in his eyes died.

"So," he said. "You know the truth about the man I killed. He was my father."

The color in his cheeks had fled once again, leaving them pale. There were shadows under his eyes I hadn't noticed before, and his lips were pressed together tightly.

"Yes," I said, feeling as if the word were being wrung out of me.

"I guess you know now why I didn't want to talk about it," he said, lowering his gaze. "It's a shameful thing. Have you known all along?"

I shrugged. "That he was your father? Just since last night. But I always knew you must have had your reasons. You said he was a monster. That's what you said about your family." I kept my gaze on the front cover of the book. "All except your mother."

"I hated the way he treated her," John said. "The only times I ever remember her being happy was when he was away at sea, and that was when I was very young. After I got older, he ruined that, too, by forcing me to go with him on his voyages, so I barely saw her. She was his second wife. He drove his first to an early grave with his" — he glanced at me, and said, looking embarrassed — "philandering and drunkenness."

I think he'd have chosen less polite words if he'd been speaking to a man.

"Oh," I said, in a small voice. I knew my family wasn't perfect, but I was realizing how lucky I was to have them . . . Grandma notwithstanding.

"The sons he had by his first wife," John went on, "they were no better than he was. I was the only *son* employed at Hayden and Sons, though I had three older brothers. My father never forced any of them to work at the family business. They were too brilliant at spending all its profits — on women and cards, as it turns out. I realized someone had to support my mother, or she'd end up in the poorhouse. They don't have those now, but they were terrible places they sent people, primarily women and children, who couldn't support themselves. The *Liberty* was the only ship my father hadn't managed to lose to my brothers' creditors. Can you understand any of this, Pierce?"

I nodded, swallowing hard against the lump forming in my throat. He looked so ashamed.

"I didn't even realize we were carrying the Persephone Diamond" — he ran a finger along it, and I shivered as his skin touched mine — "until my father showed it to me when we were already on our way to Havana. One of my brothers had won it in a card game, and found a buyer for it in Isla Huesos. Very convenient, since we could drop it off on our way back to England. I didn't like the plan, but there was nothing I could do about it once we were out to sea. I knew the necklace was probably stolen, but I had no idea from where, or what it was worth. I certainly didn't know it was . . ." He paused.

"Cursed?" I offered, my voice croaky because of my unshed tears.

"It isn't cursed," John said deliberately, rearranging the chain around my neck, "if you're wearing it. It's blessed. It wasn't until we were halfway from Havana to Isla Huesos that I found out my father had hatched his own little scheme, with William Rector —"

I raised my eyebrows at the name.

"Yes," John said grimly. "Of the famed Rector family. My father had contacted Rector, and agreed purposefully to wreck the *Liberty* on the reef —"

This I didn't understand. "Wreck his own boat? *Why?*"

"It was done," John said, his tone bitter. "Not often, but there were rumors. Captains would wreck their own ships, pretend it was an accident, then split the salvage award — they could make thousands more in one night than they could in *years* at sea. They'd arrange the site of the so-called accident with a particular wrecker in advance. Most often, no one was wiser."

"Like an insurance scam," I said.

John nodded. "My father was in debt to his ears. The *Liberty* was a new ship, a good one. Her hull could take a good ramming, and recover. But most important, he could pocket the Persephone Diamond and claim it was lost at sea. No one would ever know the difference, including my brother . . . and the buyer."

"Steal from his own son? Oh, John." My heart went out to him.

He shook his head. "No, Pierce," he said. "The necklace isn't why we fought . . . or why he died. I didn't care about any of that. My father could have taken that necklace and disappeared forever and I'd have wished him well. It was the fact that he was going to put the *Liberty*, and her crew, at risk, all for the sake of a few extra thousand dollars . . . that I couldn't allow. *Henry* was on that ship, Pierce. Little Henry, and three dozen other men, including Frank, and Mr. Graves, and Mr. Liu. What if something happened to them? What if something went wrong? Ramming a ship purposefully into a rock isn't ever the best idea, but it was October . . . October is never a good month in that strait. Those waters are churning, hot from the long summer. Storms can come sweeping in from nowhere."

I remembered my dream. A storm *had* come sweeping in . . . and John had been the one lost in it forever.

"I begged my father not to go through with it. I knew Rector. One of the only obligations a wrecker has is to rescue the crew first, cargo second. But Rector would sooner have let a crew drown than risk losing a single bale of cotton, especially if they were selling high. Never mind what would happen if it was proven in court that Hayden and Sons had colluded to sink its own cargo. The business would be ruined forever. But I saw the gleam in my father's eye." John's own eyes grew hard at the memory. "So we fought. Things got violent, as they often did with him, because he was a drinker. This time, for the first time, I fought back . . . and he lost. But it turned out most of the crew was as greedy as my father — which makes sense, since he hired them — and wanted to continue with the wrecking scheme. And you know the rest."

"But the *Liberty* wasn't wrecked," I said. "It made it into port."

"Because when that storm whipped up, there was only one man who was a good enough navigator to strand it without killing half the men on board." His grin was rueful. "And they'd tossed him overboard. The men who were for the wrecking scheme decided not to go through with it."

"John, I'm so sorry," I said. "No wonder you hate the Rectors so much."

"They're bottom-feeders," he said, the grin vanishing. "They've always preyed on the weak and helpless, taking advantage of those who can't help themselves. My father and William Rector were hateful men who were blind to everyone else's needs but their own —"

He was interrupted by a muffled chime. It sounded, of all things, like the ring of a cell phone.

"What was *that*?" I asked.

"I don't know," John said, looking as bewildered as I was. The tone sounded again, just as urgently. "It sounds like it's coming from . . ."

He bent down, then found my book bag on the floor. He lifted it to the bed. The chime rang again, this time sounding much closer.

"That's my cell phone," I said, finally recognizing the tone. I grabbed my bag and began rifling through it.

"Pierce," John said. "That's not possi —"

I pulled out the phone as it was ringing for a fourth time. "Yes," I said to him, irritated. "It *is* possible, if you're the queen of the Underworld. I get special privileges. Haven't you noticed by now?" The screen said *Unknown Caller*. I pressed the green OK button. "Hello?"

The caller was not unknown. At least not to me. It was my cousin Alex. I recognized his voice right away.

"Pierce," he said. "Pierce?"

It made sense that the connection was terrible . . . so staticky and distant that I could barely hear him.

What I could not figure out was why he sounded so out of breath.

"Alex?" I put my finger in the ear to which I was not holding my phone so I could hear him. Hope chose that moment to come swooping into the room and land on the bed, where she proceeded to waddle across the comforter, then butt me in my bare foot with her head, cooing extremely loudly. I ignored her. "Alex, I can't hear you very well. Can you speak up? Where are you?"

"Pierce," Alex said, in that same ghostly voice, as if he were speaking from a grave. "I —" I heard only static. "— something so stupid. I don't know how much longer I can hold on."

"Wait," I said. I flung a panicked look in John's direction. "*Where* are you? You sound awful. I thought Frank and Kayla took you home."

John was already pulling out the tablet he kept in his pocket. His fingertips flew over it. I had no idea what he was doing. I was fairly certain those tablets only worked for looking up the names of the dead, or in John's case, checking up on my activities on earth. But maybe he was texting Frank.

"There's no air in here, Pierce," Alex said. I could tell he was crying. "You've got to come, quick . . . can't call the cops, because I think some of them are in on it, and if I call my dad, he'll just get in . . ."

I felt goose bumps break out all over my arms. "Alex," I said. I was already scrambling off my bed and looking around for my shoes. "You're breaking up. What's happening? Did you go out again? Did you go look for the coffin? Because they haven't even finished building it yet."

"Not *that* coffin," Alex said. His voice was growing even fainter. His next words sounded like cries from the beyond . . . except *I* was the one in the beyond. "I figured it out . . . I know where they're hiding it all."

Then there was nothing. The call died.

"Hiding what? Alex?" I cried, pressing the phone so closely to my ear, it hurt. "*Alex?*"

I turned towards John, panicked, holding out the phone. "He's gone. He's in trouble, and he's gone."

Mutely, John held his tablet towards me. The screen showed the same picture I'd seen on my cell phone earlier: Alex, trapped inside what looked like a coffin.

"Why are *you* seeing that?" I demanded, slipping on my shoes.

"Pierce," he said somberly. "You know why I'm seeing it. Think about who I am."

Cold horror gripped me. "Is he dead? He can't be. I thought we saved him!"

"I did, too," John said, his frown so deep I felt my heart give a double flip. "But this says he's at the cemetery."

"The cemetery?" I burst out. "What's he doing at the cemetery? I thought Frank and Kayla took him home."

"They did," John said, looking down at the screen. "He must have gone out again. Pierce —"

"What?" My heart was thumping at twice its normal speed. "Come on, John, we've got to go. Where is he exactly?"

John turned off the tablet and put it away, still not meeting my gaze. "He's inside the Rector Mausoleum."

"*Inside* it?" None of this was making any sense to me. "That's impossible. What would he be doing there?"

"I don't know," John said. He finally lifted his gaze to me, and when he did, I saw the regret etched in his eyes. "But, Pierce, I'm afraid it's too late. He's already dead."

Then we arrived within the moats profound,
That circumvallate that disconsolate city;
The walls appeared to me to be of iron.
DANTE ALIGHIERI, *Inferno*, Canto VIII

He can't be dead." That's what I kept saying.

"He can't be. You're wrong. Just because you're the lord of the dead doesn't mean you know everything. You were wrong about the Furies being indestructible. So you could be wrong about Alex."

"Fine," John said, looking as if he were longing to punch something. "We'll go down to the beach and find him, and then you'll see that *this*, I'm right about —"

"*No.*" Maybe I was being hysterical. I don't know. It just didn't seem possible. The last time I'd seen Alex, he'd been alive. Standing there stiff as a board because I'd been hugging him and saying I loved him, too proud — or damaged — to tell me that he loved me back.

But he'd been alive. It didn't make any sense. How could he be dead?

What John kept saying — that we didn't have to go back to earth to find Alex — made even less sense.

John gave up insisting that if anyone was going to go back to Isla Huesos to look for Alex, it wasn't going to be me. He gave up reminding me what had happened the last time I'd gone to Isla Huesos — that everywhere I went, there'd been a Fury waiting to harm me in some way. He had basically given up saying much of anything at all, except that Alex was dead.

"He called me. Out of everyone, he called *me*, John. I'm going to help him."

"Pierce," he said, compassion and sympathy in his voice, but hard reality in his eyes. "There isn't any point. He's dead."

I whirled on him fiercely. "So was I. But my mom pulled me out of that pool and gave me mouth-to-mouth, and the EMTs gave me CPR, and I came back to life. Remember? So stop arguing and take me to him while there's still time."

That's when John stopped arguing, took my arm, and one . . . two . . . three . . . *blink*.

We were in his crypt. But we weren't there alone.

In the dim light of dawn, I could barely make out the shapes of two men wearing what appeared to be pirate costumes lying crumpled on the floor. They were semiconscious, their hands and feet tied with strips of what looked like their own clothing. Frank was sitting with his legs crossed at the ankles beside them, his back up against the wall, an empty bottle of Captain Rob's Rum in his hands.

"Oh, hello," he said with a wave when he saw us. "Welcome to the party."

"What happened?" John demanded. He did not sound pleased.

"Got here to meet you, as we planned, and found *them* waiting." Frank gave the bottle a toss, catching it expertly by the neck, then tossed it again. "Looks like they were planning to ambush you and Pierce when you showed up. As hired muscle goes, they don't seem to have been the best choice. It's usually not the brightest idea to drink on the job . . . but I suppose they got started at the festival and didn't see any reason to stop. I simply hurried things along. Didn't I, my fine fellows?" Frank gave one of the unconscious men a little shove with the toe of his boot.

"Go 'way," the man murmured, before rolling over on his comfortable bed of poinciana blossoms and red drink cups. "We're waiting for someone."

"Find your own tomb," the other said. "We've got dibs on this one. Nice 'n' dry."

"In my experience, challenging a total stranger to a drinking contest never works out well," Frank went on, with a wink at me, "especially when the drink in question is the one his former employer used to force his entire crew to drink on a daily basis. Remember, Captain? Ah, memories."

Frank held up the bottle. For the first time, I noticed that Captain Rob's Rum had a picture of a ship captain on the label. He bore a slight resemblance to John . . . if John had been much older, with a long mustache, side whiskers, and a repulsive smirk on his face.

It was only then that it hit me: Captain Rob of Captain Rob's Rum was *Captain Robert Hayden.* I wondered which of John's ancestors had turned the tragedy of his father's alcoholism into such a lucrative business. It obviously hadn't been John.

I saw him grimace with distaste.

"Probably acquaintances of our old friend Mike," he said, looking down at the two drunk men. "I doubt they scaled the cemetery fence in their condition."

Frank nodded. "Not with those spikes on it. Someone had to have let them in through a gate."

"The way he did the night of Jade's murder," John said, thoughtfully. "Mike, probably."

Frank brightened. "I didn't think of that. We could torture them a bit to find out."

John threw me an uneasy glance. "I think we'd better leave them here and move on for now. . . ."

I wasn't really listening. On top of the fact that I was so tortured with worry about Alex, it didn't smell so good inside John's crypt — one or both of the two men had apparently been sick on himself.

"Right," Frank said, eyeing me. "They're trussed up nice and tight. Not like they're going anywhere . . ."

I was relieved to see that the chains around the gate to John's crypt remained broken. This was evidently how the two Furies had gotten inside it. Not waiting for John to do it for me this time, I pushed open the gate and stepped onto the cemetery path outside his crypt, relieved to smell the fresh morning air.

It had stopped raining. The rising sun was putting in a valiant effort to burn off the fast-moving clouds, streaking the sky in the east with brilliant stripes of orange, red, and lavender. This was good, since it meant we had light to see by — the city had started turning out all the streetlights in and around the graveyard in an effort to combat what the newspaper said the police department was calling acts of "teen vandalism."

Some of us knew vandals had nothing to do with it, and turning out the lights wasn't going to do anything to improve the situation.

"— all the way to the door," I could hear Frank saying behind me as I moved quickly along the gravel path. "I gave him his phone and his keys, just like you told me, then we waited until he went inside. We *watched* him."

"I believe you," John said, in a calm voice. "What about his vehicle?"

I knew what they were talking about. Alex. Frank was defending himself, insisting he'd completed his assignment of making sure Alex got home safely.

I was certain Alex *had* gotten home safely, but then he'd snuck out again. *Why?* Why hadn't he listened to me? Why hadn't he listened to Kayla?

My heart was thumping as fast as a rabbit's as we moved along the path towards the Rector mausoleum, easily visible amidst all the tombs, as it was the biggest one in the cemetery. Two stories high and made entirely of shiny taupe marble, it had its own little fence around it, a low chain like the kind at a fancy art museum, warning patrons not to touch. Beyond the chain was a grass lawn, probably one of the only ones in all of Isla Huesos. Tropical climates, my mom's landscape architect had explained, were inhospitable to grass. The Rectors had to pay a fortune to maintain that grass.

"— however he got here, it wasn't by driving," Frank was saying. "I put the knife from my boot into every one of those tires —"

Alex didn't need a car to get to the cemetery, though. My mom's house was only a few blocks away from here, and Grandma's house, where Alex lived, was even closer than that. He'd probably walked.

"— didn't want to go home." Frank's voice drifted towards me, carried by the strong wind that was also stirring the tops of the palm trees around us, planted at periodic intervals between the tombs and the statues of weeping angels.

"*What?*" John's voice was sharp.

"She didn't want to," Frank said. He sounded defensive. "You know what girls are like these days. They do what they want. She didn't want to go home. She said it wasn't late and she wanted to stay out."

"Then where *is* she?" John sounded alarmed.

"I don't know. She dropped me off here. I don't know where she went after —"

"She dropped you off *here?*"

I realized they were talking about Kayla. I wasn't too alarmed. If anyone could take care of herself, it was Kayla. Alex was the one I had to worry about. Wasn't that what Uncle Chris had said? My eyes filled with tears as I remembered the conversation he and I had had in the driveway of my mom's house. I was never the one he'd felt he had to worry about, he'd said.

I was supposed to have taken care of Alex, because he was the one Uncle Chris had always worried about. And now I'd let him down.

I saw the birds before I saw the mausoleum doors. They were just like the ones I'd seen in the Underworld, black ones, wheeling around high in the air, dozens of them, circling in a flight path directly above the Rector mausoleum. They were silent as death.

"Oh, God," I said, and started to run.

John got to the doors first. They were gates, just like on his crypt. But the Rectors' weren't scrolled wrought iron, decorative and rusted, and kept closed by a bike chain and lock. They were thick black steel, modern and new, like doors to a prison cell, with the lock built in.

I flung myself at them, gripping them with both hands and shaking them in panic.

They didn't budge, of course.

"It's all right," John said soothingly. "Pierce, it's all right, I'll open it."

"How?" My voice had a hysterical edge to it. *"How?"*

"Stand back," he said, and pushed me gently towards Frank, who put his hands on my shoulders and steered me aside.

Then John did something that completely astonished me . . . but it shouldn't have, after everything I'd been through with him, and already seen him do. He turned around, and, just as he had done to the cemetery gates that terrible night we'd fought so badly, and he'd thrown my necklace away, he kicked those thick steel doors, causing a noise so loud, I threw my hands over my ears, and turned around worriedly to see if he'd woken anyone.

Of course he hadn't. We were in the middle of nineteen acres of tombs. There was no one to waken . . . except the dead.

The gates crashed open.

John strode inside, and I followed, my pulse skittering. The mausoleum was made up of wall after wall of burial vaults, one stacked on top of the other, with shiny brass nameplates beneath each, starting, at the top, with William Rector and his wife, then their sons and their wives, then their children and grandchildren, and so on, six to a stack. The Rectors were evidently as skilled at producing offspring as they were at building profit-making businesses. As the vaults reached eye level, the dates on them became more recent, until finally came a dozen on which the nameplates were empty.

In the center of the mausoleum was an elaborately large fire pit, in which burned an eternal flame fueled by the open air . . . the building had no roof. A copper hood shielded the dancing flame from the elements. On top of the hood was a hideously ugly bronze statue in the modern style. The statue was of a couple, dressed in togas, wrapped in an embrace. Cupped in their hands was a piece of fruit. I couldn't be sure, because realism did not appear to be the artist's specialty, but it looked to me like a pomegranate.

"Good God," Frank, who'd trailed after us, said when he saw the statue. "Rector's even sicker than any of us thought. I've never wished I was blind before, like Graves, but I do now, because then I'd never have to look at *that* again."

"Frank," John said, his gaze on my face. "Be quiet."

"But what do they *do* in here?" Frank wanted to know. "Have picnics with their dead relatives and admire their ugly art?"

Ignoring Frank, I stood in front of all the vaults, my fingers balled into fists. I was having trouble catching my breath. I felt as if the statuary were watching me . . . *laughing* at me. "Which one is Alex in?" I asked. "How can we tell?"

John stood at my side, helping me scan the nameplates. "He's in an empty one."

My heart lurched. "Of course he is." If they'd stuffed him into a coffin with a corpse — I didn't want to think about it. "But there are so many empty ones. . . ."

I became distracted by the fact that Hope was pecking something on the stone floor . . . something that clearly wasn't edible, because it was an unnatural shade of red, and not shaped like a poinciana blossom.

"Hope," I said to her. "Stop that."

Of course she didn't. She looked up as I approached to take whatever it was away from her, then waddled out of my reach, as if annoyed with me for disturbing her meal, and began to peck elsewhere. I leaned down to examine what she'd been trying to eat.

It was a long, thin red streamer . . . exactly the kind that might fall from the pom-pom of someone dressed as a cheerleader, then stick to the bottom of her boyfriend's shoe.

In front of the streamer was a vault at ground level. It had a blank nameplate.

"*This one,*" I said to John, pointing. "It's this one!"

Without hesitating, he ripped open the burial vault door, even though it was locked.

Inside, there was a coffin. Why would there be a coffin in a vault with an empty nameplate?

I stood there with my heart in my throat as John and Frank rushed to pull it out. It wasn't a homemade, four-by-eight plywood coffin, painted in the IHHS school colors. It was a *real* coffin, a casket, actually, made of glossy black lacquer, man-sized . . . and sealed airtight.

I gasped. Was this some relative of Seth's whom his family had just buried? Maybe the nameplate hadn't yet arrived. Had we made a mistake? Were we disturbing the final resting place of Seth Rector's grandfather?

It was too late, though. Because when they finally dragged the coffin all the way out of the vault, Frank accidentally dropped his end. The coffin fell over and the lid came unlatched. There was a hissing sound, like something decompressing. . . .

Oh, no, a voice inside me whispered. *Oh, no, oh, no.*

Then someone who'd been sitting up inside the casket, the better to lean against the lid and try to suck whatever fresh air he could from the cracks around it, landed on his back on the hard stone floor of the mausoleum, his dark hair sticking up from his head in sweaty tufts. His eyes were closed.

It was Alex.

He was dead.

"It falls into the forest, and no part
Is chosen for it; but where Fortune hurls it,
There like a grain of spelt it germinates."
DANTE ALIGHIERI, *Inferno*, Canto XIII

L etting out a soft cry, I fell to my knees at his side. Sharp rocks bit into the bare flesh of my knees, but I hardly noticed. Alex's face was red and burning to the touch.

There's no air in here, Pierce, he had said. *You've got to come, quick. . . .*

Alex could be a pain, it was true. He'd refused to let me in about whatever it was he was trying to do — get revenge for what he perceived Mr. Rector had done to his dad — until it was far too late.

That still didn't excuse what they'd done to him. Frank had said the Rectors were sick. But what kind of sickness would make anyone do *this*?

"Alex." I grabbed his shoulders and shook them. "Alex!"

He didn't move.

I was too late, I realized, my heart slowing down to what felt like a beat a minute. I was too late.

"Where's my cell phone?" I asked, feeling as if I were in a dream. "We need . . . we need to call an ambulance."

"Pierce," John said. His voice was the saddest I'd ever heard it. "I'm sorry, but it's too —"

I was too late.

"Call 9-1-1!" I shouted at him.

John shrugged, then reached into his pocket for the phone I'd made him put there. My dress had no pockets, and I hadn't wanted to lug my bag around during a rescue mission.

Except it was no rescue. Because I was too late. Alex was dead.

I turned my attention back to Alex, pounding him on his chest. I knew CPR, of course. You can't die and then come back thanks to someone performing CPR on you without grasping at least a rudimentary knowledge of what they'd done. I'd taken a first-aid course.

Everything I'd learned during the course fled my mind.

I leaned down to blow into Alex's mouth, my tears falling onto his face, making new tracks in the dirt stains there. I hadn't even realized until that moment that I was crying.

I should have been kneeling there thinking of how I was going to explain all this to Uncle Chris, and to my mother, and to my grandmother, of course (although I didn't owe her anything, certainly not explanations).

I should have been thinking of Alex, of how unfair it was that his life had been cut off so soon, especially when he had been so unhappy for so long. He deserved better than this. This was no way for it all to end.

Instead I was thinking of how he hadn't said he loved me back. I knew he did love me. Probably. I also knew it didn't matter. I didn't deserve his love, because I'd been late. And I was going to be damned — yes, *damned* — before I let someone else I love die because I'd been too late.

Which was when it occurred to me that I didn't have to, because I knew someone who could make this go away, without having to count on CPR, or EMTs, or anything . . . someone who could make it all better with a wave of his hand.

Why hadn't I thought of it before?

Lifting my face from Alex's, I turned to John, surprised to find he was already kneeling next to me. He was wearing jeans, so the gravel wasn't cutting into his knees.

"I called them," he said, his face pale and tight in the dawn light. "They're on their way. If we don't want to be caught here with him, we need to go soon, Pierce."

"No," I said, catching his hand. I smiled at him through my tears, feeling suddenly joyful. It was going to be all right. Everything was going to be fine. "John . . . I had an idea. You can heal him. Like you did me, with my cut, and then my throat. You can make him come back alive, like you did the bird that day."

He stared at me, seemingly uncomprehending. "What?"

How could he not know what I meant?

"The day I met you," I prompted him. I reached up to wipe the tears from my cheeks. I didn't have to cry anymore. It was all so miraculous. "Remember? It was right here in the cemetery. The bird I found the day of my grandfather's funeral when I was seven, the one that looked so much like Hope. It was dead, and I was crying, and to make me feel better, you brought it back to life. You can do the same with Alex." I took his hands and put them on Alex's lifeless body, smiling up at him. "Do it. Do it now, then we can go. We can all go home."

John left his hands where I'd placed them, but he shook his head, looking at me like I was a bit crazy. That wasn't unusual, though. Everyone looked at me that way. I was used to it.

"Pierce," John said, not taking his gaze off me. "I told you that day when you asked me to raise your grandfather, remember? Birds don't have souls. Humans do. It's not the same. I can't do it."

This was true, actually. I remembered his saying it now. But I wasn't going to let a minor detail like this stand in the way of something I knew he could do. He could do anything.

"How do you know?" I asked him. "Have you ever tried?"

"As a matter of fact," Frank said, from the wall of vaults opposite ours, against which he was leaning, "he has."

I glanced at him, startled. "He has?"

Frank nodded, examining his cuticles. "Quite successfully. I can think of four times he's done it at least, off the top of my head."

John whipped his head around to lash out at Frank in a hard voice, *"Frank, be quiet."* In the distance, thunder rumbled.

I glanced back at John in confusion. "Well, if you've done it before, why won't you do it now, for me?" I asked. "I know you can do it." I smiled at him confidently.

"Because it wasn't right," John said. His voice was gentle, but I could see the storm brewing in his eyes. He was going to fight me on this. I didn't know why, but he was going to. "It was when I was first starting out, and I didn't know any better. I didn't understand the consequences."

Consequences again. Stupid consequences.

But if it meant Alex didn't have to die . . .

"What were the" — I swallowed, then smiled. I didn't want to let him see that I had any reservations. Because I didn't — "consequences?"

Thunder growled again, louder this time. Looking up, I saw that the birds had fled. Where had the birds gone? Only Hope remained, and she'd fluttered over to the grotesque statue and was sitting on the pomegranate.

"The consequences were *not* worth it," John said firmly.

"That," Frank said, "is a matter of opinion. I happen to be grateful I'm still alive, and I think if you asked them, the others would agree."

I looked from Frank to John and then back again. "You mean —"

"That's right," Frank said. "The captain found Graves and Liu and Henry and me, dead as doornails after that October tempest. Felt bad about it, I guess, because he brought us back to life —"

"And they were doomed to spend the rest of eternity with me in the Underworld." John's voice was a whip, his eyes looking not unlike twin tempests themselves, they'd turned so dark and furious. "So you see, Pierce? There's a price to pay. I can bring your cousin back, but not to life as he knew it. Let him go on to whatever is waiting for him on the other side. I'm sure he'll be happier, and better off."

I bit my lip. "That's not for you to say."

"Actually," John said quietly. "It is."

My eyes filled once more with tears. I couldn't believe this was happening. I had gone from the depths of despair to the heights of hope, only to have him dash that hope the way . . . well, the way I'd dashed that cup of tea in his face the day I'd run from him.

"Pierce," he said, in a voice that sounded as desperate as it did determined. "*Don't cry.* I mean it. It's not going to make a difference. I'm not changing my mind. If I had known bringing Frank and the others back to life would mean sentencing them to an eternity in the Underworld, do you think I'd have done it?"

"Why not?" I asked, letting my tears spill over. It was easy to cry. All I had to do was look at Alex's limp body, and the tears came effortlessly. "You were happy enough to do it to me."

There was a beat. Then John asked cautiously, "What do you mean?"

"The *consequences*, John?" I let out a bitter laugh. "Persephone wasn't doomed to stay in the Underworld because she ate a pomegranate. She was doomed to stay there because she did with Hades *what we did last night.* That's what the pomegranate symbolizes, right?"

John stared, speechless. But I could tell I was right by the color that slowly started to suffuse his cheeks . . . and the fact that he didn't try to contradict me.

And of course the fact that the whole thing was spelled out right in front of me by the statue Hope was sitting on. I didn't get why the Rectors were so obsessed by the myth of Persephone that they'd put a statue of it in their mausoleum, but it was clear enough they were involved in an underworld of one kind or another.

"Don't worry," I said, lowering my voice because I didn't want Frank to overhear. "I don't blame you. You asked me if I was sure, despite the consequences. I said I was. But I thought by *consequences* you meant a *baby, and* I already knew that could never happen. I guess Mr. Smith must have told you last night that he found out the pomegranate symbolized something completely different than babies *or* death —"

"Pierce." John grasped my hand. His fingers were like ice, but his voice and his gaze had an urgency that was anything but cold. "That isn't why I did it. I love you. I've always loved you, because you're good . . . you're so good, you make me want to be good, too. But that's the problem, Pierce. I'm *not* good. And I've always been afraid that when you find out the truth about me, you'd run away again —"

I sucked in my breath to tell him for the millionth time that this wasn't true, but he cut me off, not allowing me to speak until he'd had his say.

"Then you almost died yesterday," he went on, "and it was my fault. I wanted to show you how much I loved you, and things . . . things went further than I expected. But you didn't stop me" — his silver eyes blazed, as if daring me to deny what he was saying — "even though I *told* you we could slow down if you wanted to."

"I know," I said softly, dropping my gaze to look down at our joined fingers. We'd each kept a hand on Alex. "I know you did."

"I don't want to lose you again," he said fiercely. "I lost you once and I couldn't bear it. I won't go through that again. I . . . I know I did the wrong thing. But it didn't feel wrong at the time."

I raised my gaze to his. "You're right about that, at least," I said.

"So am I forgiven?" he asked.

I hesitated, confused by the myriad of emotions I was feeling. John had *known*. He'd known the whole time we had been together the night before that he was forever sealing my destiny to his.

Of course, he'd thought I'd known, too. He'd asked if I was sure it was what I wanted, despite the consequences. I might have misunderstood what those consequences were, but I'd been very adamant in my response. I'd said yes. And I'd meant it.

"Excuse me," called Frank's voice from the opposite wall of vaults. "But you might want to take a look at the boy."

John and I both glanced down. Beneath the hands we'd left on Alex, he'd come back to life.

Not without making first a circuit wide,
We came unto a place where loud the pilot
Cried out to us, "Debark, here is the entrance."
DANTE ALIGHIERI, *Inferno*, Canto VIII

It was impossible.

"Hey," Alex murmured. His eyelids had begun to flutter. He raised a hand to fight some unseen enemy. "Get off me. I said, get *off.*"

"No," I breathed, quickly removing my hand. *"No."* I lifted my astonished gaze to John's. "Did you do this?"

The eyes he raised to meet mine were every bit as incredulous. "I didn't. I didn't mean to, anyway."

John did not look happy. Anything but. His thick dark eyebrows slanted into a V as he stared down at Alex, who murmured "Stop that!" before fully opening his eyes.

"Oh, Pierce," he said, recognizing me. "I had the worst dream. What . . . what happened?"

"You're an idiot," Frank strolled up to inform him. "And someone killed you for it. That's what happened."

"Frank," John said, irritated. He looked back down at Alex.
"How do you feel? Do you think you can walk?"

I wondered why John was asking about this, until I heard it . . .
the sound of a siren in the distance. The ambulance I'd made
him call was on its way. Of course we didn't need it anymore.

I wondered how the vehicle was going to get in to the cemetery, when both gates were locked. The EMTs didn't have a key.

Unless Mike was coming back to let his friends *out* . . .

"I . . . I don't know," Alex said. "I feel strange." He looked
off into the distance. "Is that the sunrise?" he asked. "Or the
sunset?"

Frank glanced where he was looking. "Sunrise," he said.

"It's beautiful," Alex said, in a wondering voice. "So red."

I was surprised. Alex had never been prone to comment on the
beauty of things like sunrises before. Maybe dying had given him
a new appreciation for life.

Of course it had, I realized. He was an NDE now, just like me.

"Nothing beautiful about that sky," Frank said, with a snort.
*Red sky at night, sailor's delight. Red sky in morning, sailor, take
warning.* That means there's a storm coming, boy. A much bigger
one than what you've just been through."

John shot Frank an exasperated look. Alex, meanwhile, had
glanced at the casket lying next to him, the lid open. Things
seemed slowly to be coming back to him, judging by his expression. "Oh, *God*," he choked.

"Alex." I reached out and took his hand, my heart aching with pity for him . . . and for Uncle Chris. Neither of them had any idea what they were in for. "I know what you've just been through must have been horrible. I tried to come as soon as I realized. But —"

"It was them, Pierce," Alex said. He lifted his dark eyes, and I saw they weren't pain-filled at all. They were burning with rage . . . and a desire for what I could only guess was revenge. "I knew it. I went back out and followed them. They came here. Guess why?"

"Alex," I said. Now I didn't feel pity. "None of that matters anymore. I have to tell you something important." Because I realized he didn't know. He didn't understand what had happened to him, or remember —

"No, it *does* matter," Alex said fiercely, rising to his elbows. "Seth and those guys, they act like they own this island. But guess what? We have them right where we want them now. I snuck out and followed them, and I saw where they're keeping their stash these days. In here." He pointed at the casket.

"But . . ." I blinked. "It's empty."

"Yeah, *now* it is," Alex said, exasperated. "'cause when they caught me spying on them, they took it out, and stuffed me in there instead. But isn't it genius? *No one* comes in this cemetery, 'cause it's supposed to be haunted or something, so there are no security cameras, no lights, nothing. I bet *this* is why Jade got killed. She saw them sneaking around in here, so they snuffed her."

I realized Alex might be right.

"They think they shut me up, stuffing me in there," Alex said, sitting up. He wasn't listening to me. "Well, guess who has the upper hand now? They're gonna freak! They think I'm dead." He laughed. "We'll show them."

"Uh, Alex," I said, glancing at John. His mouth had pressed into a line so tight, his lips had practically disappeared. "I have to tell you something—"

I was interrupted by the sound of a woman's sob. Everyone looked at me.

Although I certainly felt like crying, I wasn't sobbing. I turned my head, and was shocked to see Kayla sitting by the fire pit, tears streaming down her face. She hadn't even changed out of her Coffin Fest finery, though she'd lost a rhinestone from the corner of one of her eyes, and her cape was missing.

"I . . . I'm sorry," she said, holding a hand towards us, palm out. "It's just . . . someone had better tell him the truth."

John whipped his head around to stare daggers at Frank. "What is she doing here?" he demanded, under his breath.

"I don't know," Frank muttered, as he hurried to Kayla's side. "Kayla, how long have you been here, honey?"

"Long enough to have figured out exactly what's going on with you people," she said, loudly.

"Kayla." I rose to my feet. The siren sounded quite close now.

She ignored me, snatching her arm from Frank's grasp when he attempted to take it, saying, "Let me explain."

"I don't need your explanations," Kayla said, her chest rising and falling dramatically in the early morning light. "I thought there was something weird with all of you, I just couldn't figure out what it was. But now I know. It all makes sense." Her dark, tear-filled eyes sparkled as her accusatory gaze traveled from one of us to the other. "I can tell you battle on the side of good, and I want to join you." She turned to Frank, brushed her curly hair away from her throat, and closed her eyes. "Go ahead. Do it."

There was a long silence as everyone stared at Kayla's shapely neck. Then Frank looked helplessly at John.

"It's no use," he said. "We have to take her with us. She knows everything."

"*No*," John said. Now the thunder was directly overhead, so loud it drowned out even the sound of the siren.

"Kayla," I said, walking over to her and giving her shoulders a shake. "No one's going to bite you."

She opened her eyes, looking confused. "Then what . . . how did you bring Alex back from the dead like that? How did John kick in that gate? How did John bring *Frank* back to life? What are the Rectors hiding in caskets? What have you guys been *talking* about?"

I realized Frank was right. She really did know everything. Or almost everything.

"Jesus Christ," Alex said, his eyes round and suddenly frightened looking. "What's she saying? Is she on something? Because I haven't come back from the dead. I almost died, but I didn't. Not like Pierce."

I threw him a pitying look. He clearly hadn't seen a light.

"She'll talk, and they'll kill her," Frank said to John. "They already killed *him*." He gestured at Alex. "What makes you think they won't do the same to her?"

Alex looked even more alarmed. "Why do people keep saying I'm dead? *I'm not dead.*"

John stormed up to Frank and hissed, "It's the realm of the dead, not a safe house for girls in trouble."

"Why not?" Frank asked, not batting an eye. "That's what you're using it for . . . *Captain.*"

I widened my eyes. I half expected John to hit him. The old John would have.

But though I saw John's fingers curl into fists, he didn't lift them. He took a deep, measured breath.

This wasn't the old, wild John. This was the new John . . . still full of unpredictable behavior, but more thought-out behavior than before I'd joined him in the Underworld.

I walked over to him and whispered, slipping a hand around his arm, "Frank's right. We can't just leave her here. They killed Jade, and now Alex. Maybe she could stay a little while. Only until things settle down." I slid a nervous glance at Frank. "We can try to keep them in separate parts of the castle."

John swiveled his head towards me, his gaze a mix of incredulity and skepticism. "And how, precisely, are we going to do that?" he asked.

"The same way we brought Alex back to life," I said. "And that we got rid of that Fury. And that we're going to get rid of the rest of them. And the Rectors, too, eventually." I raised my necklace, showing him the diamond. "Teamwork."

His jaw muscles tightened. "Pierce," he said, lifting his gaze to mine. "It's —"

Black. That's how he would have finished that sentence. If I hadn't been so preoccupied with everything going on, I would have looked down and noticed myself, or seen that Hope had taken off, and was flying in high, tight circles above us, letting out cries of alarm, frightened to death of something.

It was too late, though. By the time we realized the danger, it was already at the door.

The familiar voice crackled so loudly, I ducked, thinking it was coming from somewhere close by. So did John, at first. He threw a protective arm around my shoulders.

"Pierce Oliviera," Police Chief Santos called out. "We know you're in there. You're trespassing on private property. Please come out now, and you and your companions won't be hurt."

John was the first to figure it out.

"Megaphone," he said, straightening. "They must be right outside."

Frank ran to look, flattening himself against the wall of entombed Rector ancestors. He nodded, then slunk quickly back towards us.

"Police," he said. "Pulled their cars right into the graveyard." He lowered his voice so Kayla and Alex couldn't overhear. "They appear to be extremely well armed."

I realized the siren we'd heard hadn't been an ambulance at all.

"It's my fault," I murmured. "They traced that 9-1-1 call. I can't believe it. I'm so stupid."

John's arm tightened reassuringly. "It's not your fault," he said, pointing. "Look."

I looked where he indicated. I hadn't noticed before, but in each of the four corners of the open area where the fire pit was located were security cameras. They were pointed right at us. They'd been filming our every move.

"Again," Police Chief Santos's voice boomed, "you are trespassing on private property. I'm counting down from five. If you do not come out by the time I've reached one, we will use force to remove you. *Five —*"

Kayla's eyes were wide and frightened as she moved closer to me. "That's the chief of police," she said worriedly. "Remember, from the convocation? I'd know his voice anywhere."

John laid his other hand on Kayla's arm, as if to comfort her. Frank took her hand.

It was in that moment that I knew that John had made his decision . . . or that he'd realized the Furies had made it for him. There was no going back.

The rhyme Frank had said earlier popped into my head. *Red sky at night, sailor's delight. Red sky in morning, sailor, take warning.*

The sky in the east, I noticed, had turned bloodred.

Kayla looked down at Frank's hand, confused. "Wait," she said. "What's going on?"

"Four," the police chief boomed into the megaphone.

"Rector is going to press charges for defacing his property," Alex said, climbing to his feet. "I know it. No one's going to believe anything I say, because of who my dad is."

"You're probably right," I said, following John's lead, and taking his hand.

"I'm not going to jail for what those guys did to me," Alex declared.

"Three."

317

"Don't worry," I said. "You won't have to."

"Wait." Alex looked at me bewilderedly. "How do *you* know?"

"Two."

I looked up at John. He looked down at me, then tightened his hold on my shoulders.

"Forgiven?" he asked, his gray eyes glowing.

I smiled. "We'll see," I said.

"One."

Blink.

THE ABANDON TRILOGY
A New Young Adult Fiction Series from Meg Cabot

— BOOK THREE: AWAKEN —

*D*eath has her in his clutches. She doesn't want him to let go.

Seventeen-year-old Pierce Oliviera knew by accepting the love of John Hayden, she'd be forced to live forever in the one place she's always dreaded most: the Underworld.

The sacrifice seemed worth it, though, because it meant she could be with the boy she loves.

But now her happiness — and safety — in the realm over which John rules are threatened, all because the Furies have discovered that John has broken one of their strictest rules: He revived a human soul.

Now, if the balance between life and death isn't restored, both the Underworld and Pierce's home back on earth will be wiped away by the Furies' wrath . . . and not even a necklace forged by an ancient god can stop them. This time, the Furies are out for blood — and they'd prefer John's, if they can get it.

But if all they want is a life for a life, Pierce is willing to volunteer her own. John won't hear of it, but Pierce has already cheated death once before. What's she got to lose?

Except her life . . . and, if she fails, the thing she loves more than anything else in this world, or the next:

John.

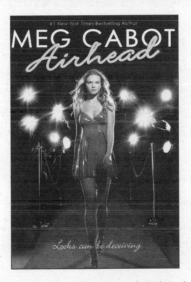

"Oh, God," Frida moaned, dropping her head into her hands in mortification.

"Come on, Free," I said, elbowing her chummily. "We aren't *that* embarrassing, are we?"

"Yes," she murmured. "You are. You really are. Don't you realize that you guys look down on everything normal people like? Like Nikki Howard and her friends —"

It was kind of funny that as Frida said this, Nikki Howard herself actually appeared — along with some of her friends — in front of us.

Except that Frida didn't notice right away.

That's because Frida was too busy defending her idol to me.

"You're always going on about feminism, Em," Frida continued. "Well, do you really think Nikki would have gotten where she is today — the Face of Stark, currently one of the highest-earning models — if she weren't a feminist?"

"Uh," I said. Because I couldn't believe the person we were arguing about was so close to us.

"And I don't see how you can even call yourself a feminist, Em," Frida went on, oblivious, "when you are so totally mean about a member of your own sex. I mean, Nikki's just a girl, like you are."

Except that I could see with my own eyes that Nikki was very far from being just a girl — let alone a girl like I am. For one thing, she was about a foot taller (thanks to a pair of five-inch heels, but even without them, she had to have been about five foot ten) and about half as wide as me. Seriously. Two of her would have fit into my jeans.

And for another, her shiny blond hair flowed smoothly down past her elbows, not a strand out of place, even though she was practically running — despite her heels — across the store. Strangely, her filmy dress seemed to cover everything it was supposed to, too . . . despite the fact that it was the lowest-cut thing I'd ever seen — aside from what Whitney Robertson wore to school last year on Picture Day. How did Nikki keep those thin straps of material over her nipples, anyway? Double-sided tape? I'd heard about that kind of thing, of course, but never had a chance to observe its use in real life.

And it was a good thing, too (that Nikki had thought to use tape to hold in her breasts, which weren't huge enough to need their own zip codes, or anything, but — unlike my own — definitely stood at attention when called to duty).

Because she was carrying a tiny ball of fluff that appeared at first glance to be a pom-pom and at second glance to be a small dog, trying frantically to burrow its head between her boobs and get away from all the crazy lights and sounds in the store. If it hadn't been for the tape keeping him out, well, that dog would have dived right inside Nikki's dress.

Frida was still going on about what a bad example of feminism I am (about which, can I just say, *Hello, Pot? This is Kettle. Yeah, you're black*), completely oblivious to what was going on behind her — even though everybody else in line was staring, slack-jawed, at the rapidly approaching supermodel and her entourage of dog, some kind of agent or publicist (red-haired lady with a briefcase, jabbering into a headset), hairdresser (man in a silk shirt and leather pants, carrying a can of hair spray), and the number one F.O.N. herself, Lulu Collins, an equally skinny, equally pretty seventeen-year-old girl in a faux snakeskin-print wrap dress, who couldn't seem to stop looking at her Sidekick, even to watch where she was going.

I swear, it was just like at school when Whitney and Lindsey and the rest of the Walking Dead start their morning prom-enade from the front of the building to their lockers. Every single person in the vicinity just stops talking and stares as if transfixed.

And not just the people all around us, either. I noticed that Nikki had caught Gabriel Luna's attention, as well. He was still smiling at the girls clustered in front of him, thrusting CDs (and their phone numbers) at him.

But he was also keeping a pretty close eye on Nikki . . .

. . . as, I might add, was Christopher.

It was at that moment that Frida finally turned around to see what Christopher — his mouth slightly agape — and I were staring at.

And completely lost it.

"Omigodomigodomigod," Frida cried, waving her free hand (the other was still clutching her cell) in front of her face as if she were fanning tears from her eyes. "Omigod, it's her. It's her. It's HER!"

"I don't know what you're talking about, Free," Christopher said. "That Gabriel guy may be sensitive and all of that. But he is *totally* staring at her chest."

"Um, he wouldn't be the only one doing that," I muttered, noting — with dissatisfaction — the direction of Christopher's gaze.

He realized what I meant and began to turn bright red. But I noticed he didn't look away.

Funny how, all of a sudden, I wasn't feeling so *fine* anymore.

"Omigod, you guys," Frida said, clutching my arm. "Lulu Collins is with her! I have to get their autographs. I have to!"

But at that very moment, the line in which we'd been standing for the past hour reached the very table that, mere minutes before, had seemed so very far away and out of reach. Gabriel Luna himself was within autographing distance. Heck, he was within TOUCHING distance.

Not that, you know, I was going to reach out and grab a big hunk of his shirt or anything. I'm just saying I could have. If I'd wanted to.

Up close, he looked even better than he had when he was onstage. Up close, I could tell he definitely didn't have any tattoos. Nor was he wearing eyeliner. His eyes really *were* that blue. And his gaze really *was* that piercing.

Except that it wasn't looking anywhere near mine. It was, in fact, still glued on Nikki.

"Frida." I found myself as unable to tear my gaze from Gabriel Luna as he was apparently unable to tear his own away from Nikki Howard. "Uh, Frida?"

Except that when my sister didn't reply, and when I finally forced myself to look in her direction, I saw that Frida had actually stepped from the line and was heading toward Nikki and her entourage — not like she meant to be doing it, but like she simply couldn't resist the pull of Nikki's celebrity . . . kind of like how Leander was drawn into the Dark Castle by the beam of the Ring of Ashanti in the *Journeyquest* movie (which sucked).

"Frida?" I called after her. Then, realizing that Gabriel Luna had finally stopped staring at Nikki and was instead looking curiously at me, I turned toward him slowly and heard myself murmur, "Um. Hi."

"Hi," Gabriel said back. And then he smiled.

And — I'm not kidding — it was like reaching another level in *Journeyquest*. No, it was even better than that . . . it was like waking up in the morning and hearing your mother go, "Guess what? They just canceled school. It's a snow day." Seriously, that's what his smile did to me — gave me a jolt of pleasure that was almost physical, it was so strong.

Which is weird because I'd felt something very similar just minutes before when Christopher had called me fine. Boys are confusing.

Of course I couldn't say anything. Of course I could only stand there gazing at him with my mouth hanging open, wondering how anyone so beautiful could be real and not a product of airbrushing or computer animation.

"What's your name, then?" Gabriel asked, in his gorgeous English accent.

"Um." Oh, God. He was talking to me. He was talking to *me*. What should I say? Why was this happening? Where was Frida? Where the frack was FRIDA? "Em."

"Em?" Gabriel smiled some more. "Short for Emily?"

"Um," I said. Oh, God. What was wrong with me? Normally, I had no problem talking to cute boys. Because normally, all the cute boys I met — Christopher excepted, of course — were sexist creeps who needed to be taken down a peg or two. They weren't sweet British hotties with a voice like an angel and blue eyes that seemed to pierce my soul. "No . . ."

"Do you have a CD you'd like me to sign?" Gabriel wanted to know, looking questioningly at my empty hands.

Oh, no.

"Hold on," I said, my heart pounding. "My sister —"

I spun around to find Frida and ran smack into Christopher, who was still staring at Nikki. Only now he wore a look of concern. "Uh, Em," he said. "Look —"

What happened next seemed to unfold as if it were in a dream. Or more accurately, a nightmare. I saw my sister walking toward Nikki Howard and her posse.

At the same time, I saw a guy standing nearby suddenly throw open his trench coat to reveal an E.L.F. T-shirt . . . along with a paint gun. A Megastore security guy with an earpiece, seeing this at the same time I did, grabbed Nikki by the wrist and jerked her back. Meanwhile, Paint Gun Guy, grinning balefully, raised his rifle and fired at the plasma TV hanging directly over Nikki's head, leaving an enormous yellow splotch across the screen where Nikki's boobs had been. Actually, it looked like she'd been eating a hot dog with mustard that had slid out onto her chest . . . something that happens to me not infrequently.

Only this time, the plasma screen came loose from the wires suspending it from the ceiling. First one wire popped. Then a second one.

And standing directly beneath it stood my sister, Frida, still holding her pen toward Nikki for an autograph.

"Frida! Move!" I yelled, my heart giving a lurch.

I darted forward to push her out of the way just as the last wire holding the giant television in place broke with a pinging sound that was easily audible, even over the music blasting from the Stark Megastore's speakers.

And then the whole thing came crashing down.

On me.

And — just like in *Journeyquest*, when I make a mistake and my character loses a life — everything went black.